DEATH AND LOVE AT THE OLD SUMMER CAMP

DEATH AND LOVE AT THE OLD SUMMER CAMP

DOLORES MAGGIORE

SAPPHIRE BOOKS

SALINAS, CALIFORNIA

Death and Love at the Old Summer Camp
Copyright © 2017 by Dolores Maggiore. All rights reserved.

ISBN - 978-1-943353-77-4

This is a work of fiction - names, characters, places, and incidents are the product of the author's imagination or are used fictitiously. Any resemblance to actual persons living or dead, business, events or locales is entirely coincidental.

All rights reserved. No part of this publication may be reproduced, distributed, or transmitted in any form or by any means, including photocopying, recording, or other electronic or mechanical methods, without written permission of the publisher.

Editor - Kaycee Hawn
Book Design - LJ Reynolds
Cover Design - Michelle Brodeur

Sapphire Books Publishing, LLC
P.O. Box 8142
Salinas, CA 93912
www.sapphirebooks.com

Printed in the United States of America
First Edition – July 2017

This and other Sapphire Books titles can be found at
www.sapphirebooks.com

Dedication

To Terrie, for her belief in me and in this work...and for her enduring patience.

Acknowledgment

To Chris Svendsen of Sapphire Books, for championing this project and to all the warm, beautiful women writers in the Sapphire family. And to my editor, Kaycee Hawn, and my cover designer, Michelle Brodeur.

To Emily Whitman for her inspiration and to the women in our class who evolved into my fantastic critique group. Thank you Leann Elwood McLellan, Kylie Schachte, Elena Wiesenthal, Mary Rose, Suzanne Frank, and Lori Ubell. And a special thanks to Kylie for her pep talks and her fine edits.

To my friends who read the first ragged version, I so appreciate your support and encouragement.

To my parents, Sebastian and Josephine Maggiore, and my sister, Mary Schmidt, thank you for having been a part of my summer world in Maine.

Dolores Maggiore

Chapter One

YESTERDAY AND TODAY

Yesterday

What if I had been born a boy in 1939? I was just cooling it outside the latrine at the boys' camp. The camp had been abandoned since the '30s; now it was just some place to finally split from my folks. We were vacationing at the stupid Lodge across the road, and I felt completely trapped. Being a sixteen year old girl – well, almost sixteen – in 1959 was kind of like being in prison.

The sun was high and hot now. Flies swarmed around the latrine's screen door. Hanging from one hinge, the door gave a dry creak as I pulled it open. The air changed. All was still, a stillness that seemed baked in time – thick, dense, and dank – making it hard to breathe deeply. The urine scent caught in the front of my throat.

A drugged state took over my mind and body. I seemed to float all the way to the back stall. Penciled names wiggled on the walls.

Uncle Sam Wants You!

I stumbled into a cubicle and landed on the dried-up toilet. I sat on the cool porcelain rim and pulled my feet up under me.

Sweat poured down my straggly hair, framing

my clammy-cold forehead. My eyes clouded over. That old, faint feeling returned; I was being pulled into a waking dream. I tried to focus. I started to count. To name all the colors I could think of. I attempted to read the poem Katie and I used to laugh about. There it was on the wall, worn away, words fuzzy, but still readable.

Here I sit,
to take a shit,
paid my dime
to take my time,
but alas my heart,
I only fart.

I heard voices, different voices. At least two or three. Boys. Not one of them still alive.

"*Hey, got there first.*" Pushing and shoving. Tinkling sounds. Water running.

"*Shush! Tonight, behind the crafts cabin; we'll do it tonight.*"

"*Yeah. I'll get the rest.*"

I tried to open my eyes. The light faded in my vision again. A shirt disappeared and reappeared, a name written on the back: Roger. A taller, older blonde was squishing a small boy up against the wall. Faces were Dali-like. Slithery oblongs.

"*Ya like it, Billy Boy?*" snarled Roger, grinding into Billy's pelvis.

"*I swear, I won't tell,*" said Billy.

A deep voice boomed in, "*Stop punking around. Pick on somebody your own size.*"

Billy's blurred figure scattered, wet shorts knotting up around his thighs.

Roger turned, ready to block or punch. "*Yeah, stud, why aren't you balling the chickies? Got stood up?*"

"*Shut up, fag. It's early.*"

I heard a scuffle. Lights went out. Pee pinged chime-like on porcelain. Doors shut; springs snapped and reverberated. Screams pierced the air. A lone bugle horn, muffled and warped, played a sorrowful "Taps." A hand slithered along my throat, rubbed my clavicle, and rested a minute on my chest before the imprint puffed back out.

Today After Breakfast

As we pushed through the screen door of the Lodge dining hall, I nudged Katie gently in the direction of my cabin. We had to get away from the hall; too many guests liked to chew the fat out front. We could be alone behind my folks' cabin.

We sat on a bed of dried pine needles, leaning up against the cabin wall. I studied her face. Katie had been my best summer buddy these past seven years that my family had been vacationing at the Lodge.

"You can't say anything to anybody," I said after I told her about the dream. I swam in her blue-eyed gaze. She looked worried. "I don't know what that dream was about. My Sicilian grandmother, Francesca, she could dream the past and the future. Ha! I guess I inherited it."

"Are you…do you see ghosts?" Katie twisted her Peter-Pan collar.

"Not really. It's only happened once or twice before."

"Well, are you…?"

"Looney tunes? No. I'll tell you more if it happens again. Please don't go away."

Katie rubbed my shoulder, her pageboy hairdo falling across her freckled face. I could tell she was trying hard not to look worried.

"I care about you," she said, "and I don't want you to cut me out of this!"

"I know or feel things. I mean, yesterday, I dreamt…I know this is crazy, but I think someone is dead. In the latrine, well you know how creepy it is. These guys, I could feel the vibration of their banging around, and they were plotting something against someone. The air turned ice cold. I just knew in my bones…"

"Jeez!" Katie hopped to her feet, rubbing her hands up and down her downy Irish arms. "Okay, got it. No more for now. Okay?" Katie's eyes were pleading. "Promise we'll be all right."

"Promise."

"Good." She pursed her lips, and then nudged me with her elbow. "Goose, you know how much I dig hanging out with you. Besides, you really get me." She let my ponytail glide through her fingers. She pulled me to my feet; her soft look lingered a moment on me.

We traipsed through the field across from the cabin, Katie oohing and aahing at the chill dew of the weeds wrapping round her tanned legs. I joked and sang "Great Balls of Fire." We ran, tripped on mole holes, and forged our way to the old camp rec hall, a good place to start our morning wanderings. As we drew closer to the rec Hall, we became almost solemn. We walked more slowly, wondering what we would find today.

Katie and I entered through the glass double doors of the rec hall. This was sacred space, encased in small, paned windows, which allowed the shifting rays of the sun to filter through the pine trees and dance across the floorboards. Photos, carvings, and trophies lined the pine board walls, like icons waiting for our devotions to begin. The building was perched atop the slope overlooking the shooting range, and the whole precipice threatened to erode into the lake below. Katie didn't know it yet, but I sensed something evil – the smell of mold, maybe dead animals, but the smell of death for sure – had already begun to shift the slope beneath our feet.

Katie and I dared to turn our backs to the drop-off of the land. We hoisted ourselves up onto the window seats lining the room. With the scent of mildew and thirty-year-old sweat in our nostrils, we believed we could see boys suiting up for games, pulling on shin guards, and catcher's masks, and cleats. The trunks beneath the bench seats held all the necessary gear: mice-gnawed, brittle leather still reeking of sweat-won games. Dirty socks, a stray cap, and cups – those weird boy things – lay about.

"Hey, Katie, let's do it," I said, gesturing to the pile of gear. "You game?"

"Yuck. You really want to put it on?" Katie asked, fingering a cob-webby sock.

"Yeah. Kinda. Can you reach that thing?" I asked, turning a deep shade of red.

"That thing? It's a cup. I've seen my cousin's." Katie picked one up, passed it to me, and rubbed her hand off on her shorts.

I giggled at the feel of it in my hands. I poked it down into my underpants and created a nice, big bulge in my shorts.

"Hey Katie," I said, imitating a husky boy voice. "Wanna be my girlfriend?" I strutted over close to Katie.

Katie let loose a high-pitched squeal and patted

the bulge in my shorts. "God, take that out! It's like too real. Here, put a mask on, at least."

As soon as I put the mask on, the action began – the crack of the bat, the scuffle of dirt, a streak.

I wondered if this was really happening. I made the creaking door sound from the new, spooky TV show *Inner Sanctum* but stopped; I wasn't ready for Katie to think I was totally crazy.

It was all coming back. I didn't want to go through all that again – doctors, my father crazy with worry, and my mother cursing my grandmother's gift of dreaming. Back then, everyone finally decided that I was just a bit kooky over my grandmother's death, and that I wasn't really seeing things. Well…sort of decided.

These visions of the past lurked around the camp, drawing me to the rec hall today as if to a funeral memorial.

After an hour of goofing around a` la 1939, Katie and I went to the beach and dashed headlong into the chilly water, Bermuda shorts, polo shirts, and all. We made our routine canoe ride to the float and dove for stray golf balls.

Lying on the float, Katie slapped me on the back. "One more dive?" The twinkle in her eye suggested a dare.

"Okay. I'll bite." I hesitated, hoping just to bake a little longer on the float.

"Well, we dive in together and see who touches the bottom first. Then we grab something…"

"Right. Whoever gets back on the float first – with something in hand – wins. Got it," I said.

"But something, well, something really far out," said Katie putting on flesh-colored nose plugs.

"Not a rock?" I poked her gently in the ribs.

"No," she smiled, "something special."

Toes wrapped around the edge of the float, we sprung off and dove straight down. I touched powdery, lake-bottom dirt. Katie had something solid in her hand, I could tell.

We used each other's bodies like ladders to ascend. I reached around and wrestled Katie's prize out of her hand. We struggled for a moment, but I was stronger.

I spouted bubbles as we broke the surface. "Winner!" I raised my hand with the object. "Got something."

"Mine!" Katie snarled.

"Like heck," I said. For the first time, we both got a good look at the item in my hand: a four inch lacquered penknife. I pried it open, then flicked off encased mud and rust, scraping it with my nail to shine up my treasure. It was engraved *BC, anodized special.*

Katie swore she had touched it first. I wouldn't let her have the knife back. It felt alive and vibrating in my hand. I knew this knife was the real thing.

"Katie," I blurted out, grabbing for her arm. "Stop! This knife, it's real. It's telling me something, like, like the dreams. Please."

Katie jerked her arm away. "I'll tell you something – you're a real drag!"

She jumped into the canoe and set off for shore, leaving me on the float. Katie looked back with pure disgust in her eyes and shouted, "You stink!"

Her words stung but didn't take away the excitement of holding treasure from the deep. I didn't know why I had been such a creep to begin with, stealing the knife from Katie. I hadn't even thought about it. I started the slow, cold crawl back to shore.

As my arm cut through the water, a split-second icy freeze almost stole my breath as well as my artifact. My high spirits disappeared, and my upside-down stomach told me something about this knife. Something dark. Yeah, my death if I didn't get back to shore.

In my panic to speed up, I had swum off course, into the "narrows" area of the lake. Something wrapped itself around my ankles. Was it seaweed? It slithered up my calves. I didn't dare break my stride to feel for it. I tried to focus. Was I going into a dream? A distorted shape loomed ahead of me in the shaded, murky light. Something rotten and decomposing. Something dangerous still, though no camper had been here in twenty years.

I threw myself on the shore, petrified, at the foot of the camp shooting range. Not hard to imagine a practice gone wrong in that dark, cut away bank, the lines still strung to pull shooting targets back and forth. The soft, rot-damaged wood in the platform still held .22 shells shining among the otherwise darkened stains of seeping earth. A grave for casings.

Padding along the pine path up from the lake, I remembered the last time I had a waking dream. My parents reassured me it was only Grandma Francesca saying her dying good-bye to me, because we were close and she wanted me to know my heritage.

She showed me those things, like a dream – a very real dream of what had happened centuries before in Giuliana, Sicily, as if I had been Queen Constance living in the castle there. Ha! Me living in a swanky, old castle. Maybe more like hanging out in a cold dungeon. My dreams were part cool, part creepy.

What would Katie think about my dreams? I couldn't tell her everything yet. Shoot. I just wanted to get lost in Maine, its incense, and Katie.

I couldn't shake the feeling that this was a life or death thing, but I didn't know why yet. It would be my death if I didn't get back to the cabin to change into dry clothes—and to the dining hall before my parents flipped out about my lateness.

Chapter Two

Lunch

Made it to lunch, clean Lacoste shirt and Bermudas, dry Keds and ponytail. My parents, Barney, short for Bastiano, and Giusy, for Giuseppina, Mazzini just looked at me that look. They wouldn't make a scene, not here in the dining room.

I pretended to listen to my mother talk about me wearing my "nice, little sundress." I craned my neck to catch a glimpse of Katie down the other end of the dining room. She looked all normal, with her shiny Breck-girl pageboy, one ear poking out, wearing those red pedal pushers and her saddle shoes with the pink gum soles. She was laughing with her parents as if nothing was bothering her. Her face was open and warm, just the way I loved it when she was smiling at me.

I got away from my parents as soon as I could; I was afraid Katie would disappear.

Outside, she grabbed me by the arm right away. "Boy, I'm confused. First, you yell at me if I don't show to meet you before breakfast, and then you pull a stunt like that?"

Katie pulled me behind a massive yellow pine to shield us from the other guests leaving the dining hall. "What gives with you? We've been friends seven years now, and you still don't trust me?"

"No, wait. I should have explained better. I mean I do want to clue you in on the dream thing. I just got scared to let you see the knife. It was…buzzing. It felt electric!"

By now, I hardly dared to meet Katie's gaze. "I am so sorry. I was a real jerk."

I knew all was forgiven when she wiped my tears with her navy blue neckerchief. The smell of 47-11 cologne really perked me up too.

"Yeah." Katie sighed. "Hey, I've gotta tell you. My father was a real pain."

"What else is new? My neck is so sore from my mother!" I flipped back at her, chewing on a pine needle.

"C'mon, my father's usually cool."

She was right. Dr. Ron McGuilvry, Doc to me, was really neat, for a dad. I even liked his white bucks and madras Bermudas – something my father wouldn't be caught dead in.

"Okay, what'd he do?"

"Man! He almost had a cow when I asked about the old boys' camp. I just thought it'd be a blast to hear his stories from when he was a counselor there."

"Really? I don't know, Katie." I was getting that squirming feeling in my stomach like this might be quicksand Katie was pulling me into.

"When I asked him to help us get into all the old cabins, he really blew his stack. I swore we hadn't been poking around." Katie bit her lip. "I didn't mean to give anything away."

"Shoot! Listen, don't say another word to him. It's kind of our thing. Got it?"

"Well, he kind of flipped, like out of the blue," Katie said with a roll of her eyes.

"Like I said, 'mum.' But let's get out of the sap we're sitting in and back to the scene of the crime." I slapped Katie on the back, laughing, but I wasn't really joking.

In a few minutes, we had slipped into my parents' cabin to grab a composition notebook. We had to search for it a bit, because my family's things were always helter-skelter. My room was the sitting room, having the luxury of the Ben Franklin wood-burning stove in this budget, bare-walled cabin – not like Katie's folks' almost palatial deluxe cabin.

Notebook in hand, we dated the first page, Wed., June 26, 1959, 1:57 P.M. On the cover, we printed in bold letters 'The Case of the?'

We decided to go to the latrine to study the latrine walls. Of course, we named the log 'The Writing on the Wall.' Katie started taking notes. Her handwriting was a better "Catholic school style" than my left-handed hieroglyphics. We scanned the warped walls of the latrine inch by inch. Katie copied everything.

"For a good time, call Butch."

We saw the Brylcreem ad, *'Brylcreem, a little dab'll do ya.'*

"Yeah, a little jab'll do ya, yeah, like Butch."

"Butch, my ass."

"Yes, little one, watch your ass!"

Then there was the heart - *'Ron and Regina'*

"Do you think that's your dad?" I asked with a raised eyebrow.

"Nah. I don't know." Katie tucked her chin in and yawned. "But we could write in the margin, 'who are Ron and Regina?'"

We scooted away from the latrine through the wooded slope, gliding in the dried needles, moccasins skidding on the terrain.

"Whatd'ya think - not too dark today to go down the channel by the old beach?" Katie asked.

"You mean all the way to the dam?" I stretched my neck and yawned, feigning exhaustion. I didn't want Katie to know I was scared of the water over there.

"The creepy dam…with its wonderful collection of arachnids."

"Stop," I said. "You know I hate spiders."

"Spiders, nothing…" said Katie, waving me off.

"Bug off, or I will never show you the knife." I tried to bargain with her.

"Let's get going, and you can show me the knife in the canoe in case I have to stab a big, bad spider." Katie straightened up, and pulled her hair behind her ears.

"I'm going to dunk you," I threatened as I started singing Splish Splash.

"Nah, c'mon."

I eased the knife out of my pocket. I rubbed the initials B.C. and handed it forward to Katie.

Katie put the notebook under her jacket to accept my offering. The knife seemed to throb and jerk forward in my hands. She opened the blade slowly, uncrumbling some dried gunk and tested the blade.

"Ouch!"

I sat up instantly. I thought Katie had really hurt herself. She turned too quickly and—oops, girls overboard. Katie and I both splashed into the lake.

I gurgled, tasting the swampy water. "Save the book!"

Katie grabbed onto the gunnels. I swam and steered the canoe through the somewhat slimy, oil-slicked water back to shore. We were both safe, the book and knife too. We got back in the canoe and retrieved the paddle with a deep sucking sound from the clay muck.

Phew! What a stink! Flotsam and jetsam swirled in the water when I pulled up the paddle. Old, rotten leaves and shreds of canvas, a shirt? I prodded at the debris with the paddle. No, not a shirt…something solid, but spongy. Fighting back the urge to puke, I finally pushed and jabbed until I discovered parts of a raft.

"Huh? That's weird," I said. It looked like the one beached by the shooting gallery, but how could one of these have sunk?

We paddled slowly and rested a bit. I was not happy to be all the way down here at this end of the channel, full of years of rotting leaves, scum, and parts of motors. Dark branches cloaked the sky; they snagged at our clothes and limbs, drawing blood. Bugs appeared to feast on us. We were both scummy from our tumble in the lake, still wearing our clinging, mud-encrusted clam diggers and spongy, squirting Keds. My humor was dark, at best.

"Why are we going this far down the channel, Katie?" I hoped she was bored and uncomfortable. I was cranky because I hadn't confided more of my grandmother's story to her yet.

She replied, "Still too much sun and heat where we are. We'll go to the hatchery at the very end. Besides, we can wash up there."

"I'll take the canoe out just this side of the dam. Okay? Go, get onto the bank and tie us up," I said.

Katie was definitely off-kilter. She had slipped her footing by about a yard. One foot pressed into the dark sand on the bank and the other, about six inches lower, into the thick, oozing water.

"I, uh, can't move, I can't, my foot is stuck," said Katie.

Pushing and knocking rocks away, I helped Katie pry her foot out as some flotsam rose to the surface. It was a shirt cuff. We yanked; the material shredded and gave way. It kept on coming – first, a sleeve. It was plaid and gray-green, caked with mud and rust.

"That's strange. Who left their shirt?" Katie asked me.

It was strange, but we were filthy and slimy. I couldn't think about the mysterious shirt just then.

I shrugged. "Let's go to the hatchery. There's a drinking fountain and a faucet there."

We stowed our book and the shirt in the canoe and walked the two hundred feet to the hatchery. The parks guy greeted us. He saw our mucky clothes and joked about fish that live in the muck. Maybe we were leeches, he said. We used the hatchery's water to clean ourselves up a bit.

"Hey, when do you want to look at the shreds?" Katie asked on the ride back, referring to the shirt we'd found.

"Maybe it's an old-time trapper's or…" I knew it was something important when each thread seemed to wiggle in my hand, just like the peculiar aliveness I felt in the knife. "Let's look at it when we get back to the beach."

Anxious to investigate the piece of plaid history, we immediately beached, dried off in the sun, and stretched out with our wiggling toes in the sand. Carefully we unfolded the pieces of the shirt. The right front panel was all in one piece; also, the right sleeve. The right pocket was partly torn off, but a shredded hole went clear to the bottom of the panel. Weird, like it was all rust colored and brittle, but not oil-slicked like the rest.

"Katie, could you sew it, or just attach the parts? We can see how big it is and ask someone how old the material might be."

"No sweat. I'll dry it first and ask to borrow the treadle machine. I love that thing. Did you ever notice the pattern on the treadle? Like snakes," said Katie.

"You and your snakes."

I gave Katie a playful shove. She shoved back and started massaging my ribs.

"Ha! I'm the sewing machine, vibrating through every part of your body. Your teeth will begin to chatter."

I rolled over, doubling up with laughter – and maybe more. I just adored Katie's silly side.

Chapter Three

AT THE REC HALL

Y ou here?"

Katie's voice woke me, almost jostling me off the back window seat at the rec hall. I had fallen asleep after breakfast.

"Life just seems frozen here," I said, yawning.

"Frozen? Maybe it's the chilly fog this morning. Lake's almost got a veil."

"Doofus, I mean, like everything stops, everything is the same. That dart board looks like they were just in the middle of a game in 1939."

"We weren't even born yet. It's like your dream stuff."

"No, it's just I'm 'sensitive.' At home, I can feel, well, I know how things were in my house when it was built in 1917 – I've seen the owners, the Hamiltons, but not in real life. Real old fogies, tall and bony, and uptight. They had a child who died. I kind of heard the crying. I also saw my parents going to buy it in 1949. It's as if I knew how things had gone on and what would happen next." Uh oh. I saw Katie's eyes dart about.

"Katie, please don't think I'm weird."

"I don't, but it's kind of scary too. I do want to know. I want to be in on it, too."

I watched her grimace, a tender, dear smile, distorted by something else, the remnants of fear, disgust?

"Oh, Katie, it's just me, the same me as before."

Same as before? Yeah. I didn't like when things changed. If this new part of me scared her, what would she think about my other…changes? I couldn't deny that I had this…crush on her. What would she think of a queer? I mean, queers were like bloodsuckers, like that girl Janet who came to my sleepover last year. Man, she was trying to smooch all over me. Lucky for me, we locked her in the bathroom. Jeez. I wasn't like that. Was I?

"Where'd you go?" Katie asked. "You went Sleeping Beauty on me…I know it's the same you." She tried to soothe my thoughts from before.

"Sorry, I was just thinking about our case," I lied. "Let's grab the log; we've got to keep track of what we know."

"Right," said Katie, still staring at me with huge question marks blinking in her eyes. "I'll get the log."

Our Notes:

-Some boys, older boys: one, a bully, the other, a lady-killer

-younger, scared boy

-hearts and pictures of Katie's father (on the rec hall walls)

"Leave him out of this," said Katie.

"You said he was being really weird about this camp," I reminded her, "and the heart? It did say Ron."

"Shut up! He's my father," said Katie. "Besides, he never loved anyone but my mom."

"Okay, okay, and the tooth fairy?"

"Quit it," said Katie.

"Right. Hey, maybe we need a break. I'm feeling kinda sleepy." I decided to change the subject and the mood. "Wanna take a nap or just lie out in the sun?"

"Gosh, Pina, you really are becoming Sleeping Beauty." Katie laughed as she pushed me out the creaking door.

Baking in the sun, I pretended sleep. Something bugged me. Katie's dad was all over this camp, and Katie was intentionally keeping him out of the picture. She seemed afraid that her dad might actually know something about all this.

Pretend sleep drifted towards the real thing. This mid-afternoon grass felt warm and safe. Even the dirt felt right. The sound of golfers on the other side of the white pines grew distant. I lost track of Katie, who had gone off to gather berries. The sun was like a big purple blotch under my eyelids, and soon I forgot everything.

I was aware of the earth thumping, of pounding, like a bunch of people running hard. Giggles and words like "jerk" and "jackass" and a stronger thump. Two ten-year-olds were play-wrestling at my feet. One called the other Billy, tickling him. Billy squealed and shoved "Wolfgang" playfully. Sitting up, Billy jerked Wolfgang's head.

"C'mon, seriously, would you stick up for me? Like not let me get hurt?" said Billy.

"Who's going to hurt you? He's a jerk, but he won't do anything really bad."

"Hey, Wolfie, what if he's already doing something bad?"

"Well, tell someone, someone important, like the director."

"Director's a pervert."

"That's a rumor. C'mon let's get ice cream."

Wolfie got up, and Billy followed.

I woke with a start, feeling a cold dribble down my chin. I dreamt about butter crunch ice cream. No, I dreamt I was wrestling. I felt the pebbles and heard the hollow banging of the rec hall door as the old panes rattled in their casements, most of the putty gone. I opened my eyes to see Katie coming at me with the catcher's mitt full of blueberries.

"Pina! You all right? You're absolutely white."

Katie was down on her knees by my side. Her hand on my forehead felt so good, and the heady smell of the blueberries roasting in the sun made me hesitate to break the spell.

I ran my fingers on the stubble of the dried weeds and looked into her eyes. I had to trust her.

"Katie," I started. "I just had a…well, you know, I saw things."

"Yeah?" She extended the mitt of berries towards me. She looked nervous.

"The little kid, Billy…" I said.

"Yeah, go on."

"Well, maybe someone…" I munched some blueberries. "Maybe someone is really bugging…I mean…" I stumbled and blurted the words out all at once, "Pervert – maybe there's a pervert."

Katie blanched and stared blankly off to the view of Sebago Lake on the horizon. She patted my wrist and mumbled, "It was a dream, Pina, just a dream."

She muttered about having to do something before lunch – I couldn't quite make out what – and ran off, leaving me alone to chew on grass and worry.

Outside the dining hall a few minutes before the lunch gong, Katie bounced in front of me, balancing from foot to foot.

"Pick a tree," she said, pointing to the big yellow pines by the tennis court directly in front of the hall. "There's a hidden message for you after lunch."

I had been looking at Katie quite a bit lately, and with her dancing in front of me like this, there was a lot to look at. Her pullover top was bouncing too. I didn't know if the message I was receiving was the hidden message she had intended to send.

The BLTs never went down so quickly. I was out of the warm, pine-smoked dining hall in a hiccup. Katie followed and snatched the bundle from under the tree. The bundle unfurled into a plaid flag-like shirt; it was a bit sappy from its time under the tree. Katie had reattached the pieces so it actually looked like something to be worn again. Without blinking, I pulled it out of Katie's hands to examine it closer.

I started to slip the shirt on, but just as I was buttoning the top button, Katie lunged for me.

"Hey, me first," she said.

I jerked away, but Katie just managed to snag it. I felt her nails dig into my chest, drawing blood and a sharp pain. I heard a slight tearing sound where she had grabbed me.

"Look," I said. "You made me stain the shirt." Droplets of blood started to seep through the chest.

"It kind of matches the rust stains on it." Katie grimaced. "I really hurt you."

"No, I'm okay." The blood – and the rust – confused me. "Here," I said, almost ripping the shirt off. "Try it on."

As Katie put the shirt on, I stared long and hard.

"Katie, look, did you cut it by the pocket?" There was a hole right over the chest again, just like when we'd found it.

I looked down at my chest, where Katie had drawn blood. There was a large welt now, only it didn't look like scratch marks from Katie's nails. It looked more as if a sharp branch had poked deep into my skin. I was overcome with uneasiness at the sight.

"Katie, can we just put the shirt away for now? It's kind of creepy."

Katie took it off slowly. We looked at each other and, without a word of explanation, just started running. I think we just needed to do something really physical.

We chased each other over to the camp cabins. Finally exhausted, we dropped to the ground in front of the older cabins and decided to explore one we didn't know at all.

Getting down to this cabin was tricky. The door was locked, so we had to slide down the slope to crawl through the lattice that surrounded the basement. Spider webs were all over and glass shimmered all over the dirt floor. The cupboards pulled away from the frame. We hesitated to go much further. It looked spooky. I saw a mouse and froze in place.

Katie noticed that the "basement" connected two cabins. Light came from some more latticework on the other side. As we drew closer to investigate, something fell from a nook in the lattice.

"What is that?" I pointed to the whitish object on the ground.

"A piece of paper. It's all balled up. Yuck. It fell next to something awful. Is that dog poop or people poop?" Katie pointed to a petrified white and brown turd.

"Oh, yuck! Hey look, there's a trap door in the floor above it. Here, use the stick. Did you get it?"

Katie started getting nervous. "Got it. Can we get outta here now? Let's go to the other cabin."

"Shoot, Katie! It's gotta be a clue. Don't go all scaredy-cat on me now!" I scrunched up my face at Katie. Why was she backing off?

"Can't we just go someplace else? I can't breathe here."

"We've got to read this now. Look, if it's about your dad—"

"No. It's not that. I promise." Katie shoved the paper in her shorts pocket and sighed loudly.

Before I knew it, Katie pulled away from me. I had to follow her—and the note. We crawled out from under the crafts cabin and scrambled up the hill, scraping our way through pine needles and dried branches. We found ourselves on the deck of another one of the cabins. The place was overgrown with shrubs and new baby pine trees. Katie continued to wriggle her way in between trunks and branches. She found a door that was cracked open that she was determined to enter; I was determined to follow her.

The door squeaked and stuck, but finally, with both of us banging into it, lurched open. A long, plain table was in front, and some stools scattered around. A funny metal thing with a dried up, skinny rubber hose sat on the desk. We would definitely have to explore more later, but for now, it would be a great hiding place for the shirt and the paper!

Katie said, "Uh-oh! I have to go to the bathroom."

"No. You can't go back to your cabin or the main house now! Sure you're not just running away from me with that note?"

"No! I've gotta go now. Look for something, Pina."

    Dolores Maggiore

Convinced that Katie wasn't escaping with the note, I searched the ground. I saw a raised board. "Look," I said. "A trap door in the floor."

We eased the trap, found ourselves looking into the basement. I thought of the other trap door we had just seen…and the poop. Uh huh. Looking at Katie and back at the empty space in the floor, I giggled. "Well, why not? No one will know."

"I don't care, I just gotta go now!"

Katie lowered her shorts, turning around to see if I was watching. I turned away for a second and then snuck another sheepish glance. She tugged at her panties urgently. I heard her let out a light sigh. Her whole body seemed to ease itself down in a flowing movement when she exhaled.

"I hope you're not watching," she mumbled, as a burpy, gas-passing noise escaped.

"Hey. It's just natural. Nothing to be embarrassed about." I stifled a giggle. I was afraid she would fall through. Now, that would be ugly. That thought made me realize I had to go too.

Although I was afraid of splinters and spiders, as soon as I squatted over the hole in the floor, I was overcome by the rising smells of damp earth, rotting leaves, dank mushrooms, and mice.

"Please, no jokes about spiders," I begged. I did my business, then stood and pulled up my shorts.

"Umm. What a cute doolie you have." Katie smirked.

"Katie!"

"Hey, sweetie, it is cute. I'm only playing around with you."

We had just emerged from some rite of passage. We were now members of a wilder group. Maybe the camp was really drawing us in.

"Was that like sick?" Katie asked.

"It was weird. I really felt like a boy, a boy doing what a boy would have done."

"You think? Kind of like an initiation?" Katie stroked her chin.

"Should we put on skins and loin cloths? Like, where are the vines to swing on?" I joked, but I had to admit to myself that I did feel different.

"Quick, close the hatch," said Katie.

As we attempted to cover up the wafting reminder of our brave new world, we returned to the past. "Let's look at the paper now," Katie said, handing it over to me. "I promised you, didn't I?"

We pulled stools up to the long table and sat. She said, "Unroll it, spread it out. Easy, it might break."

"There's a date, 7-9-39. It's a calendar page," I said.

"It's a bunch of scribble." Katie looked at the page and shook her head.

"Let me see. Um…it's ripped. I can make out words like 'all cut' and 'square.' Then, a drawing of a box." I scratched my head and chewed my nail. "This is wacky. It sounds like it's a sign, like a secret group tattoo. I mean, when I fell asleep in the bathroom, someone said something about a secret group meeting behind the crafts cabin, like, *'shush, tonight's the night. Get the rest.'* Let's keep thinking on it. But I really have to get outta here. I feel dizzy and sick – something's bad in here, like cleaning stuff."

Katie looked around the room. "I get it now. This is a science lab." Katie was thrilled. Her eyes were huge. She loved science. "We could come back with gas masks," she said.

"You jerk, Katie. You'd look like a turtle."

We reverted to poking and tickling, as we left the pungent cabin.

❧ ❧ ❧ ❧

Katie had to go for a drive with her parents the next day, which gave me the chance I was waiting for. I grabbed one of my father's handkerchiefs to wrap around my nose. I got back into the science cabin, snatched the shirt from the cupboard, and headed out to the rec hall. There it was safe; there I knew the feel of the floorboards and the waves in the glass. There, I thought I knew what was real and what was – I don't know – real, a long time ago, or real in some other world.

I took off my tennis shirt and put on the worn plaid. I buttoned it slowly and was about to sit down on the floor, back against the benches. Something threw me to the ground. Felt like my legs came out from under me, like the time my parents had to give me that medicine with codeine again. Like I was part dead, my legs useless, then more dead, up to my neck, and then it sucked in my head too, and I was really all dead.

I heard a rumbling in my ears, like being in the New York City subway, my head speeding through the tunnels with a warm, kind of prickly feeling in my stomach. I guessed that maybe I wasn't really dead. My left side felt like all these fingers were crawling over it. Then there was a gash, something sharp in my heart, as if I was being stabbed. I put my hand up to the rip in the shirt. Now I was awake and alive but hurting so bad. I felt around and tore the shirt off, sure that blood would cover my chest. Sure enough, there was a thin line, about four inches long, right over my breast. Just as soon as I looked at it, the wound seemed to zip itself up and disappear.

I screamed. It came back to me from the four walls and the rattling glass doors. The funnel canyon of the hills down to the outlet of the lake also seemed to echo back my cry. I flew to the doors, my real shirt in one hand and holding my heart as though afraid it might fall out. Then I would really, really be dead.

I cried face down in the grass for a long time. I knew that I was either crazy or something really bad happened with the shirt. I had to put it back. I had to tell Katie. I had a million ideas going on in my head. My mother would sob. My father would blanch and rush me to a doctor to have my head examined.

No. Katie and I would just figure this out. We could play detective. Only now, it didn't feel like a game.

Katie was smart and curious and wouldn't rat on me. Besides, she was my friend, she made me laugh, and I would trust her. She was tender with me, took care of me. I had even shown her my old diary where I wrote I was ugly. Katie had brushed my bangs back from my forehead and told me she thought I was cute. It was the first time I ever felt like that could be true.

Thinking about those quiet times with Katie, I felt shivers. My knees got all soupy when she did things like that. I didn't like girls; I couldn't. I mean, I knew I liked Katie, but that way? A lesbo?

I told my head to shut up. I couldn't think about that stuff now. I had had enough for the day. I'd tell Katie more when she got back. All of it. I really would.

Chapter Four

BLOOD SISTERS

I needed a break. Couldn't I just "be" for one day? The morning humidity was heavy on my skin; it matched my mood. In the dining room at breakfast, I gave Katie a lazy jerk of my head in the direction of the camp. She knew to meet me afterwards on the porch of the rec hall.

We sat on the brown, peeling porch steps, Katie just staring at me. I wanted to tell her just a little about the shirt – just that I had a hunch about it. She looked at me in a way that was becoming more familiar as I told her about the events of the day before. It was a look that said, "I wanna believe, but really?"

I told her how the shirt took over, and I "became" whoever had worn it. I was stabbed; I was bleeding. That was how it was with my dreams. Sometimes I had no warning they were coming; they snuck up like ether in a dentist's office. All of me got pulled into that cold, black, ether mask.

Katie's eyes roved over me, just for a second. I hoped it was with understanding and maybe something more. But when Katie spoke, she didn't reassure me, she just wanted to go back to the "science spot."

We walked the short distance to the science cabin. Katie pulled out some rope she had brought with her and told me to tie it around the big pine next to the science cabin. Little by little, we lowered ourselves to the "basement" level – the space below the trap door we used as a latrine the day before. Underneath the cabin, we found the science storeroom: a smashed-open cupboard and powders all over. We remembered to tie our handkerchiefs around our noses to protect ourselves from the fumes. I looked over at Katie and smiled; we both looked like bandit thieves.

The colors were beautiful: a bright blue and a soft yellow dusting on a broken bottle marked "Sulphur," and something like those silver balls you put on cookies. That jar was whole and the little ball of silver rolled back and forth, still magic after all these years. One box had a skull-and-crossbones; we left that one alone. There were also some neat glass jars and small, wooden racks of test tubes. There was a big, dried rust stain, sort of near some—oops, that was where we went to the bathroom. Now *that* was a bad smell, although apparently heaven to the flies zigzagging all around us. But that rust stain was definitely weird.

"I'm gonna get a chem set for my birthday." Katie broke the silence.

"Creep!" I teased, but I really got stuck on the word birthday.

"But we can use it together. We could figure out all those chemicals and find out what they did with them."

"Far out! I want to analyze the spots on the shirt. When's your birthday, anyway?" I tossed back as nonchalantly as I could.

"Oh, crumb. I didn't want to tell you 'cause I asked my parents if we could take you, and they're being jerks. 'Oh no,' said my mother, 'birthdays are for families.' Why doesn't she just stay in her own world!

She's always half out of it, anyway! I told her you were like family to me, more maybe.

"It's Saturday, my birthday. I'm turning sixteen, and we're going to Star Island in New Hampshire. It's an inn right on the beach. It's got these old-fashioned rockers where I curl up, so no one can tell I'm there. I used to pretend I could rock myself right off the porch and go flying out onto the water. No one would know." Katie sighed. "Privacy, at last!"

I heard her say I was "more than family." So that's how she thinks of me.

I was already thinking about what I could make for her birthday and decided on a pine needle basket. I'd need to go down to the library to get a book on old Indian crafts.

"Hey, where'd you go?" asked Katie when I didn't respond right away.

"Nowhere. C'mon. Let's see if we can get into the crafts cabin. Maybe they're connected. Or here," I said as I picked up a small sledgehammer my foot had dislodged from the loose, dried dirt. "We could break the hasp on the front door."

We hoisted ourselves up and around to the front of the crafts cabin. I swung the sledge once, the rotten wood let go of its screws, and the lock flew off. We were in.

Again, the still air, closed off for twenty years, greeted me, but there was a sweetness too, like dried flowers. Lavender, maybe, and berries. A can of rubber cement, all dried up, still held that gasoline-like smell nestled among balls of yarn. Bright yellows, royal blues: the colors of the camp.

As I started to rub strands of the wool through my fingers, memories of my old childhood blanket, tangerine and green wool, started to flood me. Not for long. Katie burst in, letting out a war hoop, triumphantly waving what appeared to be a six-inch bone.

"Cool! Look what I got!" She laughed and hooted while baring her teeth like a wild woman. I quickly clapped Katie on the back. Another discovery!

"My cavewoman!" I teased, but my stomach had started to turn. "What do you think…?"

I stopped short. I couldn't tell if I was scared about the bone, jealous, or what. Maybe so lovesick over Katie, this silly, gutsy version of Katie, that it hit me like a club, hard as this bone. I was missing her already, waiting for her to leave for her birthday celebrations.

Katie let out just one big guffaw. Then she started to chew on her lower lip. "Don't know, maybe a dog, maybe…Man! Promise to wait till I come back from my birthday to find out?"

"Like I'm going to be able to analyze it…" My sarcasm came out sharper than I intended. Probably from my lonely place.

"Shoot, Pin. I wish you were coming with me." Katie laid the bone aside and gingerly placed her hand on my wrist. She raised her eyes to meet my gaze. "It'll feel weird without you."

My knees were water. I knew I was already missing Katie. We belonged together. I realized we were still holding each other by the wrists, and our smiles were slipping into somewhat sad grimaces.

"I uh…I uh…I'm gonna miss you," I managed to get out without totally turning fuchsia.

Katie turned away as if looking for something to wrap the bone in. Still, I managed to get a quick glimpse of her blushing face. Together, we creaked open a crooked, warped drawer containing some scissors and razor blade-like knives. There were some bits of cloth we could use to wrap the bone. I started to reach in, and then my hand slipped.

"Ouch!" I screamed.

Katie spotted the blood pooling on my finger. "Is it deep?"

"I don't know. Do you have a hanky?"

The hanky turned pink and then a deeper red, then brown. No, I wasn't going to faint.

"I'm okay," I said. "Hey look, I have color-changing blood." I tried to stay light and airy, so Katie wouldn't worry. I was fighting back the hint of nausea I felt. I just couldn't pass out, not now.

"You sure?" Katie took my hand and made as if to kiss my boo-boo. "Wanna be blood sisters? It won't hurt; you're already fatally wounded." She smiled a warm smile that reached into my heart and held it tight. Yes, I was fatally wounded!

"Here, watch!" She pricked her finger and sucked the bead of blood. Katie was humming *Everyday* by Buddy Holly and bouncing around in rhythm.

"Yes! I am yours; you are mine in this co-mingling." I had read that someplace. I was desperately trying to stop myself from blubbering, "I think I love you."

"I am yours; you are mine." Katie gave me an open and vulnerable look that I drank in.

We squished our bloody fingers together, trying to laugh even though the moment felt serious. We took turns sucking first the other's finger and then our own. My stomach got all the more squishy. Good squishy, with a little bit of "uh oh" bad.

I heard the last lyrics to the Buddy Holly song Katie had been humming; "love like yours will surely come my way."

Chapter Five

BIRTHDAY PLANS

This was going to be a painful day. I knew it from the time I got up. My mother was calling to me from her room on the other side of the cabin bathroom. She was telling me I should wear my "nice plaid pleated skirt" to go to the library with her.

"Right, Mommy, like the books will care," I shot back.

"You listen, miss," she called back in what she thought was an affectionate voice. "Someday you'll be happy I made you pay attention to your clothes."

"Right, Mommy. What would people say about my pedal pushers?"

"Don't be so smart. You know what I mean."

I was tired of shouting through walls, but I couldn't resist, "No, mother, what do you mean?"

"It's time…"

"Eight a.m.?" I thought I'd help her out a bit.

"It's time," she said with an authoritarian edge, "you stopped acting like such a tomboy. Grow up!"

Ouch! This library jaunt was going to be a real blast. I just couldn't wait. Sigh.

My father passed through my room to turn on the radio. Winking at me, he hummed notes of "Sugartime" as the McGuire Sisters drowned out my mother's complaints.

After a near-silent breakfast, my mother and I set off. Her litany of complaints started as soon as we were on our way. Chief among them was all the time I spent with Katie.

"You know I like the McGuilvrys, and Katie's just lovely, but..."

"But what, Mommy?" Oh God, why did I have to bite?

"People might talk." She stopped to wave at fellow guests walking on the other side of the road. "Say 'good morning,' Pina."

"Good morning, Pina," I said.

"Stop it this minute," she snapped, "You're getting too old. You should be dressing more like your cousin Mary Grace. More, well, lady-like."

My guts were churning. Don't say one dang word, I said to myself.

She continued to ramble, most of which I tuned out, except for "lovesick puppy dog."

We arrived just in the nick of time. Five more minutes and I could have been accused of matricide! I immediately got the book *How to Make a Pine-needle Basket,* so that I could make my present for Katie. After that, I hung out in a quiet corner of the library and avoided my mother. When I was with her, I could block out the sound of her voice, but it didn't completely block the sting of her words. By now, I felt as if bees covered me. I was a tomboy. So what! That didn't mean anything. I knew I couldn't scream in the blooming library, but dammit!

So, did my mother think I was 'that way'? If I... were, I mean I didn't think so, but...that would go over like World War Three. I remember my schoolteacher aunt's friend. What was it my father called her? Spinster bulldagger?

I had to clear my thoughts and be a blank slate so my mother couldn't read anything on my face. I would have to talk about food or plants lining the road on the walk home. Something boring like that.

After an uneventful, semi-quiet stroll home along the elm tree-lined road, we arrived back at the cabin before lunchtime. Pleased with our outing, my mother allowed me to change into my blue jeans and my favorite red pointed-collar shirt. I also stashed the library book in my drawer before she could snoop. Yet another thing to hide.

Lunch came and went. My mother chatted about the food; my father made sure his mouth was full. Apparently, neither of us felt like talking.

Afterwards, I had a few hours until dinner. I scooped up pine needles on the way to the camp latrine. I had brought a cup to scoop some water from the lake. I made my way back up the slope, trying not to slosh too much water over the sides. I put my pine needles in the water to soak, then slumped against the wall of the latrine. I tried to read the next set of directions in my book, but started to nod off in the stale heat of the latrine. The next thing I knew was the brassy sound of far-away voices.

"Hey, swine! You, Romeo, better be careful. One of 'ems gonna get a big belly."

"Shut up, you don't know anything."

"Well, maybe your cock will get big, oozing, bumps."

There was a thud, and the door swung hard. Sweat filled the air and something else, urine as someone screamed about *"pissing on him"* and *"cutting off his dick."*

I jerked awake in terror. Were they still there?

Who was Romeo? What was he up to? I'd do more of the basket another day. Grandma wasn't just saying "hello" from the past. Maine and this camp were telling me a whole story.

My mind went to the bone Katie and I had found the other day. The one I had promised not to touch… yet. What did a "cock" bone look like? Katie would have to look up info in her father's medical books.

Chapter Six

BASKET MAKING

Next morning, the weather was perfect – not too chilly, but still that crisp bite that made me pull my nose back under the covers of that half-itchy, over washed plaid wool blanket. My ears were awake enough to hear my father puttering around the room. He was trying to make a fire in the stove, to tempt me out of bed. I breathed in the sulphur, heard the whoosh of the first papers taking flame, and, soon enough, the spitting and crackling as the sappy kindling caught. I waited for that familiar incense-like fragrance, always powerful enough to take me over, body and soul. This was my church-like moment.

I played my morning ritual with my dad.

"Is it warm yet, Dad?" I said.

"A steam bath," he answered.

"No, really?"

"So warm I can't put my socks on yet."

"Is the bathroom empty?"

"Your mother's still snoring. It's all yours."

I loved the ritual, always the same. I think my father never got tired of playing pioneer, making the homestead ready and safe for his 'young'uns and missus.' Sometimes, just to get me up laughing, he'd recite an old limerick or ballad. He'd put on this big actor-voice and start in:

"...a bunch of the boys were whooping it up..."

Eventually overcome by the woodsy warmth, the laughter, and my father's fresh smell in his athletic shirt, I'd swing my feet onto the chilly floorboards and start my day.

I managed to sneak out of the cabin with a good chunk of time before breakfast. The basket was where I'd left it in the latrine. The needles were pliable and those I had already formed still held their shape. I threaded in and out and over and between rows and the contrast of the black thread and browned needles was quite attractive. I knew Katie would love it. Now I just needed to let it dry in the sun. The latrine would be a perfect place to dry it, but Katie and I were going to go there after breakfast to talk about the 'bumps and bellies' and 'dick bones' I had heard about in my dream the day before.

If I could put it up on top of the light fixture, Katie would never notice it. My feet almost slid out from under me because of the dust. I finally managed to slip it above the fixture, but something fell. It fluttered to the ground, folded so small.

Shoot! By now, I didn't have a whole lot of time before breakfast, but I just had to open it up. The paper was yellowed and brittle. Several pieces crumbled and fell apart as I tried to unfold it. The bits of the note on the floor seemed more like a jigsaw puzzle. What I could piece together left me pretty stumped.

I was able to decipher, "He did it" and "We threat to cu off his dic." I found some shreds with parts of names, but I couldn't rearrange them to spell out a whole name, just "Ro" and "Bi" or "Bu."

I was totally frustrated. The first gong for breakfast rang out through the pines. Without thinking,

I shoved the remaining parts of the parchment-like note into my pocket. When I pulled my hand out, I left behind a wad of confetti.

Chapter Seven

BONES

On my way back from the latrine, I slowed my pace at the last minute as I approached my parents, who were entering the dining hall for breakfast. We ate mostly in silence, blueberries in cream, pork sausages, and eggs. Across the room, Katie motioned to me, miming as though she were flipping through pages. I figured Katie had had the chance to search through her father's med books. I couldn't wait for an update on cocks and chicks.

Katie and I both rushed to the latrine to go over the newest clues. I told Katie about all the strange things I had heard in my dream. 'Big bellies' meant pregnant, obviously. The 'bumps' were sores on the genitals, a word we didn't usually include in our vocabularies. We read what Katie had copied from her father's book. Apparently she'd found it under "penis – diseases and disorders." Based on what Katie had copied from the book, we figured the big guy from the latrine dream had put his thing in somebody (or bodies). He'd gotten some kind of disease, and the girl had gotten pregnant. So who was going to have a baby?

I showed Katie the tattered bits of the note that fell from the light fixture. We couldn't figure out any more than 'He did it' and the threat to cut off 'his dick.' What about 'dick bones,' I wondered.

"What were you doing on top of the light fixture, anyway?"

I made a stupid face to avoid answering.

"A feeling, a dream?" Katie asked. "I'm definitely going to talk to my father tomorrow. I'll say that sometimes it's like God talks to you. You know, Saint Teresa talked to God. Look at Joan of Arc."

"What am I looking at?" I played along.

"She wasn't lady-like either. Listen. Teresa got blood on her hands."

"She was a killer?" I joked.

"No, you're not listening. She had the wounds like Jesus." Katie had become quite serious. I almost felt as if she were going to search my skin for blood.

"The stigmata. See, I listen to the nuns, too," I said.

"Remember the blood on your chest when you had the shirt on?"

"Now I've got the stigmata?" This was actually kind of fun. I then turned serious. "Hey, we've got to write up what we've got so far, and what do you think, take a peek at the bone?"

Katie nodded her agreement, then ran her fingers through her curled bangs, and flipped her shirt collar up. She looked tougher than she was, and I found it adorable.

We walked in silence to the crafts cabin and stared down at the drawer where we'd hidden the bone before gently easing it open. Katie unwrapped the bone. We took a step back as if before a museum piece. Perhaps, in a way, it was.

The cloth was a small, thin square, plaid, almost shredded. The bone offered us no information, other than its size, six inches. It had a jagged end, and a greyish, whitish color with thread-like black lines. Katie hesitated, tilting her head, eyes mere slits.

"Pin, I've really gotta tell my father. You know, during the trip. Can I?" Katie was almost begging.

"Um. Hold on. Let me think." I stroked my chin almost raw, blew out a huge sigh, and said, "Kat, I really do trust you. You know I do—"

"But…?" Katie pursed her lips.

"Your dad, his name is all over this blooming camp."

"Crap, Pina, he *is* a doctor! He would know what the bone is."

"Okay! Okay! But the bone stays here." I shrugged and started to turn away.

Katie nodded and put her hand on my shoulder to reassure me.

"It'll be okay. You'll see. Now let's go get the log."

Her touch made everything okay, much more than okay. I'd go anywhere with her!

We retrieved our logbook from its cache. It now contained information:

-Roger, who was physically abusing Billy
-Wolfgang, who wanted Billy to tell someone in charge
-Romeo, who got girls pregnant, had 'bumps' on penis
-The homosexual Camp Director
-Ron (probably Katie's dad) and Regina, who were boyfriend/girlfriend
-A group met to do 'it,' and they made a 'square'
-Hard evidence: the B.C. knife, the shirt, and now the bone.

We wondered about the possible pregnancy. I asked Katie if her father had gotten anyone pregnant.

Katie's filthy look told me she didn't want to go there, but she still said, "No. Mrs. Robinson, the owner of the hamburger joint, is always saying my dad was a great camper, 'sweet' on someone but not on 'townies.'" Katie said.

"Another camper?" I asked. Katie poked me for teasing that her dad liked a boy.

"Doofus," she said, "You know it was Regina, and the Ron had to be my father."

A bit cranky, I cut to, "Don't leave before breakfast? I have a surprise for you."

"I'm going to sneak into your cabin tonight and find it."

"I'll lock the screen door; besides, it's not there."

"Now I know what you were up to with the bathroom light."

"You rat!" I said.

"I love you too."

"You know I do, but you're still a creep." I was giggling again.

Chapter Eight

EVE OF BIRTHDAY DREAM

My old bed, with its lumps and creaky, uneven springs felt cozy that night. I fell right to sleep, even though I was excited about giving Katie her basket the next morning. I wished my parents would lower the radio playing that corny Pat Boone song. The walls in our cabin were paper-thin, the cheap stuff. The bathroom wedged in between our rooms also allowed little soundproofing. I rolled over and hugged the pillow. It smelled of pine and fire, and it felt good against my cheek. I started to drift, losing sensation. I lay suspended, as though on a ship. Adrift.

I thought I heard an engine, like nuts and bolts grinding against each other, gears getting their teeth into each other. There was a banging, like a screen door and a breaking, crunching sound. Was it Katie, sneaking in like she said she would? Or someone else?

Rough hands grabbed me and tore me from my cradled spot. I struggled to free my arms and managed to get one hand got loose. Something jerked me, wrenching my whole body. It had me now by my hair. I hit the floor hard, and I felt hands under my arms as I got dragged and burned along splintery floorboards. Then nothing. I couldn't breathe. I was screaming and crying, but it all came out choked.

Suddenly, I was outside. Pressed against a tree.

My hands, clawing and cutting, got roped tight; my flesh burned against the rough bonds. I couldn't move. My head spun. I was clammy. My body was at once lost and alive with a screaming, tearing pain.

I thought I had died, but I heard panting and something said, *"I've wanted to get you."*

I felt broken, and this beast was saying he had gotten me. My hands came loose then, and I was tearing at the gag in my mouth. Shrieking. Flailing. I got the beast's eye in my claws and ripped. I reached up to dig my nails in again. This time I felt nothing but dirty, brittle paper.

I opened my eyes to see wallpaper and sheets all knotted around me. I was back in my own cabin, breathing hard. Luckily, my parents were loud snorers; they had heard nothing.

I hurt all over, and I was petrified. What, dear God…what just happened? I got up and crawled to the bathroom to pee.

There was blood on my thigh.

It was almost dawn. I needed to swim – to feel the cool water around me – but I wasn't sure if I even could in this condition. I had never had a dream like that. My legs were like Jello when you suck it and it turns liquid. I felt like I had a big hole in me. I wanted to puke. Had to get down to the water.

Slowly, I walked and sat and sat and walked some more. My body ached so much. I needed the breaks to rest and gather up my will again. I reached the beach and slipped into the ice-cold water. It lapped over my shoulders and burned my thighs. I let myself be pulled in, dunked my head, and took a few strokes. I could swim. I felt clean again, finally. When I emerged from the water, I wrapped myself in two towels and changed out of my suit, pulling on my heavy crew sweater. Bundled and cleansed, I made my way to the latrine.

Entering the latrine felt the same as before; the boxed-in air was still hot from yesterday's sun even though the floorboards had started to cool. I knew this well. Somehow, it soothed me. I sat up against the wall for a while. I closed my eyes.

More *Billys*, more *farts*, and "*your mother wears Army boots.*"

The old heart and Ron and Regina were yet in another spot. No, the *Ron* was crossed out, and I could barely make out *Butch*.

I didn't know…I didn't know anything. I felt like I was slipping out of myself again, and after the terror of my dream, I did not want to go. I tried to latch onto something I knew, anything. I had made a basket. That was real. Katie was real, it was her birthday, and I had to give her her birthday present. I hauled myself to my feet and stumbled to the light fixture. Yes, the basket was there. I got it down and decided not to tell Katie anything about my dream.

Somehow, I made it back to the dining hall area, clothes and all. I had to be okay for Katie, for her birthday. If I told her, I knew she'd want to take care of me, and it was supposed to be her day.

My steps were mincing in the slippery pine needles in front of the dining hall; I didn't dare jerk my body too much. I still hurt. I practiced my smile before coming any closer to Katie, who was slouching in an Adirondack chair, waiting for her folks. I slipped up behind her.

"Happy birthday!" I held out the pine basket for Katie to see. I managed a slow smile.

"Oh gosh, Pina, it's gorgeous! I love it. I love

it. Come here, I'm gonna give you a big, slurpy kiss." Katie pulled me closer.

I felt her big, warm hands on me. This was the first, safe touch since my dream. I burst out in tears and sobbed and sobbed.

"Pina, my God, what's wrong? I really love it. I love you, and you're my best friend!"

I recovered and lied. "I just like you so much. I was afraid you wouldn't like it."

A part of me registered her words "I love you." I felt a warm tingle at the thought. But mostly I was really scared to let her go for a whole day.

I watched as Katie's parents' Lincoln drove away. I got that hollow, black feeling, like all of a sudden, I walked into a deep, empty, cold room. It smelled of old plaster: cold, chemical, dank. I was all alone, and it was my prison. The feeling seemed like it would go on forever. My stomach flipped; I worried I'd give myself away to my parents.

First, I had better get the heck back in the cabin and under the covers before my father made the fire. I was going to spend the day fishing with him so he would have plenty of time to grill me if he found out I had been up to something.

ChapterNine

OUT ON A FISHING EXPEDITION

My father and I walked slowly. We made our way in silence, but for the crunching stones along the path to the boat dock. My father's cigarette pulsed between his lips as he breathed heavily. He smoked too much. His ugly gray Dickies work pants or some cheaper version blew in the breeze against his skinny bowed legs.

"*Rickets*," he explained to me once. He was one of seven children – second generation, poor Italians – and didn't get enough fresh vegetables and fruit. We never talked much, but somehow our steps were in sync. I fell into my nature-state, that's what I called it when I was one with the pines and the loons and the fresh water lapping. We were all in sync, that way.

My father helped me down to the boat and threw me a life vest. Loosening the bow tie line, my father took the stern and pushed out. The small Evinrude caught, and we sputtered away. The oil and gas odors drifted into pine and seaweed scents, and the breeze drew us out beyond the float to more open water.

"There's Maidenfern." Cigarette in the left hand, my father indicated a point to the south. "If you were a little rich girl, you could go to camp there too."

"I wouldn't want to," I said. "They're stuck up."

"How do you know?"

"I saw some of them on an outing at The House That Jack Built."

"Well, your friend Katie's dad was talking about sending her there."

I said, "She'd never go."

Inside, I was panicking. Was that a possibility?

"You wouldn't want to go?"

"No!"

But what if Katie did go? A yucky sense of betrayal was creeping over me. I feigned asphyxiation by gas fumes to justify my tears. Katie and I never talked about money or what it did and didn't bestow upon us. Yet, we were strangely aware there was a difference between us that focused or clouded our dreams.

Dreams. I was trying to avoid thinking about mine, but my body ached. Why did a dream have to hurt so much? I just wanted to die to make it stop hurting, both in my body and in my soul. I felt nausea rising up and realized that I had to focus on my father if I didn't want to lose it completely.

He looked so sure of himself and in command in this boat. Strong and gentle.

"We don't belong to part of this world up here in Maine," he said.

My mother certainly wanted to, which caused my father no end of pain. Was he a failure? Would Katie really go to this camp?

My father turned back to the motor, pushed the choke, and the engine hummed a different rhythm. A real fleet of red canoes made in Orono, Maine passed us by in formation, and I stared after the beautiful wooden boats with longing. Maybe I could go to college there one day.

The girls looked neat and tidy in those white

Lacoste shirts. New ones, not like my old hand-me-down. They probably rode horses too.

"Hey, Dad, do people ever win horses from the cereal boxes?"

"From Frosted Flakes?" he joked back. "Would you prefer a Wheaties pony or a Grape Nutty one? How about for now I take us to the lily pond bog?"

I knew he was on a roll.

"Are you going to start in telling me about the Lilliputians, again?"

"You got me. Besides, you always like the part where Swift has Gulliver 'make water in the castle!'"

"Yeah. You know, I got in trouble in school for talking about that part. According to the good Sisters, it wasn't proper for Catholic young ladies to laugh about 'bodily functions.'"

"Their loss, Toots. How about we be quiet for the fish? I'll bait up two lines, and we'll troll slowly."

I helped hook the worm as my father managed the motor with his right hand and held the pole with his feet. I watched the bait, hook, and bobbing thing gently go plop in the water. We drifted on at a snail's pace. A slight tug, and then I reeled in an eight-inch sunfish.

"Is he legal?"

"Sure, put him in the tin."

By now, we were in Paradise. We floated, swished our way through the lily bog, surrounded on all sides by yellow and white flowers. The long leaves separated before our prow.

I leaned over and just stared. My father gathered a bouquet for my mom. My eyes looked into the water, murky, but still clear enough that I could see my reflection. I looked tired, messy, and scared. It all came back to me…the dream, the hurt. As the pain of my nightmare came rushing back, reality slipped around me. What was real? I couldn't be sure. I let my hand stroke the water. Cold. A slimy lily pad tendril wrapped itself around my wrist. I started at the sensation.

"What?" My father's voice brought me back.

"Nothing, just a lily pad."

I looked at the beautiful bouquet we'd gathered. "Think that's enough?"

The flowers wouldn't last long. My mother would see the wilted, puffy, round heads and put them in water just to please my dad. Their anniversary was August fifteenth. Tomorrow.

As we started to oar our way out of the bog, my line caught on something. A huge fish judging from the weight, and it wouldn't budge. This was unheard of, something this big in this little lake. My father took over to help me pull in my fabulous find. It wouldn't budge; we wound up drawing the boat closer to my catch.

"Hey, hey, you did it!" He laughed. "Come over here."

"What is it?" I looked into the water and saw that I had hooked an old tire.

"Here, honey, let me cut the line."

As he bent over the water, my father asked me to get his glasses. "Something shiny, here. Get me the small net too."

He was tugging and pulling, but nothing worked.

"I think we hit pay dirt, really," he grunted as he lost his footing and gracelessly flopped into the water, rubber-soled canvas shoes and all.

When he turned back to me, he was clutching something, but his demeanor had changed. He was white. Dad held his hand away from me as he heaved himself up and into the rowboat.

"Start the engine," he yelled.

"But Dad."

"Just do it!"

"What about the pay dirt?"

He slowly opened his hand. I saw the shimmer of something. A ring. A big signet ring, but something else. I couldn't see well, and my father was turning to vomit off the side of the boat.

He said quietly, "Someone has been badly hurt."

"I don't understand."

"It's not just a ring, Pina. Someone lost his finger."

"Daddy, you're scaring me."

"I'm sorry, honey. Don't be scared; it happened a while ago." He put his other arm around me.

My father still clutched our macabre sunken treasure in his hand: the unmistakable bones of a finger still wearing a heavy man's ring. I began to sway, and a cold sweat broke out on my forehead. He held me up as we motored back very quickly.

"Don't tell your mother."

"But what are you going to do? You can't keep it."

"I'll worry about that."

"How could someone lose a finger?"

"Must have been a fishing accident," he said as he took a long, pained drag on his wet, filterless Raleigh.

Dad seemed someplace else, and his color was only slowly coming back into his normally tanned cheeks. When we got back to the dock, I saw him wrap up the bones and the ring and put it all the way down in his wet, baggy pants. He would have to tell my mom some big story to explain his sodden clothes, the kind he could usually weave so well when pulling someone's leg.

But this time was different. I held the lilies, which now felt more like funeral flowers. Maybe it was a burial at sea, although this was not like any Robinson Crusoe story I had read.

I wished Katie were here so badly, or that I had gone to Star Island with her. I tried to make my thoughts go there: helping Katie celebrate, unwrap presents, and blow out her sixteen candles. I could do that so well, just go away, make my thoughts take me elsewhere.

I felt better now. The bog was behind us, and I was laughing, showing off my sunfish.

My mother was busy "tut-tutting" at my father's wetness. "Oh, your father has done it again. At least you're dry. Surprised you didn't both drown."

"Look at the wonderful flowers Daddy got you. For your anniversary tomorrow."

"Yes, that's likely all I'll get," she groused.

"No, Mom, Dad has a real surprise for you," I said.

I knew my father planned to take us to the local lobster pound. Normally, I'd be delighted, but I just wanted to be with Katie. I had to talk to my father about the bones, and I really wanted to see the ring. Signet rings always have initials.

I suddenly felt tired. I just wanted to sleep now. Maybe if I went to bed early, Katie would be back before I knew it.

Chapter Ten

BREAKFAST REUNION

Katie was back. I could see her through the thick morning fog still shrouding the pines in front of the dining hall. I had dreamt about her during the night, visions of her taking the small ferry to Star Island with her mom and dad. I even imagined Katie on the rocking chair she'd told me about, rocking and rocking as if she could just take flight into the ocean from the wrap-around porch of the old hotel. Now that she was here, I felt a bit shy.

After breakfast in the overheated dining hall, we stood around out front of the dining room, kicking at pine needles.

"I don't want to ruin your birthday, but I'm scared," I said finally.

"How'd you know?" said Katie.

"Know what? I can't keep it all to myself."

"So you didn't find out about my father?"

"Your father?"

"My father has the scar, or square. Jeez, you think he's really bad? I saw it on his arm, the square, the scar. You know, the sign of the secret group."

She described her father carrying the birthday packages, shirtsleeves all pushed up, almost like a hood's, she said, but without the Luckies rolled up in his undershirt. Then she saw it. She saw the shirt ripple up, his somewhat flabby muscle wiggle and distort the mark on his arm. It was a square, all uneven and faint, kind of like an old tattoo. The edges were ragged, as if it was made with a knife and blue-black pen ink.

Katie said she tried to act nonchalant, questioning him about hurting himself, but he made up some story. Then, as Katie's dad pulled away from her to bring more presents, he tugged his shirtsleeve all the way down and put on a cardigan as if he was trying to cover up.

"Holy crap!" I said.

"Exactly what was the square about?" asked Katie, scrunching up her face.

"First, I've gotta tell you about…so much that happened while you were away. I dreamt I was attacked."

"You mean, for real?"

"It was in my dream, but I woke up with welts on me."

"Slow down. You're really scaring me."

I started from the beginning. "In the dream, it was like I was at the camp, back in the '30s. Like, maybe this stuff really happened."

"Attacked? Oh my God…what can I…my father… oh my God!"

I felt myself being folded into Katie's soft arms.

"I'm hurt and achy," I said. "You feel so good." For the first time since the dream, I just let myself go. All the feelings I'd tried to get under control finally released. I felt every part of me overflow like a dam, up and over the barrier of my body.

After a long, quiet time, Katie whispered, "I don't understand how…I don't know what to say. Did you tell your folks?"

"What's to tell? That a twenty-year old story is

happening to me? Mom will die."

"Damn! Pina, we really have to tell someone. Really."

"First time I've heard you curse," I couldn't help but giggle. But then I sighed. "There's more. My father and I went fishing, and we pulled up another bone...a finger in a signet ring."

"Gross. What's he going to do?" said Katie.

"He hasn't decided."

"Do you think it's connected to our bone?" Katie asked.

"Well, there's a way to find out: signet rings have initials. My folks are going out for their anniversary this afternoon. We'll take a look when they're gone?"

"Creepy, but yeah."

"My father tried to say it was a fishing accident. That doesn't make any sense. See, some real heavy rocks were holding it down in an old tire. Katie I don't know what to believe. I'm even afraid to go to sleep tonight."

"Can we cool this till after lunch? When your folks leave, we can find the ring, the initials, and the bones—all of the bones." Katie stopped short. She put her hands on my shoulders and just looked at me. Her face softened. "What about your dream?"

"I don't know, I don't know. I can't go on crying like this. Distract me...just tell me about your birthday presents." I sniffled and dried my eyes.

"That seems so...I don't know...babyish now. But I did get this one thing—"

"You didn't?"

"Yup. The biggest chem set ever *and* the microscope."

Katie and I managed to hang out without talking about dreams or scars for the whole, chilly morning.

We strolled over to her cabin, where we could be alone because her parents had gone to the main house to play Bridge. The embers were still alive in the fireplace.

We built up the fire with some sappy kindling and dried pine. We mimicked the firedogs in the hearth, curling up on the floor to watch the blaze together. Katie leaned back on her elbows, knees bent. She pulled me back against her, her arms around my shoulders. She seemed to help contain the craziness and confusion burning inside of me. All of the things I'd been feeling, our fears, our warmth, this inexplicable thing catching fire between us felt easier, somehow, when we were alone like this.

I tried to say more about the dream, but Katie just shushed me. We were quiet, listening to the pop and sizzle of the blaze. It seemed like her birthday added more than just a year to her. I felt the wisdom and warmth of age radiating from her.

Her cabin, with its new woven rag rugs and folk art pictures on the wall, felt safe. I was in the most comfortable place I had ever been, seated on the hard pine floor propped like that against Katie's knees.

My cabin was just across from Katie's, even if it sometimes felt like a world away, so we listened for the sound of my parents' car. Once they drove off to celebrate their anniversary, we crept over to my place. I saw Katie take in the whole place: the ramshackle bridge table set up with a small, plug-in radio and papers, bills my father had been working on. The rag rugs on the floor in our sitting room, which doubled as my bedroom, were tattered but homey to me.

Katie must have seen my stuffed Siamese cat on the bed. In an instant, her face softened, her dimples made a rare appearance, and she threw herself with abandon across my bed.

I loved this side of Katie, this flitty, childlike behavior, but I couldn't help but worry. Maybe she chose not to ask more about the attack in my dream. Maybe her father came first in her book—

"I'm scared about my father. What if he was part of...of the attack in some way?" Katie looked devastated at the thought.

"No way, not your father." I tried to act confident, for her sake.

"But if he's got that mark, he met with those other kids," Katie said.

"Katie, we don't really know anything yet. We don't know what happened." I couldn't let myself wonder about her father now. There were too many other questions.

I jumped off the bed and crossed the splintering floor to my parents' bedroom. I dropped to my knees and opened my father's lower dresser drawer. Katie was at my side in an instant.

"Is this your father's underwear drawer? I've never seen ugly boxer shorts like that." She giggled.

"I suppose your father's are silk?" I said, throwing a pair of his shorts at her.

"Stop it, you goof. They just have snaps." She actually put the shorts over her head.

"Shine the flashlight here," I said. We couldn't take all day even though it would have been unreal to play with my parents' dowdy clothes. My parents were a good ten years older than Katie's and many years less comfortable.

"Eek!" Katie jumped back at the sight of something in the drawer. Once she got over her shock, she reached her hand in to grab the object I had just revealed.

"Don't poke." I tiptoed my fingers to the ring to avoid touching the bone. I managed to shift it a bit so we could read the initials.

"There they are...B.L." Katie lowered her head almost into the drawer.

"Careful, I don't want to touch the bones," I said, pulling away.

"Any chance B.C. on the knife is really missing a letter?" Katie was up and zoomed way ahead of me.

We closed the drawer and sat in silence for a moment. Katie jumped back on my bed. She threw the stuffed cat for me to catch.

"I really don't want things to change. Gimme my kitty."

I threw it back at her. "You scared about your father?"

"For lots of reasons," Katie said as she snuggled the cat a minute and then sat up and stared at me very seriously.

"I'm so lucky you're my friend." Her voice trailed off as her eyes seemed to focus on something far away.

"Me too." Why did I get so tongue-tied when it came to letting Katie know just how much I liked her? I broke the heavy moment by pushing her back on the bed with a playful shove.

"Let's have a slumber party tonight for my birthday!" Katie laughed breathlessly.

The thought of sleeping next to Katie was overwhelming.

"Okay," I agreed, feeling kind of nervous. "But only if you come with us to the lobster pound tonight."

❧❧❧❧

Later that night after the lobster pound, Katie's cabin again felt safe with its thick, knotty pine walls (not just panels like mine), and wide, braided rugs. Katie had her own bedroom, separate from her parents, and the separate sitting room had over-stuffed wingback chairs and three Hudson Bay throws in front of the second fireplace – a real one, not just a stove.

Katie and I scrambled into bed; we both gave off the lingering, sweet smell of buttered lobster. The fragrance of lavender wafted in, fused with the aroma of pine, which permeated the whole cabin.

"Brr! Stay under the covers, I'll get your pajamas." Katie offered as she got out of bed to get undressed.

I snuck peeks at Katie's ivory creaminess as she changed, at her smooth freckled skin.

I heard myself say, "What kind of bra is that?"

I almost dove under the coverlet in embarrassment. I didn't know where to hide myself! I couldn't take back the question or pretend I hadn't been staring at the rainbow satin bra, both before and after she removed it.

"Oh, this?" Katie seemed unfazed. "My crazy aunt shops all the time and finds these far out things. You were peeking, you rat!" She threw my pajamas, worn flannels with a cat and dog design, but she was smiling coyly.

"I couldn't see a thing. But..." I smirked. "It almost glowed in the dark."

I was glad to have the excuse of dressing under the covers. I could hide the blush I felt spreading up my cheeks. It wasn't that dark in the room.

"It's a kick, isn't it?" She giggled as she slid under the blanket with me.

Cuddling, we both fell asleep quickly. It was

more than just the cabin making me feel safe. I felt so at home in Katie's arms. Tomorrow, we would get to use the chem set to find out more about the bones. Answers would come. Maybe answers to dreams, too.

In the morning, Katie and I woke up still glued to each other's side. We lay in bed for a while, reading bits and pieces of the manual that came with the chem set. There were tests for blood and ways to differentiate bone from antler or petrified wood. It was distracting to see Katie's pale, soft skin close up, and all the more distracting for a strand of her thick, dark hair to tickle me. She didn't have any idea, did she?

I wanted to stay in bed with Katie forever, but hunger for pancakes and blueberry syrup won out. Still, as soon as we had put in the right amount of time with our families at breakfast, a different kind of hunger came over us: hunger for answers.

We crossed the road opposite the dining hall, sliding on pine needles and snapped branches and twigs. We carried the chem set between us, and its bulkiness made it hard to scoot under and between overgrown shrubs and thick, bushy pines.

All of our finds awaited us: the knife, the shirt, the bone from the crafts cabin. The only thing missing was the finger, still in my father's dresser. Equipped with chemicals, slides, and the microscope, we tested and waited. A drop of solution here, a shake there, and wait, wait, wait. It seemed like we would be standing there forever, and then the results came in.

Just as we thought: blood, human.

Silence bounced back from the walls of the science cabin as the two of us let this new information sink in. This definitely wasn't a plaything anymore. If these objects had been used in a crime, what about the tools we found near the cabin? Shoot! Was there more evidence just lying around?

I jerked Katie. We had to go see.

Dust from the cabin and old things gritted and smeared our faces. We held each other by the hand, stumbling as if someone were pushing us ahead with a gun at our backs. Down, down between boards and in dirt, we found ourselves on our knees, clawing in the dirt, oblivious to splinters and small shards of glass. Clawing, digging through, for what we didn't exactly know. Yet, somehow, we knew. We raked up a hammer, a plane, and the sledge we used to break the lock.

"We've got to test all of it. Bring them in."

"Get the drops," said Katie.

We went through the same process of mixing and stirring, smearing water, chemicals, rust, and dirt. Our hands and faces were soon coated in this mixture. We looked as if we were being tested.

"Yup. All three," I said as the results appeared.

"Holy…!" Katie said, putting her hand to her mouth. She made tiny, retching sounds when she heard everything was covered in blood.

"Gross!"

"Yeah, you said it, Kat."

"So…who…what? Were they used as…weapons?" Katie stepped away from the tools.

I saw Katie blanch through the smears of dirt and grime on her face. I tried to think fast so we could get outside – now.

"The B.L. finger…cut or removed; the shirt slashed; and the bone?" I was frantic. Katie had split. I was alone with the empty sound of my voice asking, "Why?"

Chapter Eleven

MORE THROUGH A LOOKING GLASS DARKLY

After our discoveries, we tried to lay low for a while. Hanging out in her cabin, we pretended to be just goofy sixteen-year-olds who didn't have a real thought in our heads. It wasn't difficult; both of us knew tons of girls like that at school. We spread cold cream on our faces and made big lips with Hazel Bishop lipstick. Three hours of this stuff, and we started to avoid each other so we didn't have to ask those hard questions.

"What the heck, Katie, we can't just let this be!" I jabbed at her with some blood red lipstick. I was half joking, but we had just uncovered major clues.

"Don't you dare!" Katie pushed back with a hand full of cold cream. "I'm sorry, I really am." She turned so I wouldn't see her tears.

"It's okay. It was a joke." I gently wiped the lipstick off Katie's face.

"No, I mean…I'm kinda chicken about the case." She held onto my goopy hand. "Just give me some time."

I looked into her eyes and read fear. But there was something more: a glimmer of curiosity. I would soon find out this was one of Katie's winning character traits. She had a deep desire to know the truth.

Several hours later, we both noticed my father

quietly pulling Katie's father, Ron McGuilvry, aside. We both perked up. We snuck out of the cabin and wandered around the nearby pine trees, pretending to look for stray kittens that roamed around the grounds. We slithered and slid into earshot and saw my father unrolling the handkerchief. We heard the clink of the signet ring against my father's own bloodstone ring. The doc cleared his throat with a strange cough. Katie frowned.

"Barney, where'd that come from?" Dr. McGuilvry must have been sucking on his pipe. We could smell the smoke.

"Fishing," said my father. "Pulled it from an old tire. What do you make of it?"

"It's a finger, all right. Old one, too. Maybe fifteen or twenty years in the water."

"And?"

"And what?" asked Dr. McGuilvry, pulling at his button-down collar. "Maybe belonged to an adolescent. It's a bit small for a grown man. The ring is smallish too."

"Was it cut, caught in a motor blade?"

"Hold on. I'd have to examine it better to see if there are marks on the bone. Would you let me have it a bit?"

"Should I notify the police?" My father asked.

"I wouldn't bother them. There's no indication of anything foul. I'll take care of it."

"Thanks a million, Ron." My father clapped Doc on the shoulder and walked off, a Raleigh cigarette stuck in the corner of his mouth.

Katie wore a glazed look.

"We could go to your cabin and see what he's doing," I suggested.

"I don't believe my father's bad." Katie stomped the pine-cushioned ground.

"I didn't say that," I soothed. "I just want to see what he does and what he finds out."

We watched from the window outside her cabin as her dad spent a great deal of time twisting the ring from hand to hand. He turned it over and over, as if looking for answers. He put his hand to his brow and leaned on his elbow. Again, that strange cough. Then, he took the bones, and he pulled over the microscope. Katie's father played with the focus and shook his head. He put everything away and sat himself down heavily on the edge of the bed. Katie's mother entered the room, and he barked at her to leave him some peace. He propped himself up by the pillows, legs up, and hugged his legs.

Beside me, Katie whimpered. It was a strange position to see your father in.

Now, her dad was up. He rolled up the handkerchief with the bone and left the cabin, walking with a robot-like determination toward the Lodge's main house.

We followed behind quietly. We followed his movements through the lace-curtained windows to the living room and hid underneath the window by the phone. We watched him pick up the receiver and heard him ask the operator for a number in New Jersey.

We overheard him talking, but it was muffled. Just a few words here and there came through.

"Your cousin…ring…get your bottom up here."

Katie's dad slammed the phone down and coughed that strange cough. He threw the ring across the floor, muttering under his breath, but immediately retrieved it and shoved it in his pants.

Tears were streaming down Katie's face, and she let out a little whimper. I had to drag her away from the window before her father heard us.

"What did he do? Is he really involved?" Katie asked.

"We don't know he did anything."

"He knows something," Katie said.

"We have to find out more. We could try to get to the tire and maybe to the girls' camp, you know, where Regina was a camper back then. I just have a feeling there's a connection there. Maybe I could pick up something about Regina."

Chapter Twelve

AT SEA

Katie and I knew we had to be cool and not jump to too many conclusions. Just paddling and splashing around in the lake usually calmed us down, so we decided to take a break. We suited up and stumbled along the rocky path to the beach. We took the last hill running and sprinted for the beached canoes.

"Let's take the small canoe."

"Stern!" called Katie.

The gentle lapping of water against the bow and Katie's irregular J-stroke carried the small canoe forward, closer to the girls' camp. The rhythm lulled me and I faded. The smell of Canoe Cologne helped me drift deeper.

I began to hear things. Sounds from another time.

"Ring" – and then – *"Regina"* and again *"Regina,"* and finally, with kind of a question at the end *"Regina?"*

My whole body lit up with pain.

I screamed. My wild tossing shook the boat. Something else was shaking me.

Katie leaned over me, her paddle pulled in so she could shake me awake. "Are you crazy? Do you want to tip us?"

I said, "Someone was attacking me! It was a dream…another dream! Like the one in the cabin."

"Who?" shouted Katie above the rumble of a nearby outboard. "Who was attacking you?"

"The same guy. The ring was his. He was wearing it."

"Are you hurt?"

"No, but I feel like puking. I think I have blood on me. It felt like a blade was slicing me open. I felt ripped apart. Oh, God, there's more blood on my dungarees on my thighs. God. My grandmother…it's happening…"

"What? What'd'ya mean? God. Let me take a look," said Katie.

"My grandmother. She's the source of the dreams. She sends them to me, like visions. She wants me to pay attention and do something."

"Here, let me help. I'll wash you off," Katie said. She drizzled some cool water on my forehead too, holding me close to her.

I continued to tell her what he said. "He kept on calling me *'Regina,'* and I remember saying *'Regina?'* And he said, *'Yes, o saintly one, Regina Coeli—'*"

"Like the church song?" said Katie.

"Yes, but his face was twisted and ugly. He was so close to me, with this look in his eyes. Like he was mocking."

"What were the initials on the ring?" Katie asked.

"B.L. The same as the ring we found."

"In the latrine, 'Regina and Ron' was crossed out for 'Regina and Butch.'" Katie recalled, "Was it Butch, the man in your dream I mean?"

"I'm going to be sick." I vomited over the side of the canoe. I washed my mouth and sat in a fog for what seemed forever. "Remember what we heard your dad say on the telephone? *'Your cousin's ring!'*"

"Whose cousin? Who's Regina? I thought she was my dad's girlfriend." Katie was almost whining. "We can't very well ask my dad."

"You want us to stay stuck?" I snapped back. "You don't care about what's happening to me?" I'd been feeling anxious about this for a while, and it finally came out.

"Wait a minute. You're just so sure my father's done things—"

"If I thought he had done something wrong, I wouldn't be talking to him." I started to whimper. "I'm hurt, Katie. Can't you pay attention to me?"

"Stop. I'm sorry." Katie gave me a quick hug. "I'm so confused."

We stayed quiet for a little while.

Then Katie popped her head up, as if she had realized something. "You know what? Claudia! She owns the cabin down the road, and she went to the girls' camp. She's the same age as my dad. She might have a yearbook."

"A Maidenfern Yearbook?" I asked, getting caught up in this new possibility.

"Yes." Katie took a shaky breath. "Do you always have to push my nose in things before I'm ready?"

"You're not ready for me or your dad?" Oops, I didn't mean to say that. I might have given my growing feelings for Katie away.

I tried to backtrack, hoping Katie wouldn't notice. "But you always want to know things."

Katie flashed me a strange look. Her look went deep into me. I felt my whole body go soft. She hugged me hard, but I was still afraid I'd gone too far. We paddled back in complicit silence.

❧❧❧❧

After we had returned to our cabins and gotten cleaned up for dinner, Katie and I met by the shuffleboard court in front of the dining hall. A crowd of people was already milling about.

Katie looked nervous. She tugged on my shirt and pointed to the porch on "Shawnee," her cabin, located across from mine, in the better "neighborhood." Soft patio furniture coddled those in need of coddling. Katie's parents and some other folks were enjoying drinks over there, clinking ice cubes in their glasses. I smelled whiskey and cigar smoke.

Katie put a finger to her lips and motioned for me to follow her. She hid me under her cabin's porch overhang so that I could eavesdrop without being spotted. Katie joined her parents on the porch, begging for an olive from her mother's drink. The adults' alcohol-coated voices carried as they introduced Katie to her old "Aunt and Uncle, Sandra and Bud Lawyer" whom she hadn't seen since she was two years old.

I guessed this Bud had gone to camp with her father! Bud Lawyer, his initials would be B.L. – or maybe B.C.L., which would explain the initials on the knife. Butch and Bud…were they cousins?

Chapter Thirteen

CLAUDIA'S "CAMP"

The next morning was a bit chilly and damp. We exchanged only a few words before going into the toasty dining hall to eat. Katie's blue eyes were downcast and dark.

She whispered, "So Bud and Butch are cousins," as she slipped past me on the steps.

Right after breakfast, I put my arm around Katie's shoulder. She quietly said she heard her father refer to Bud's cousin Butch. She would say nothing more about the cousins. Her tense body said it all. I led her along the path to Claudia's "camp," what year-round residents called their summer cottages.

At Claudia's red, rustic door, we changed our attitudes into the regular girls everyone wanted us to be. We became all smiley and giddy. Claudia liked us this way. Upon opening the door, she burst into a big grin, welcoming us in, as we knew she would.

Inside the cabin, I looked around. I loved the feel of the Maine artifacts, the Hudson Bay blankets and the smell of balsam as you leaned on them. This incense really made my head dizzy, I guess like drunk, even if I didn't know what that felt like. It was better for me than church. This time, though, we had important things to focus on.

We chatted with Claudia and told her we just

loved Camp Maidenfern. I knew she would want us to see photos of her in her glory days. Claudia showed us the Yearbook, offering narration and commentary on all the girls as she flipped through the pages.

"Of course I knew Regina Gallo. Everyone did, and how!" Claudia shot us a coy smirk. "I'm surprised your father never said anything, Katie. After all, he was crazy about her. Swore he'd go to whatever college she did, that they'd get married. But then…" Claudia licked her lips, as if she was savoring the taste of a big, juicy story to impress us, or scare us. She lowered her voice to a gossipy whisper, "The scandal! Regina Gallo was whisked away. A tragedy, everyone said. Some people thought she was only sick. The story was, someone snuck into her cabin. If you ask me, maybe she invited them in. Who knows, it could have been your father."

Katie turned pure white and shouted, "No!" Katie shook her head back and forth, "No way. My father never talks about other girls he dated. It's one of the rare things mother teases him about! She calls him her late bloomer."

We were spooked. We said hasty goodbyes to Claudia, who looked a little proud to have rattled us like that, and left the cabin as fast as we could. We headed for the shade of the big yellow pine. We threw ourselves down on the ground, burying our faces in the dirt and pine needles, like maybe we didn't want to see any more of the outer world.

"I think I get my dreams," I said after a while.

"What happened to you in the dreams? You mean it really happened to Regina?" Katie said. She turned away from me and started to pound the ground with her fist.

I touched her shoulder and turned her back

around. "It's not your dad, Katie; it's Butch." I rubbed my chin, trying out my theory. "Okay, Katie, here's what I think. Yeah, your dad and Regina were going out. Butch was jealous, a real creep. Not just a creep but crazy. Let's see. He tried to flirt with Regina, but she told him to get lost. He got drunk and decided to get even. He snuck into her camp and tried to assault her. It's gotta be."

The clearer some things got, the harder the rest was to understand.

Katie's jaw dropped. She muttered, "And my father? Didn't he know? Or protect her?"

I rocked her a bit and finally risked saying, "But your dad does seem awfully nervous about the ring."

"I'm not liking this very much," Katie mumbled before sitting straight up. Her eyes were set, her body tense.

After Claudia's, Katie wanted more answers. We would shadow her father and Bud. The early morning crispness had already turned muggy and warm. Despite the heat, we crawled under the screened porch and sat in a pile of sticky sand in the small, cramped area created by the cabin's support stilts.

We caught Doc and Bud reminiscing, reclining on the cushy rockers on the porch above our heads while their wives played bridge in the main house.

They were drinking from a bottle of whisky, and after a few swigs, decided to go over to the old crafts cabin flanking the rec hall. Katie and I couldn't remember everything we had stowed away there, and in an effort to prevent the inevitable, followed them over there.

Bud and Katie's dad moved as if they were already a bit tipsy. They crossed the road in an older man's rolling jog. The volume of their laughter was up a few decibels, so we trailed behind, hidden by the trees. I stroked Katie on the head, sensing her delicate state.

Katie and I slipped under the scaffolding into the basement space beneath the main floor of the crafts cabin. Down here, we could hear Bud and Katie's father better, and there was less risk of being caught.

At first, the only noise they made were guffaws and gloo-gloo, gulping whiskey straight from the bottle. Then, slurred conversation, but loud and telling.

"Damn!" said Bud, "it's good to be here. Seeing you, my old pal. And, b'jesus, that girl of yours, sure something!"

"Dunno, Bud...too many memories." Doc coughed. "Gimme the bottle, will ya?"

The floor creaked with the heavy movement above our heads.

Doc continued, "Yup! Katie...I darn near jumped down her throat the other day. She was singing that church song, you know the one." Doc hummed a few bars of *Regina Coeli.*

"Regina was all I had to hear. I snapped, 'be quiet' at my poor daughter. Tell you the truth, Bud, I haven't thought about Regina Gallo in ages. Too ashamed, I guess."

Katie looked at me and nodded in recognition.

"R – E – G – I – N- A! Wow!" Bud whistled, "You fell hard."

"Not hard enough. I never got the whole story, didn't have the stomach."

"C'mon, guy, you said yourself your old man wouldn't let you," Bud said.

"Hah! No one let me...She-it! I was a coward. I did try to phone her at home once. Put on a phony voice and all. Got her Mafioso father, Fifi Gallo. He cussed me out but good."

"Eh, c'mon. No one wanted to mess with him after the…uh…what happened to Regina."

We could hear the flimsy stools scrape against the floor.

"Uh, I cringe when I think I lacked the balls to find out what really happened to make her leave." Katie's dad's voice was all choked up.

"Whoa, Ron, all I knew for sure was that a guy was seen leaving Regina's bunkhouse. Maybe Butch, maybe you. The Square group kept me in the dark."

"Gimme some more of that stuff," Doc slurred. "But you were part of the Square too; we were supposed to be protecting the little kids, no?"

"Yeah, but sometimes they left us out of the smaller loop. Remember all that crap about our 'old, monied families' and how the Square group didn't want to ruin our 'Ivy League destiny?' C'mon, you gotta remember all that elitist crap." Bud belched.

"Maybe…maybe I had a vague idea someone was hitting on Regina. Maybe everyone did, and no one wanted to tell me…to protect me? Or…? What'd they think I'd do?"

"Easy, guy. It was a different time. We're the good guys, remember. Jack Daniels, 100 Proof says so." We heard Bud take a gulp of that Jack Daniels.

"Yeah, yeah. What about your cousin, Butch?" Doc hiccoughed.

"Right. The bad guy. My family said my cousin Butch never came back from camp, that he ran away because there was a warrant out for his arrest in New York. He was such a thug, really a slick, mean son of a gun. You know, his family, the Judge's friggin' family was ousted from the Bedford Country Club. People talked."

When they were slurring their words and totally blotto, we heard Doc stretch out on the floor.

Then we heard a few loud clunks as something fell to the floor. Katie blanched; I froze.

Bud screamed, "That's my knife; it's my knife that was stolen and an old shirt."

I felt sick. I could hear more scrambling above. The sound of pages flapping. Oh God! Our notebook.

"What is this?" Bud asked, and we heard more pages turning. "It's some kind of book...'*what we know*', and...ah damn! It's your daughter's. Look, here. '*Signed super sleuths, Katie McGuilvry and Pina Mazzini.*'"

We'd been found out. Katie and I traded looks, planning a silent getaway, but we stayed just long enough to hear the rest.

Doc was cursing, saying he had a lot of explaining to do to Katie. The slur was gone from his speech, and he coughed that strange cough again.

I gave Katie a tight hug as she began to cry. Then, I quietly strong-armed her out under the cabin, carefully guiding her down the slope to the lake. Maybe there'd be some relief there.

❧❧❧❧❧

I left Katie down by the lake, a bit off to the side of the guest beach. She had calmed down, but she wasn't ready to face her family at lunch. I concocted a plan to find both of our parents and beg them to let us have a picnic day. Occasionally, the cook would prepare a box lunch for us, and our folks usually welcomed the break from our "teenageness." I knew I could convince

Catherine, Katie's mom. Her father was probably recouping with Bud some place and hadn't returned yet.

Catherine, dressed in a proper white crepe short-sleeved blouse and a straight, linen skirt, sat smoking her Kent and flipping through "Ladies Home Journal" on her porch. She lifted her pale eyes from her magazine with a blank look, a look that was ready to agree to anything as long as it left her alone. She said yes to the picnic immediately, as did my mother. The cook liked me; the rest was simple.

Within a half-hour, I was back at Katie's side on the sand with a picnic box of tuna fish sandwiches, chips, lemonade, and chocolate chip cookies. Katie smiled and briefly touched my hand as I finished showing off the spoils of my "hunting and gathering."

Leaning up against the grassy slope, head in hands, Katie said, "We can't not do this."

I also knew we couldn't stay away from the thick of things. The mystery was bound to get messy.

"You sure?" I quickly wiped the smudge of mayonnaise off my cheek.

"Blasted square tattoo or whatever the heck! I mean, he's involved."

"Katie, eat something, please."

Katie slowed down. She squished up bits of soft white bread and popped them in her mouth, wiping off her hands on the grass.

"Katie, it sounds like your dad, well…he kind of wasn't…" I tried to be careful; I needed just the right word.

"Wasn't what?"

"Well, he sounded really upset. Not like he killed or attacked anyone or…" I just wanted to eat my cookie and rest.

"Sorry, Pin. I gotta know how much of a liar he is…" Katie bit her lower lip.

"They've all got their heads in the sand. All our folks." I kinda hoped we could stop. I was tired and afraid of what other horrid things I might have to experience in my dreams. Tired…but I knew I needed to help clear her father in her heart.

We finished our food and Katie decided that maybe the tire held more answers. We launched the nearby canoe and started to paddle out to the spot where my dad and I found the tire. I was weary. I needed rest. What was I thinking, agreeing to pursue this now?

We paddled out to the lily pond where yellow and white petals embraced us. Rubbery, sweating lily pads swirled in widening circles around us. We were weak and wrung out from the humidity, and our paddling got sloppy. Katie's paddle got stuck on something underwater, and I had to hold onto her to keep her from falling out of the boat while I tried to yank the paddle free. It was then we spotted the chain attached to the tire.

The last links of a chain clunked against the wall of the canoe, making that hollow thumping sound I knew so well. Sometimes it meant cool, fresh water and a great swim with splashy games. Sometimes, it meant I was too close, dangerously too close to jagged rocks.

I looped my paddle around one of the chain links and started to pull the tire in. Katie grabbed on to help. We both heaved for a bit, with little luck.

Katie brushed a sweaty lock of hair out of her face and sighed. "I can't. It's too heavy."

We had lifted part of the tire. I was straining, my muscles burning from the effort.

I saw something, canvas, no, leather. A glove. I tried to reach it. God, there was something in it.

"Grab it." Katie was leaning over the edge of the canoe, but it was too far away.

"Dang." I made one last lunge. I felt everything give. The glove and its contents in my hand, I pitched forward, my body following my chest out of the canoe. The canoe tipped after me. Katie, in the stern, managed to right the canoe, but got dumped in the water in the process.

Water overcame us. We thrashed around, occasionally kicking the tire in our struggles. We couldn't find our way out. There was a ringing in my ears as panic and loss of blood pressure took over. We both knew we had to get back in the canoe. With whatever willpower and consciousness was left, I pulled the glove free of the tire. Its contents spilled out, several bones drifted back down into the deeper water. I grabbed the gunnel, glove and all, and hoisted myself into the canoe.

I turned to look for Katie. I could just make her out below the surface: her legs were stuck in the rocks inside the tire. I managed to pull her by the hair. Her hands reached up to find mine, and I braced my legs against the wall of the canoe to yank her in.

Neither of us spoke for quite some time as the canoe drifted lazily. A light breeze dragged it closer to shore. The familiar short boardwalk came into view, and the underside of the canoe grated along the gravel alongside the dock. We pitched headlong onto the sand and simply allowed ourselves to let go of outside things: sights, sounds, smells, sensations. The glove lay tucked inside my short's pocket, some nubby contents inside, intact.

Chapter Fourteen

GIVE ME A HAND

Alive in the sand next to Katie, I felt my eyes rolling about unfocused in my head. Nothing else seemed to be functioning up there.

I sensed myself slipping into another dream. My chest was burning, and someone was pinching me. I rolled over on my back. A faraway part of me, the one in the real world, twitched with sand fleas, but otherwise didn't move.

In the dream world, I scrambled backwards over the sand, my hands clutched at my chest, cupping my throat. I was pierced over and over again. I was mutilated, carved. My hand was severed from my body, and I was wet with blood. I screamed. My bone protruded from my wrist; I screamed again. Hands pulled at me. They dragged me back across the sand. Sounds faded, only a vacuum in my ears. My body was rolled over, and something hard slapped my face. Then only blackness.

"Wake up. Wake up." Katie shook me.

I tasted warm, salty drops. This was not blood. Katie lifted my eyelids, one at a time. Water splashed my face; Katie had poured it on me, trying to rouse me from my stupor. I stared at my hands, struggling to focus. They were both there. My left hand was wearing the glove. The glove that held the hand, the bones...

were they mine? It was all coming back. My eyes sought Katie's with a plea to tell me the truth. Katie looked as crazed as I felt. We embraced.

"You were screaming that it was your hand."

"They cut my hand off, cut my chest, cut me…"

"We've got to get help. No more secrets, I'm begging you."

My fog took over. I passed out again, and again. Katie managed to drag me a bit, hoisting me upright. I shuffled along, my dead weight leaning on her almost the whole path back from the beach. I started to feel calmer. Katie's touch was the best medicine.

As we got to her cabin, Katie yelled for her father. He entered the room and looked me over, interrogating me with his stare.

"What happened here?" he asked Katie, "She's bleeding. What are these welts on her face?"

"I don't know! She kept scratching at herself and muttering about 'clearing the fog.'"

"It's okay," Doc said. "I have you, Pina." He carried me over to Katie's bed. "I'll get your parents. Katie, what happened?" Up close, in his arms, I saw him blanch when he noticed the faraway look on Katie's face.

My parents seemed to appear suddenly at my side.

I just sobbed, repeating over and over through spasms of choking, "Mommy, Mommy, Daddy, Daddy." I let myself be hugged, but their questions didn't make sense. I just stared ahead. I stared at Katie's dad as he told my parents he would observe me overnight. He said some doctorly things about knowing better in the morning. What? Knowing what? Needing to go to the hospital?

My mother protested, "But, but, but."

My father answered, "Let's do as the doc says." My eyes tracked the doctor pulling my father aside. Their whispering wasn't low enough.

"Barney, come here a sec. The girls have been messing around in this Butch story. I don't know what they've done or what happened, but calm, quiet, and rest will help, and we'll be able to get some info tomorrow. They've been traumatized, not physically, but emotionally."

Doc gave my mother a sedative, and Dad managed to convince her to go back to their cabin and lie down. Once she was gone, my father hesitated to leave. He debated with Doc about the ER, but relented when Doc reminded him that the nearest hospital was two hours away.

Doc took my father by the shoulders. "Barney, I promise, at the first sign of distress, I will call you and we will make the trip to the hospital. Right now, the jostling of the two-hour drive would do more harm than good."

I felt my father brush his lips against my forehead, and then I faded.

I awoke the next morning with Katie lying next to me, buried under tons of comforters on her bed. The sweet smell of sweat and Dove soap combined was a heady perfume. I felt Katie's arm next to mine. I stroked it back and forth, loving the sensation of her dark, soft hair.

Everyone was just letting us sleep and wake and sleep and wake. We had the radio on with tons of Everly Brothers and Buddy Holly songs and often dozed to the notes of *Dream*. Everything now seemed as calm as the morning air, soft warmth drifting in through the window behind the bed.

We attacked the food Doc had left: blueberry muffins and sausages, as well as Katie's mom's pancakes and my mom's chocolate. Our appetites pleased them all and they left us in peace for a bit. Neither one of us was thinking or remembering, just stuffing and slurping. We did overhear Katie's dad outside the screened windows telling my father to put off talking to anybody. No police, no one until he could find out what happened to us. I heard my father agreeing.

Katie and I licked our fingers and gobbled crumbs off the flannel sheet blankets with their pinecone motif. We felt the presence of Doctor McGuilvry, Katie's father in all his official capacity. He seemed huge, blocking the doorway with his full head of thick, wavy white hair. He had a kind smile, but we knew there'd be no getting away from telling it all.

I recounted my hysterics. I really and truly physically felt my hands cut off. I felt those boys' bodies, hands, and blades, but could not see their faces. As I relived it all again, I began to weep. Katie's dad wrapped an arm around me as I wailed and wailed.

As my sobs began to ease, I felt lighter. I heard a chickadee and a finch outside the screen. They felt extra *real* somehow, as if I was done with that confusing dream world once and for all.

I snapped out of my reverie when I felt Katie's tears. She was begging her father to tell her he wasn't involved, and tell her about the square tattoo…

Doc ran his hands through his thick hair. He appeared almost disheveled, which was unheard of for him. He let himself sink into the easy chair next to Katie's bed. He told us about the scar. Back at the camp, a group of older boys had banded together to protect some of the younger boys who were getting beat around.

"Katie, I swear to you," he said. "I didn't know anything about any violence. Some of the guys tried to keep me in the dark, knowing I was supposed to be going to Harvard in a few months. I want answers now too. I need to find out more about this, but you two absolutely need to stay out of it."

Doc wrapped his arms around Katie and buried his face in her hair. He pulled away and turned her face to him. Holding her that way, just inches from his face, he whispered, "I love you. You're the most precious thing in the world to me. That's all you have to know."

Convinced for the moment, a tear-stained Katie urged me to tell her father about the dreams. I did, starting with more details about that one on the beach.

When I started talking about the hand, my eyes felt like they were sinking back, back, into my skull, back away from the room. Noises became distant, muffled. The room smelled like a hospital, and I started screaming again.

I came back to Katie's room once more, but the pain didn't stop. I ripped open my pajama top and made the Doctor look at the stab wounds. He held me tight, stroking my hair away from my forehead.

"There's nothing there. I'm looking, but I see nothing," he said. The kindness in his voice made me start weeping again. He stroked me, and Katie's mother brought me a glass of water. He leaned forward, cradling me in his arms.

I was back again, totally cool. I saw that there was no blood. I spoke one word at a time, as the courage to look deeper came slowly.

I looked up at Doc. His face was calm, his light blue eyes the same as Katie's; the eyes I could swim in. He could have been Santa Claus, maybe God. I let myself go.

"I didn't know…" I examined my hands, hoping my lifeline would supply answers as I tried to explain. "I did not know whether these were mine. They felt, really felt cut…cut off. A blade…something sharp, but not too, was sawing away at my hands."

"Go slow, Pina." Doc stroked my hand as much with his voice and his words as with his soft touch. I pulled my hand away with no explanation.

I spread out the fingers of my right hand. "Then my other hand, this hand, became different. I felt it grip a knife. I…was cutting into something…I was slicing. I could feel the tip of a dull blade through…well, like a tough piece of meat. I became all these people, a whole cast of cutters and victims." I looked back up at Doc. A part of me felt almost normal, as if I had just told him about my favorite food.

Then, Doc asked me about Regina. I hid my face in my hands. It was too real again.

I told him, "My body hurts." I muttered something about boys bothering me. I cleared my throat and tried to spit out. "A boy did stuff to me." My face felt like stone again; my stomach, a quarry. Cold.

"There's no rush," he whispered. He continued to rock me. He pushed himself up and off the bed and puttered around the room a bit. He padded out of Katie's room and into his own, returning with chocolates and another big pillow, all the while checking to see how I was.

He told Katie, "I want you to sit with Pina. Do something; comb her hair, paint her nails. Just…just hold each other," he said. He looked the way I felt.

Katie managed to get my foot, paint my big

toe nail with her mother's True Crimson polish, play this little piggy, and distract me. The chocolate and chocolate chip cookies helped too.

We were smiling again. I felt as if this was a fever dream, everything slow and warm honey, tea and Social Teas. We smelled smoke as Doc opened the door to the porch. My father must have been outside smoking. We heard Doc explaining something about a pill. They agreed on half a pill and chamomile tea and more sleep.

Catherine knocked on Katie's door to see if we were still awake. She served us tea in two beautiful china teacups, brought from home, filled with warm water that tasted like lemon and pee. Still, it felt good to drink.

From outside, I overheard a lot of hushed 'hms' and 'ahs', but nothing made sense. Katie was jumping for joy, bouncing up and down on the bed. Maybe she drank the pee water and the pill too? It wasn't supposed to wake you up though. She said we were going to have another pajama party that night.

We ate lots of ice cream, butter crunch to be exact, with big pieces of nougat. This sick thing did get us lots of goodies, and that chamomile made everything seem better, as if we didn't have a care in the world. That night, Katie and I slept side-by-side, warm and sweaty and melting into one another. That is, until Katie unwrapped her arms and her legs from around me. She tapped roughly on my shoulder. I awoke immediately and saw her stare down at me.

"Do you think he helped kill Butch? I mean, he had a crush on Regina," she whispered.

I didn't want to get sucked back into the mystery, but I couldn't help myself. "According to Claudia, he had more than that," I said. I was back...back to normal, I thought.

I couldn't believe Katie's energy; she was wide awake and alert.

She went on, "Do you think he knows about Butch and Regina?"

"It does look bad," I said, but I really didn't want to be awake. "C'mon. Go to sleep. Remember, he swore he wasn't involved." I sighed and pulled her head back under the covers.

Chapter Fifteen

ANSWERS AND MORE QUESTIONS

We woke the next morning physically refreshed, as if nothing had happened. A soft breeze cooled us and swayed the gauzy curtains behind the bed. In our absence, since we had slept the better part of two days, lots had happened. We learned about what had transpired through the cracked door to Katie's room.

Katie and I heard Jeremiah Chandler, the owner of the Owl Lake Lodge and former camp cabin boy, come into the McGuilvry's. Leaning forward, we peered through the doorway and were just able to make out Jeremiah planting his overalled bulk into a rocker. He pitched forward on his kicker boots and spoke of his great respect he held for Doc and the mistrust of Bud Lawyer and his uncle, the Judge, Butch's father. Jeremiah was relating how the Lawyer's had paid off his family to make sure that Butch never returned. Jeremiah believed that the Lawyer's really had Butch put out of his misery.

We heard Doc raise his voice. "What the heck are you talking about?"

Jeremiah said, "I saw you all messing around out there by the lake. Mr. Mazzini, the girls, and then, Mr. Mazzini again just yesterday. I went out to see what the heck was going on and found that damned tire. I got it out of there and buried the bones. But I want answers."

Katie said her dad's face looked even more upset as he informed Jeremiah that he too wanted answers and that Jeremiah had now implicated himself by removing evidence. Katie and I were still drowsy from the pill, and we drifted back to sleep.

The next time we awoke, the sun was already high, brightening Katie's already cheerful cabin. Sun danced off her turned up nose, and for a second, I thought she was Annette Funicello. Obviously, my head was still cloudy. I knew I needed to sleep some more. But Katie swatted at a gnat and flipped back the stifling covers.

She slipped out of bed, leaving our door ajar I heard her flop herself down in one of the chairs in the sitting room.

"Hi, sugar, you feeling better?" Doc asked.

"Yeah," she yawned out loud. "Dad, I need to know. I can take it. You've gotta tell me more about camp."

"Can you believe I didn't do anything?" he asked.

"I want to," Katie said. "What about Regina?"

"We didn't call it dating, but I had a huge crush on her." He hesitated and then added, "We teased about going to the same college."

"So, she wasn't a floozy? But it sounds like the other boys..."

"Katie, what is it? Why are you crying?" I could hear Doc shift his considerable weight in this chair. I assumed he was hugging Katie. I didn't dare peek.

"I think something bad happened to her. Why'd she go away?" Katie asked.

"They said she got sick and had to go home early."

"Didn't you write to her?"

From where I lay, supposedly sleeping, Katie's

tone sounded like an accusation.

"No." Doc coughed. His tone became more doctorly. "My father was very strict." Doc stifled a yawn and continued, "When he saw I was mooning over Regina, he forbade me to try to track her down. He lectured me about college and how I had to be serious, that I had a brilliant future, following in his footsteps as a doctor. He was very strange, and inexplicably angry about that summer."

I stumbled into the sitting room where Katie and her dad were talking. Their faces told me everything. Doc was telling a nice story which Katie didn't believe. Or did Katie think he lacked the courage to do the right thing? Either way, she was acting as if she had made up her mind that he was guilty of something.

Katie was biting her lips and sniffling. She seemed to will me back into the bedroom so that she could continue her private talk with her dad.

Doc looked more and more puzzled. Puzzled, but maybe too much so, as if pieces were sliding into a place he never expected them to go, a place he had unconsciously fought all his life. He was seeing his youth come to life through Katie.

"Good morning," Doc greeted me and seemed glad for the interruption.

"I've been asking my dad about Regina. You ready to talk about her?"

Again, Katie's tone…

"You don't have to talk," said Doc.

"Just don't be angry with me. I hurt all over, and I feel dirty," I said.

"Go slow." Doc coughed and adjusted himself in the chair. It looked like he was trying to get more comfortable, less uptight maybe.

"Well, it's like my dreams, but not. He hurt me and did things to me. I could hardly breathe, and he touched me all over."

I heard my name as if through cotton. My face was hot and cold with sweat and heat rising up from the neck of my pajama top. Then, cold water, and Doc was holding me still, sitting me up, and putting my head between my legs.

"I think I'm okay. I'm back."

"Take your time. Who did this to you? Where is he?"

I watched Doc's face twist with anger. I thought I saw pain in his eyes. It matched what I was feeling. The physical pain was gone, but the picture I had in my head made me feel dirty and wrong. Doc softened his face, leaning over to me and touching my arm.

"Butch. It was Butch," I told him.

"But Butch…Butch is, I mean, should be, an old guy, like me," said Doc.

"Yes, but I was Regina in the dream, back at her camp, back then." I wrinkled my face. I knew how weird this sounded. "I know she was assaulted a long time ago, but I'm reliving it now."

"What?" asked Doc.

"He sang that church song, *Regina coeli*, but slurred the coeli, like it became Jayli or Gayli or Gaylo. He woke me up from my bed."

"This can't be." Doc was up on his feet, pacing. "In your dream, did you kill Butch? I mean, did Regina kill him?" Doc's eyes were darting all over. He was no longer calm.

"I don't think so. I don't know," I answered. Doc tried to get his arms around me to hold my fists. I had begun to pound the arms of the chair.

Doc was up pacing again. As if he were arguing with himself, he said, "Of course you didn't hurt him. Butch got hurt a long time ago."

"So did Regina. But I feel like I got hurt a few days ago," I added.

Katie, who had been sitting, looking small in the nearby rocker, came over to comfort me as her father turned to go. Now rather pale, he left the sitting room to go into his room like a man with a mission. He closed the door a bit too hard, and it crept back open.

We could see him and hear him. He punched the wall first, then threw his head back, and squeezed his eyes shut. He didn't know we were watching. He did know about Regina, but not enough. He had asked me if I – or Regina had killed Butch. We saw him drink a glass of water and pull out a small bottle of whiskey. The smell came all the way into where we were sitting in the sitting room. When Doc came back out to the sitting room, he bent down to give me some water. The strong, sweet-like smell of whiskey seemed to jump out of his mouth. He told us not to think about this, to go play.

Chapter Sixteen

I AM SPECIAL

We scuffed around that day, coddled by our mothers. We piled pine needles and flopped in rocking chairs. Half bored, half scared to talk about anything, we swiped ice cream bars from the kitchen in the main house, rolled on the barn floor under the pool table, got bored with that, found the kittens, and teased and tickled until that grew stupid. All the while, floating, eating, smacking flies. Not a word.

We were in one of our "flop" states, sprawled out in front of the dining hall. There was always a bunch of umbrellas outside the hall, at the ready for one of those sudden downpours. We had rounded the umbrellas up in a circle and covered them with a blanket. While we were in this makeshift tent, we heard Katie's dad talking to my father. We lay real still so they wouldn't see us under the umbrellas.

The Doc told my father I needed tests. I didn't know what he was talking about, but he mentioned my dreams and wondered about hallucinations or a "conversion" disorder. I was totally confused. Did he think I had changed religions? That I was a witch or devil worshiper? The more I heard Doc tell my father not to be scared, the more frightened I became. My father didn't seem worried, but maybe angry or ashamed. He mumbled something about his mother and before her, his "damn grandmother," Vincenza Daidone. About experiments with her father, the Doctor Daidone. About herbs and local lore in Giuliana, in Sicily.

"We've always called Pina 'sensitive'," my father told the doc. "She seems to be an old soul. Somehow, she knew how to chat in French with her teachers in kindergarten and first grade, and by fourth, she was mumbling some Haitian prayer. It seemed harmless."

"Seemed? You no longer feel this way?" said Doc.

"My mother died in fifty-three. Pina took her death really hard. She walked around in a fog, her eyes glazed, didn't wash, didn't eat. One night, she woke up screaming, ranting on about her dead sons. She raved about 'that damn castle.'"

"My sister Maria, a bit of an historian and psychic, asked me if Pina had said Constance, Constance of Aragon and Frederick II, fourteenth century Norman rulers of Sicily."

"She also said the shock of Mom's death had opened up a death field, a kind of region of negative energy. Mom had to return to her roots, the white stones of the castle in the village of Giuliana, a life-giving energy field. In this way, she was able to stop death from sapping the life of her spirit and that of Pina. Pina had tapped into those energy fields."

Katie opened her mouth as if to speak, but I placed a finger over her lips.

Dad was still talking. "We took Pina to the doctor's after a week or so. Then, she was back to her normal self."

Doc spoke, "Well, Barney...both girls have had a shock, and the more we can surround them with warmth and safety and no more talk of severed hands…I don't know if you know this, but they found the ring hand in a glove in the lake…"

"Jesus! And the police?" asked my father.

"Listen, Barney, Bud Lawyer wants to call his family first, and I need to find Regina Gallo. Pina had dreams, where Butch attacked her, and Butch molested Regina Gallo. Regina Gallo was a real person. My girlfriend, in fact, at the girls' camp, and she had to leave unexpectedly. We knew she was sick…that's all. Pina said it was as if she was Regina in her dream, and…I'm sorry, Barney, this may be difficult for you to hear…but Pina told me in her dream she was assaulted by Butch. Barney!" Doc had raised his voice. "I want to be clear: Pina was *not* physically harmed."

"God damn bastard!'

"I am sorry. She's okay. I want to reassure you," said Doc.

"You call what happened to Pina the last few days okay? Come on, Ron." My father choked up. "I know one psychiatrist I contacted did say that if she truly is intuitive, episodes like this might return around puberty or in instances of extreme emotion. But she's my daughter, for Christ sakes. Take it easy."

"Cut off fingers, scenes of violence, I think that qualifies for extreme emotion. Should I stop?" Doc asked.

"Just slow down."

Doc continued, "Psychologically it is as if she's been beaten, while physically there's not a scratch on her. I would like to call some colleagues, with your permission, and just check some things out."

"You've got it," said my father, lighting up his second cigarette. Katie and I started to slap each other around playfully when we heard footsteps going away from the dining hall. We added tickling and pinching.

Katie stopped abruptly. "Dangit, Pina! Why are we doing this? This is serious. I am serious!"

"I know..." My voice trailed off, small and quavering. "I don't want to panic. Don't want to think. Please, just hold me."

Chapter Seventeen

A MAN FORSAKEN

It was late afternoon now, grayish and cool outside for a change. We had been grounded to Katie's cabin so that Doc could continue his observations, but he hadn't done a terrific job. We had been able to sneak out to our umbrella tent and back inside without being noticed. Playing Monopoly in Katie's room, we were in a perfect spot to witness major communications between her dad and other key players.

This time it was Bud on stage. Katie's father took him into his sitting room, poured him a drink, and offered him the old leather-seated rocker to talk privately. Yet, despite the thicker walls of Katie's cabin, voices carried, especially those primed with alcohol.

"I called my father," Bud announced in a flat tone.

Doc tapped the side of his glass with his ring. "Well, what've you got? Your father spill the beans on your cousin Butch or his father?"

Bud sighed as he rocked back and forth. "The long version or—?"

"Cut to the chase," Doc said, clearing his throat.

"You've got it. According to my father, my uncle, Judge Reginald Lawyer couldn't whitewash all of Butch's dalliances with under-age girls, and certainly not the problem with Regina."

"Problem!" Doc raised his voice.

"Easy, Ron. Fifi Gallo had accused Butch of molesting Regina. Butch definitely had to disappear. My uncle paid Fifi off big time to shut up and to scare the crap out of Butch so that he would never come back."

"Ha! Scare? And Fifi wasn't going to kill Butch? What the—?"

"No. Listen! Fifi supposedly had some religious vision and—"

"Yeah, right. Saint Jude, I suppose, Patron Saint of Lost Causes." Doc snickered.

"Ron, my uncle firmly believed Fifi wouldn't kill Butch. He placed a lot of faith in money and his own corrupt power. He even paid off Jeremiah Chandler, the owner of the Lodge. Gave him his share of all this property."

"How's that?" Doc shifted his weight in his chair.

"Jeremiah was also supposed to keep Butch away and to notify my uncle if he did show up. End of story!" Bud rocked back heavily in the rocker and poured himself another drink.

"No, not quite." Doc blew out a long breath. "I called Regina. After some awkward small talk, she admitted that Butch had attacked her. I told her Butch was dead...murdered. She had no reaction. I heard something in the background, her father, I believe, and then there was silence. The phone had gone dead."

"No news...they say..." Bud sighed.

"Shut up!" Doc scraped his chair back. "Bud, can we forget about this for a bit and hit the lake? Too much old crap..."

Katie looked dazed. I was wondering how a smart

man like the Doc could have buried his head in the sand so deeply. Of course, I couldn't say that to Katie, but I think she was having a really hard time knowing what to make of him. She closed her eyes and leaned against me, hard. It felt good, as if she could trust me and needed me.

Her touch felt more than good. I felt other stirrings too. A big part of me wanted to explore that mystery. I had been ignoring those clues. What if I put them under a microscope? What would they say, and could I pretend I didn't get the message?

Chapter Eighteen

BOYS WILL BE BOYS

The next morning after breakfast, I twiddled my thumbs as we hung out on Katie's porch. I was devising a getaway. Our parents had eased their restrictions on our movements, but we would have been tarred and feathered if they had caught us going off to the camp. It was too dreary, too wet just to sit here, and our mothers were at the main house, sewing. We didn't have a clue where our fathers had gone.

We left the cabin and slogged through floating pine needles and slick grass. The latrine beckoned us. We were half-wet, and the stuffy confinement of the bathroom had a sauna-like effect on us. The rain pinged on the corrugated roof and splashed occasionally on the plywood floor where the roof patches hadn't held.

Water seeped into the room from the window that was still wedged open from the last visit. We pushed and shoved to get it closed; the window was really stuck. Finally, we got it closed, breaking some of the molding in the process. Splinters and dust came down and frosted Katie's hair, which had already been damp from the rain. It made her look ancient and gray. We both giggled, glad for the chance to laugh and be silly twits again. I smeared dust on her face, and she pushed me down to the ground, pinning my shoulders and threatening to dribble spit on my face. We rolled around laughing big, belly laughs and holding each other tight. Safe in each other's arms, we finally let ourselves feel just how scared we were. We started to sob. We stayed like that a bit, a long bit, and then I felt Katie's hand gently touch my cheek.

"You know I love you," she murmured.

"Yeah." I kissed her forehead and just hugged her close to me. We sat up and stayed leaning against the wall a while.

"I'll never forget you or this summer," said Katie. "But it's not over yet."

"Well, maybe…just maybe, I could be sick and have to recover at your house. What do you think?" I fantasized.

Even though we'd been seeing each other up here in Maine every summer since we were seven years old, I had only visited Katie at her home in the Hamptons once last Christmas vacation. The thought of being able to stay with her for a while really excited me.

"Do you think girls can love each other?" Katie wore a look I couldn't figure out.

I said, "You mean, like *love*?"

"Yeah, don't we?" said Katie.

I was beginning to think too much. I thought I knew what Katie meant, and my mind started to race again. Did she mean love, marriage, and touching or just best friend/family love?

Then, like magic, there was a distraction. There, sticking out of the broken molding was a crumpled piece of paper.

"Look!"

"I can get it with this stick. Here, read it," Katie said, flicking it over to me.

"There's crayon on it. Something like *'pecker.'*

Wait. '*Tonight*' and that's '*cut it*'. Holy cow! I think I got it: '*Watch Butch lose his pecker. We'll cut it off tonight.*'"

"Let me see," said Katie. "It's signed – Just a square. Oh God. The square again."

"I feel a little bit…"

"Are you going to sleep?" Katie shook my arm, trying to keep me with her.

"Maybe. Just stay with me…Billy?"

"No, Pina, wake up. Wake up!"

"*I'm tired of being poked,*" said Billy. "*I'm scared.*"

"*Tell someone,*" said Wolfie.

"*Tell? He'll kill me.*"

"*Or they'll kill him.*"

"*I hate myself,*" said Billy.

"*Hey, twerps! No need to hate yourselves, leave it to us big guys. Ha! Death by tickling!*" Kevin and Peter entered the room, laughing.

Kevin ruffled Billy's hair. "*What's up, half pint?*"

"*Yes, tell us older, wiser ones. Kind of like confession,*" said Peter.

"*Now you guys are going to bug me too?*" said Billy, scooting away from the older guys.

"*Who else is bugging you? Or…buggering you?*" Kevin asked.

Peter slapped Kevin on the back. "*Leave him alone.*"

"*Hey, you two. What are you doing hanging with the little ones?*" said Ron.

"*Shush, Ron, someone's got Billy for real,*" said Wolfie.

Ron rattled the cubicle, "*Who's in there?*

"*Whoa! It's just me, Joe Gallo, minding my business.*" Joe pushed the door open. "*Where is the little guy anyway?"*

A soft, crying voice warbled from inside another cubicle. *"Maybe I am just a wanker like he said, a stupid willy…and I peed. I peed. I'm all warm and wet. Let me go. Let me go."*

Katie's voice had broken into my dream at this point.

"Pina, you didn't pee. It's wet from the rain; wake up. You're not Billy."

"I'm so wet," I said.

I had come to, wet and cold and confused as all get out. This dream was different from the rest. At least nobody got hurt. I gave Katie all the new names and the old. At least her dad seemed to be a good guy in this one, and I told her as much.

We washed my face and dried it with parts of my shirt that was dry. We spent another fifteen minutes reading the walls to see if we could locate some of these names.

Then, I heard Katie way over in the far corner. She just mumbled, "Holy cow!" over and over. I joined her, and now both of us gaped at the light pencil drawing of a square and above it in bold letters, *"Don't be a square"* and below it *"Be one (Pete) to know one (Kev) (Joe)."*

"Jeez! Katie," I clapped my hands, "we got it!"

"My father, Bud, Pete, Kevin, and Joe were 'squares'!"

Chapter Nineteen

GOING TO THE TEMPLE

Doc caught us trying to sneak back into the cabin, dripping wet. He exploded, "Where in the name of the good Lord have you two been?"

"Well, you see, in the main house…Monopoly," said Katie.

"Don't give me any of that malarkey. You two were told to stay put."

"Dad, don't be mad. We want to ask you about some names."

Katie and I had decided to ask her father about some of the new names I'd overheard in my dream, like Joe Gallo, Peter, and Kevin.

"What the dickens? This better be good."

"Well, you must know Joe, Peter, and Kevin?" Katie was obviously eager to clear her dad.

"Joe, he's Regina's brother. The others are also from camp. Friends of mine." Doc was still barking. "There was a little wimpy kid who kind of went crazy at the end of camp." Doc paused a sec and then really started to bellow, "But God dammit! I told you two to leave it. Don't bother me with this crap now!"

We clammed up about the note. We had had enough for one day and quietly asked if we could stay put together. After dinner, we brought popcorn and comic books and *Seventeen* to bed. Snuggling under the old Bean's blanket with the green, red, and black stripes felt safe, and falling asleep in Katie's arms was a delight.

First light sneaking in through the gauze curtains roused me long before I got up. Still wrapped up in Katie's arms, I wanted to make that moment last as long as possible. Why couldn't this be an endless summer?

I knew there would be other summers, just as there had been these last nine years. But we were no longer kids, and I wasn't positive whether Katie's declaration of love from yesterday was only sisterly. What I was feeling was no longer best-buddy mutual admiration. Everything was different now.

I mean we never kissed on the lips. I didn't dare. But I wanted to, I really did. What would that mean? How could I leave her at the end of summer, and not see her again for a whole year? Too much could change while we were apart.

She'd meet other girls at the Albert Academy, where she'd be attending school next year. Lots of girls, much smarter and cooler than me. She'd have a roommate. She'd really fall in love. Maybe even with a guy from Phillips Exeter. Crap! I had to talk to her before it was too late. Just not yet. I wasn't brave enough yet.

I crept out of the cabin so as not to wake her. I couldn't face her yet. The dew wet my pants and every part of me that touched a leaf, a plant, a piece of wood, a blade of grass. Through the still-shaded woods, my nostrils filled with the fresh, crisp air. I felt clean and innocent and ran all the way from the road down through the damp pine needles, my feet slipping out from under me so that I slid the rest of the way across the damp sand on my bottom. I passed other cabins along my way, but all was quiet. Everyone was still sleeping.

Someone had left the aluminum canoe upside down

on the short wooden-plank guest dock. The canoe was bone-chillingly cold and wet, but I jumped in anyway. The canoe was unstable under my solitary weight, and I sat quickly as the boat wobbled and waggled. I really didn't want to go for a dip in this morning-cold water. I didn't paddle, just let the canoe drift across the water. I lay on my back, the uncomfortable seam of the canoe digging into my spine, and let my eyelids flutter open and shut. I snuck peeks at the clouds; there was a lamb, no an angel, or a unicorn.

I just wanted everything to be pretty and light and cozy, like cotton candy holding me or down feathers from my pillow and comforter, all showering down on me. Soft and cool, gentle and soothing. I could tiptoe on clouds, dance upside down, be silly, and imagine all sorts of things that didn't hurt anyone. No one would know, and no one would care. I just laid down on that crummy seam and pulled the tarp over me. There was no wind. I was safe to float.

Everything turned white and feathery. There were chickens and turkeys all over. I was dressed in white, a long, white, confirmation-like gown. There was a long aisle, and then penguins. The noise was strange, like clucking or clapping, and I realized they were applauding me as I walked down the aisle, flowing and swishing towards? Towards? A rabbi? I could see his phylactery around his forearm.

He was calling me, but I wasn't alone. I realized Katie was also there, all in white, and she had feathers in her hair, and she smiled so sweetly at me. The rabbi was smiling too, and he said something about the hoopah and pointed to the canopy over our heads. I thought he meant a hoopoe bird because of all the fowl. He asked me about rings, and Katie had cigar bands in her hands. Our nails were shaped and polished clear; we held hands. We went back down the long, dark aisle, walking towards a shaft of sunlight that entered through a doorway at the end of the room.

Something was gritty underfoot, and outside was a big sign "Carnal's Poultry Farm and Slaughter. Carnal's, which one's best? Carnal's outdoes the rest."

I heard no more turkeys, but dribs and drabs of Havah Na Guila and The Hawaiian Wedding Song. I could see people asking to kiss the bride. Someone toasted with spritzy stuff, champagne-like, and we laughed and laughed. We were sopping wet with wine trickling into our eyes and mouths as we hugged, laughed, and cried. Katie asked me if we had died and this was heaven.

I said, "No, just Greenwich Village."

"But," she said, "did they sacrifice us? Like communion with wine?"

"No," I said again. "It's just Greenwich Village, and we got married."

I was drenched. My gown clung to me, and the music had changed to a horn, a car horn or foghorn. NYPD was shaking me. They were arresting me for lewd behavior and telling me to come to my senses.

My eyes opened on the uniform of the local game warden, shaking my very wet body. Seems the spray of a motorboat got me, and when the boater realized I was motionless at the bottom of the canoe, he got the game warden. After a great fuss, I told him I was a guest at Owl Lake and that I had just fallen asleep in the canoe. He towed me back just to make sure.

I just wanted to be alone to get back to my dream. How much would I tell Katie? I wanted to share it with her, but I just wasn't ready.

Chapter Twenty

MIND READING

I couldn't wait to find Katie. I bolted from the beached canoe and tore up the hill, still full of images of our wedding. There she was, sitting on her porch looking very real. She looked as if she had just stepped out of a shower, all crisp and clean in white pedal pushers and a blue striped top. A few strands of her hair blew gently by her cheek.

"What'cha doin'?" I asked. I knew she hadn't attended our wedding the way I did.

"Had to babysit my mother. When Dad's with his friends, she really latches on to me."

"Missed ya."

I felt my face turn a darker shade of fuchsia as soon as the words were out of my mouth. Pretending to be casual, I swung myself into a chair next to Katie.

"Any more dreams?" Katie asked.

Did she know about our wedding? A curtain of fear crept over my face. It was such a beautiful dream, but I didn't want to tell her about it yet.

"Come on, all of a sudden you don't dream?" Katie paused a second and asked, "How could you make a dream happen?"

"Do you mean do dreams come true?" I said.

"No, I mean, could we make you dream about who killed Butch?"

"Never tried that…"

Jeez! I don't want to dream about Butch.

"Could we try? If it gets too scary, I would wake you up."

I was definitely nervous to force a dream about Butch and the attack, but if I could control my dreams, then I could dream about Katie, a wedding, and a honeymoon whenever I wanted.

"Okay, let's go to the shooting range." Was I crazy? No. I needed to know what happened with Butch, and this might help.

Plus, the shooting range was always a place of strength for me. Katie and I loved to collect the leftover shell casings from the hill behind the suspended targets. We treasured the shells we gathered, fascinated by the power they gave us. A kind of might makes right. They filled us with some sort of…lust? We always looked older and wiser, almost women, when leaving that strange place. Plus, Katie was my dream woman.

"Where'd you go? Hey! What if they shot him?" said Katie, calling me out of my reverie.

"Now you want me to get shot?" Even the thought of that kind of pain made me tense up.

"No, I want you to see Butch's killer."

"So I should lie down? Then we'll say, 'Dream Pina, oh dream of being killed so you can see who murdered you.'"

"Well, how did it happen before?"

"Dunno, just did," I snapped back.

"You angry?" Katie squinted at me.

"I just liked it better when you didn't think I was weird."

"I don't think you're weird. I…uh…think you're special, like you know things. Maybe you even know what I'm thinking. I don't know. That's kind of scary too. So then you know I don't think you're weird, and you know you're my best friend and all that."

"You think I can read your mind?"

Both of us were thinking the same thing, fear of what the other might know. So what is she afraid I'll know, that she likes me the way I like her?

"I don't know!" said Katie.

Wow! She sounded kind of ticked off. I wrapped my arm clumsily around her shoulder as we got up from her porch to go to the shooting range.

"Oh Katie," I stammered, trying not to say too much, "I sort of can tell you want us to be a…team…a great team, right?"

"Yeah…right."

Now, I definitely couldn't tell what Katie was thinking. Her voice trailed off, flat and unconvincing. She squeezed my shoulder once, twisted away from my hold, and pushed the screen door open with the flat of her hand.

Once we arrived at the steps to the shooting range at water's edge, I climbed up into the raised gallery and lay down on the slimy, green bench. Lagging behind, Katie barely touched the rungs of the broken ladder with her fingertips, complaining of the green gunk all the way up. I looked up from my bench to see part of the sky peeking through the rafters and spiders.

"I'm going to put my web around you." I laughed, swiping my finger through a cobweb and brandishing it at Katie.

"Stop!" Katie poked at my shoulder. "Let's get started, it's time for you to dream now."

I wiped my webby hand off on my shorts and rolled over so that I was face down on the bench.

"Do I have my hands? Am I Butch or Regina?"

"You sure you want to do this?"

"No, but...I don't know what else to do."

"Okay? So try to imagine, before your hands got cut off. Who is holding the knife, and do you hurt anyplace else? Here, I'll massage your temples and dangle this locket. You're getting sleepy..."

Hmm. I loved her soothing hands on my face. No, I'm not in a state to see Butch, or Regina, or anybody... except Katie.

"I think you're sleeping."

Maybe I can pretend. I didn't want her to stop touching me.

"Pina, are you really asleep? I know you can't resist tickling. Wake up!" Katie played coochie-coo on my side. I lay mute...for a while. Then other sensations began to trickle in.

"My hands! Help! Gotta get the blood off. Rip the skin off!"

I frantically rubbed and wiped my hands on my shorts. They were so sticky. I tumbled off the shooting gallery, falling and tripping the last few feet to water's edge, rubbing my hands against the shells and rocks. They were still dirty. I couldn't get it off. I ran towards the water. The voices...*I'm here, Butch. It's Billy. I hear you. I can see you down there. The clean water is down there. I'm coming down. I'll just dive. How far...*

I was awake for just a second and then not. Katie's arm was around me. I no longer knew which dream I was in. I was wet. She kept on telling me not to fight her. Fight? She had her arm around my throat. I struggled to get free. I swallowed a lot of water. She slapped me and said she could swim for both of us. I started to lie back. I thought I was drowning. I kept on hearing her voice say she would save me...save me...save me. But I was gone again.

Leave me. I've gotta go back. They're still dirty. The only clean water is down there.

"Pina, stop!"

Somebody hit me. It was Katie. Katie?

Right. It was a dream. I snapped awake. Katie had dragged me out of the lake. I must have said I was Billy. I couldn't remember.

"Billy? You're Pina, not Billy," Katie said.

"Yeah. Why am I wet? Was I the killer? Tell me! I remember...my hands. They were attached."

"You weren't Butch. I think you were Billy, and you thought you saw Butch in the water, down deep, *'where the clean water was.'*" Katie continued. "You know, I overheard my dad say something to Bud or someone that Billy kind of went crazy at the end of camp and almost drowned. Well, you were acting really crazy, and you could have drowned."

"You saved me?"

"I guess I did." Katie's chest started to heave, and her eyes grew wet.

"Don't cry," I said. "I don't want to die." I tapped my chest. "Me, Pina, I don't want to die."

We held each other, wet with salty tears, sopping with stinky, sea weedy water. I rested my head on Katie's shoulder. After a while, I rubbed my face to try and clear my mind.

"Kat..." I blew out some stinky breath, "Maybe we should let the adults take over. I'm just scaring you...and me."

"But Pina, we've got the answer! It's Billy; it's got to be. He's the murderer. We can't quit now." Katie shook me.

"No, no way! He's just a wimp. He could never—"

"Whoa! Butch bullied him, no, I mean Roger… well, Billy was bullied so long and maybe more. He hated himself. He said so in your dream. He must have snapped." Katie was shaking. "If I were Billy, I'd want to kill…Roger…?"

"Wait…who?" I asked.

"Roger, right? Oh man, Pina, there are two bad guys." Katie's voice echoed up and down the lake's channel as she did a victory dance.

"Yeah. Butch and Roger, but I think we gotta go back to the latrine," I said.

"What happened to saying we've gotta let the adults finish this?" Katie imitated my earlier whiny voice.

"This part probably isn't dangerous. Besides, with you there to massage and hypnotize me—"

"I didn't."

"No, but it felt good," I said.

"I don't understand anything." Katie searched the sky for answers.

"I think you do."

"Now you *are* reading my mind." Katie was still looking at the sky, not at me.

Maybe I've said too much. Does she really not know?

"Remember the first time I saw something in the latrine? Someone was kind of protecting Billy," I said.

"More like fighting with Roger who was calling him Romeo, but we don't know for sure that that was Butch," Katie said.

"That's why we have to go back to the latrine."

We left the lake to trudge up the hill behind the rec hall. My Bermudas were almost dry by now. They'd be drenched with sweat, bites, and blood by the time we made it to the latrine.

Getting up that first cutaway bank around the shooting range was tricky. Katie took a running head start with her long legs, and once on top, reached out her hand to help pull me up. We scooted through the somber woods to the rec hall, and dashed across the old softball field to the latrine.

Chapter Twenty-one

NEW MYSTERIES

We didn't stay long at the latrine. There was no further writing hidden on the wall, nor answers to be discovered. Besides, we had to get back for lunch. After our Salisbury steaks, salads, and brownies, we wandered off to play croquet. No one could get angry with us for being less than five yards away from the dining hall and it was a perfect game for the mid-afternoon humidity.

Jostling each other through the pine saplings on our way to the lawn, we spotted a small, stooped over, older man, kind of slinking around. He was no New Englander, what with the flashy gold necklace around his flabby neck, a diamond pinky ring, and a flower in his lapel. We figured he would drive a pink Cadillac, but there was no car in sight. Katie joked that maybe he was like an Italian Leprechaun. He seemed to appear from out of nowhere, weaving his way in between the thick yellow pines between the dining hall and the main house.

We started and stopped our croquet game several times to check out what this man was up to. I was winning and two shots away from the post, but I dropped my mallet and crept close to the path to the cabins, where I'd have a better view of this guy.

It was then we saw the letters Fifi spelled out in

big loops on the gold necklace. We had heard so much about this man. He was Regina's father. We just had to follow him.

Fifi had stopped. He was standing still in front of my father. Fifi had found what he was looking for. My father just happened to be in the wrong place at the wrong time, trying to fade into the scenery to avoid irritating guests with his smoking.

"Scusi, can you light me?" we heard Fifi say to my father.

"Oh, sure. You want a match."

"You speak no Italiano?"

"Come again? Oh, not since I was a child. Why do you ask?" My father's tone seemed both curious and hesitant.

Fifi touched the side of his nose, and eyed my father with a certain authority.

Katie and I just casually strolled past them, greeting my father. Fifi tipped his hat, mumbling something in broken English about my face being the map of Sicily. He called me "Bella."

I turned briefly to smile at him and he asked me where I was from. I shot a quick look to my father to see if I should answer.

When I told him Queens, New York, he said, "No. Which town, Giuliana or Chiusa Sclafani in Sicily?"

My father answered, "Giuliana," with pride and a good accent.

As we walked off, I distinctly heard the word for police, *polizia,* and an even louder *no* in my father's voice.

When we circled back away from the main house, some hundred feet away, we saw Fifi and my father shake hands. Fifi clapped my father on the back, then casually threw his jacket over his shoulders. My father walked robot-like directly back to our cabin. The ground vibrated with the bang of the door.

I told Katie to wait for me while I ran back to my cabin, supposedly to pee. My father was sweating profusely in the cabin although the thermometer only registered sixty degrees today. He had already lit his second cigarette in the few minutes since leaving Fifi. He held his head with his cigarette-free hand.

I asked my dad if he wanted some water. His only response was a scowl and a warning to stay away from that man.

I ran back to find Katie sitting on the lawn at the edge of the croquet game. She was leaning against the main house, playing with some kittens. I told her something was definitely up with my dad. His meeting with Fifi had not been good, and Fifi was nowhere to be seen.

Katie smiled. "An Italian Leprechaun, I told you."

We played with the kittens, our hands brushing occasionally as we both stroked the same cat. We froze when we saw Doc. We had to think whether he had explicitly forbidden us to be here.

Someone else was walking with him on the broad front lawn in front of the main house. Katie said this had to be Joe Gallo. She actually remembered seeing a picture of him in her dad's study. They had their arms around each other in the picture. But guys back then, they did that…didn't they?

Katie and I invented something we would ask her father, interrupting his conversation with this dark, handsome guy. Doc would have to introduce us.

As we approached, we caught Doc saying to Joe, "Same charmer, Joe, but I'm still not charmed. You've got to be here for your father." He sneered. "Your sister must have accidentally tipped him off." Doc paused upon seeing us. "Excuse me," he said, stepping a bit to the side of Joe.

"Yes, Katie?"

Katie explained that we wanted his permission to hang out and play croquet on the nearby lawn. He hadn't seen us there twenty minutes before. Doc hastily agreed, but did not introduce us.

Although Doc and Joe moved off to the side a bit, we managed to catch bits and pieces of the story.

Joe was clearing his throat. We heard him say something about his sister. "Regina…you…hers…no…mine."

Doc mumbled, "Sounds adolescent…"

"Talked about…the future, you two…just killed me." We heard Joe sigh extra loud.

"Me?…her boyfriend, not yours…too confused…ashamed." Doc coughed that strange cough.

"You know…you wanted it…" Joe snorted.

We barely heard Katie's dad say, "Yup." He cursed and mumbled, "I…been a better boyfriend to you…"

Katie and I exchanged a puzzled look. Joe was pretty gorgeous, for a man: wavy, light brown hair, green eyes, high cheekbones, and a really warm smile. Katie and I made flirting movements towards each other, wiggling our shoulders and our heads.

We heard something about "your eyes on my ass" and then "sanctimonious prick." All of a sudden, they were struggling, slapping, and attempting to punch each other.

Neither was a good fighter, but Doc was a big man, managed to pin Joe to the ground and stared down at him. Katie and I were frightened, but we couldn't move without making noise. Actually, it looked more like a junior high fight. It was good no other guests were around, probably still playing shuffleboard in front of the dining hall.

Since they seemed rather distracted, we moved a bit closer, hidden by the huge yellow pine just a few feet from where they lay on the ground.

"I'm not fighting," said Joe. "Didn't want to fight then either."

"Me neither," said Doc.

"You're still holding me," said Joe.

"I know," said Doc.

This was becoming strange. Katie's eyes were big and round, and I think she was purposely pulling her hair, strand by strand in front of her eyes. I have to admit I was curious. I had heard about girls like that, but these were grown men.

"I've never done this before, not since the..." said Doc.

We could hear Joe saying, "I didn't understand my feelings for you. Couldn't stand it. I wondered if you messed with my sister Regina and pinned it on Butch. Guess it was my way of pushing you away, of trying to hate you."

Doc said, "I didn't touch her. Butch called me queer, said he'd teach me how to treat a lady. Scared me...all the way around. Caring for you so much, holding each other that time...I did not make it with your sister. She wanted to, but I..."

"It was a lot more than holding...and here we are. Easier to see each other as evil. So hard to admit we cared deeply for each other." Joe coughed before continuing, "I heard about Butch's ring. It wasn't me; I didn't touch Butch…don't think my father did either."

Katie and I wanted to leave, but we couldn't without being found out. Then we overheard parts of stories about their last nights at camp. Jeremiah got them booze; they got blotto drunk at a wild party with some guys running around in sheets. We had heard too much. We split in the middle of their loud guffaws.

Katie and I retreated to the back of my cabin with a lot on our minds. The warm, pine needle beds around the cabins' stilts were one of the kittens' favorite spots, as well as ours when we needed to be comforted. Right now, I could tell from the look on Katie's face she needed soothing.

Her chest rose and fell with sobs several times before she could find the breath to say, "Is he…? How could he be? I mean my mom, me…I think I'm going to be sick."

I held her hair as she leaned over and spit up. "There's got to be an explanation," I said. "Maybe, they're like brothers? They didn't kiss or anything."

"But you heard them talk about not doing this since 'that time.'"

"Well, maybe there was an accident or something, or they were drunk. Remember they were talking about being drunk? Maybe it happened then."

"That still doesn't explain things. God, my father's a pervert? He can't…it's gotta be Joe's fault."

"Must be. Doc's your dad. He's a good dad. C'mere. Here, take my hanky. I know it's weird, but he's never done anything like this before."

"Like wrestle with a guy?" Katie laughed a bit. "He doesn't have a limp wrist."

"You're awful," I said.

"I'm serious." She pushed me over and messed

up my hair with both her hands.

Sounds of Doc trudging through the nearby vegetable garden distracted us.

He passed through, carrying several bottles of beer towards a couple of broken Adirondack chairs. Joe Gallo, Jeremiah, and Bud Lawyer were already back there. They were all in on it.

Katie was preoccupied, tracking their movements and trying to catch bits of information, which left me to track my own thoughts about Doc and Joe. What they were talking about was definitely queer, but they didn't really seem like sissies. Doc was big and strong and had longish, wavy hair like the Everly Brothers. He was married. Joe? Joe was…gorgeous. Well, he lisped…a little.

I started to feel really nervous. A cold, bright light flashed on in my head. If Katie's father was like that, could Katie have it too? What if her father was really involved in the murder, should I just let it go, and never find out?

What if I was really like that? Should I just let that go too? I would be going home soon. I could just let everything be, let everything go back to normal.

Yuck!

Katie shook me. "See!" She pointed off in the direction her father had gone.

I wasn't sure what I was supposed to see, but Katie told me what she had heard. We already knew some of it. Apparently, the men all claimed they were drunk that night and that none of them remembered any violence. Now, they were convinced that that had been the plan all along, to keep them in the dark about the secret meeting.

Chapter Twenty-two

SHEDDING SOME LIGHT

After our full day, Katie and I didn't talk much before dinner. It was a bit misty and cool, and the grayness of the sky seemed to match our mood. We actually hung out in the dining hall a bit longer than usual. I studied my mother's homemade culotte-dress, the wrong style for someone as short and plump as my mother. Her chattering allowed me to drift away.

My father commented on the price of gas. I think he was calculating mileage when he wasn't striking matches to light his cigarettes. Waitresses hummed snappy tunes as they passed. All was hunky-dory until I vaguely heard my father mention a date in the near future and drive home.

I gazed across the room with all its fogged-in windows, to find Katie's table at the other end of the dining hall. Her mom was gently fanning the smoke from the wood-stove away from their table. Her father, Doc, looked perky and fresh in his madras Bermudas and high wool socks, a strange choice for the weather. Katie tried to clear the window with her sleeve. It seemed a table of contradictions.

Katie gave up on the window. She turned away from it and her family and flashed me some signals to meet her at the rec hall.

I made my way in the semi-darkness, crossing the road and ducking through trees to meet Katie as planned. Fireflies more than headlights lighted my path. Katie was waiting for me outside, and we opened the rec hall doors and let ourselves drop to the floor, out of breath.

"Katie, why are we here at the rec hall again? I don't know why we keep coming back."

"We're here," said Katie. "Well...you know."

"What, so I can dream on command again?" I asked with a pout. "Like that went so well last time!"

"Hey, you sound so angry."

"Well, this...this was ours...our game...our secret...just you and me. Now, it just feels like you're not with me."

"Wait! What are you talking about? Not with you? Who else would I be with?"

"You're just trying to help your dad, not me! Katie, my dreams...they're real. Real like the el train, and the ugly stores in Queens, and my parents talking about the price of milk in the A&P..." I was starting to ramble, I knew.

Katie looked confused. "Huh?"

"I'm not making this stuff up. These dreams are real, and they're terrifying, and they hurt! You're just in this to help clear your dad. You don't even care! If this were back in the real world, away from here...you wouldn't even talk to someone like me!"

"Jeez. What is up with you? I have to figure out what's going on with my father, and you're saying I'm superficial? What is your problem?"

"I, I don't think you care about me," I said, "I think you're just in this to help your dad, and then you're going back to your private school life without me."

"I love you. This is ours. I want to help my dad, yeah. But I wouldn't even be doing this if it weren't for you. We're in this together. I want us to find out what happened to Regina, and I want us to get Butch and… whatever happened, I want there to be justice."

"But the important thing…" I said.

"Yeah, is us, our stuff," said Katie.

I didn't know what to think. It felt like Katie was saying the things I wanted to hear, but the summer was almost over, and there was still all this business with my dreams. It was too much to think about, and we were running out of time.

"I'm, I'm so…I didn't want to cry."

"What's wrong?" Katie stepped closer, concerned.

"Well, it's almost over. I've gotta go home."

"Oh?"

"That's all you have to say?" I practically yelled.

"I wasn't…I hadn't been thinking about it. The end of summer, I mean. I lost track of time." Katie turned away, and through my tears, I saw her wipe at her eyes. She couldn't stop either.

"When?" Katie lifted her watery eyes to me.

"Next week, I think."

Katie put her arm around me. I melted, letting myself feel all mushy and weak.

"I just don't want to think," I said.

"Come here," said Katie. "Come snuggle."

We melted into each other's arms. The last thing I remember was Katie softly snoring, and the soft double thud of her heart beating in rhythm with mine.

Then, the voices:

"*Awake?*"

"*Tonight?*"

I heard myself responding. I tried to fight it, but

I was lost, lost in the boys' voices. I tried to see faces, but it was no use. Just black and blacker…

"Get up. We've got the others out of sight…just us—"

"We'll get the bastard. Ron deserves this from us."

"We've got to keep them out of this. You know their plans."

"Okay. Okay," said Billy.

"We're ready to get him."

There they all were, gathered behind the crafts cabin. The fire had been lit in front of the shooting gallery, and they were ready to go.

"I said, 'just scare.' Besides, Ron's really your friend, you and Peter's," Billy said.

"Yes, but Wolfie and us, we've kept old Roger away from you."

"Sounds like you're saying I owe you," said Billy.

"Well, not exactly."

"Yeah, yeah, I'm just scared, I guess." said Billy.

"Hey Billy Boy, I'm here. We've got the other guys out stone cold," said Peter.

"So your stuff really works."

"C'mon, we got the fire going, and Butch should be coming. Here's your sheet."

"Wha? It's too long; I'll trip," said Billy.

"Hey Wolfie, show him how – and put this mask on."

I remembered clutching my face, clawing and tearing. I was definitely in my dream, but it was as if I wanted to see as me, as the Pina in 1959, not Billy or whoever's body I was inhabiting.

"My face, I can't…" I said. "I can't breathe."

"Pina, Pina, wake up."

I snapped upright, totally alert. "Quick, let's go to

the science cabin. We've got to see about those sleeping beauties," I said.

"Slow down. What are you talking about? What sleeping beauties?"

"Sleeping pills, or chemicals! A formula to knock people out, like they're dead drunk. Like your dad and Joe Gallo were saying."

Still bleary eyed and raw from the dream, I pulled Katie off the rec hall porch and half-dragged her to the science cabin. We slid our way to the basement, and I tried to focus in the darkness. I knocked over a bunch of vials and tiny bottles in my rush to find what I was looking for.

It was clear now that certain people had been drugged. We rifled through the shelves and found laudanum, passionflower, and other chemicals that, according to Edgar Allen Poe's short story, when mixed could put you to sleep. We flicked on a flashlight to search, and I sucked in a sharp breath when the beam landed on a paper marked "secret sleeping potion" signed "Peter, the inventor."

Katie was just as shocked. "How does this all fit together? What happened in your dream, Pina?"

"Well, I was Billy again, and they all, Billy, Wolfie, Kevin, and Peter, had the others put to sleep, Ron included. They specifically mentioned Ron, that they had to keep him out of it, whatever it was."

"But who were they going to do it to?" said Katie.

"Well, they were ticked at Butch, and then the voices, not sure who each one was, they said Billy owed them for protecting him from Roger. Katie, we just found out your dad didn't know anything. Don't you get it? He was drugged and couldn't do whatever it was they did. Your dad's clear!"

Chapter Twenty-three

CHILDREN AND FATHERS: ALL INNOCENT

After our midnight jaunt last night, we talked quietly for a while. We tried to figure out how Katie could tell her dad we knew he was innocent. Tell him, but not tell him we were still messing around in old camp business. He definitely wouldn't like that.

We had just gotten to sleep by dawn, so we barely made it to breakfast. The morning mist was bracing. The woodstove usually was a welcomed morning touch, but now it only made us dopier and sleepier than normal.

By the time reluctant, morning conversations with the parents were totally finished, and breakfast completed, I was fully awake. I glanced down to the other end of the dining room to see Katie lean over to kiss her parents good morning. That was her normal M.O. before going off to play. I distinctly heard her father's professional voice tell her to stay close at hand.

We met outside the dining hall and slinked over to the back of her cabin, where we flopped down beneath the pine trees. We discovered the two Gallos, who were not guests at Owl Lake. They were sitting in the bus hut on the side of the road. The hut was usually reserved for schoolchildren, so it seemed a suspicious place for two men to meet. We were perfectly camouflaged against the green-black needles, a short distance away from the Gallos. It actually acted like a music shell, so we heard each word distinctly, even in spite of Fifi's accent.

"Dad, who exactly are you? What did you do back then? You've got to level with me," said Joe.

"Nothing. I did nothing."

"For Christ sakes, I just accused Ron McGuilvry, the only man I ever loved besides you, of terrible things, of rape and murder. You've got to tell me. Did you kill Butch for Regina? And me? Did you know about me? I confess, I would have wanted you to get Roger. He was on me, constantly. Damn near beat me to a pulp. For her, you did everything. Would you have protected me, me your sissy son?"

"My son," said Fifi. "Come embrace your father. Nothing would make me stop loving you. I know about you, all along, it's okay. As for the rest, I did tell Lawyer…papa of Butch…I scare the hell out of Butch, I promise him. I tell my boys, find him. Just to scare, maybe hit him, one, maybe two times. Nothing else! But, no trace of him. My boys, they never find him."

Katie's face looked troubled. We had to talk. About her dad, definitely, but also about us. Listening to Joe Gallo talk about his emotions with his father, I began to realize that Katie and I couldn't avoid the discussion much longer. I knew that talk might be as hard for me as for her. How to talk about love without talking about what kind of love?

But, as usual, there was no time for that kind of talk. I heard my father calling me. He had walked over towards Katie's cabin, thinking I was there. I had to get out from our hiding place, brush myself off, and act as if I had just been looking for kittens. No one could know that we were still looking into the camp mystery.

I said goodbye to Katie, who told me that she just wanted to be left alone for a while. As I approached my father, he was really acting weird. His tone was firm and cold when he told me just to follow him back to our cabin. When I got there, cartons of beach stuff cluttered the porch. Inside the cabin was already a mess of frantic piles: bunches of papers, bills mostly, a stack of Readers Digest Condensed Books, and two half-written postcards. My father told me to start packing.

I started to panic. "Daddy, why?" I tried to reach out for his arm, but he slapped his hand down on the bridge table.

"Because I said so. Time to go home." Dad's tone was still strange and harsh.

"But why can't I stay? I could stay with Katie."

"No. You can't impose on strangers. The fares are cheaper this Friday. That's when we'll leave."

I collapsed into the folding chair, trying desperately to think of ways to win.

"And the car? What does Mommy say?" I heard her bustling in their room.

"Don't talk back, Pina. I'm tired this year. The train will relax me," my father answered.

"But we were supposed to stay another week or two this year!"

"When you're older, you'll understand. Be quiet and help your mother pack."

"What about the ring and the finger?"

"That's for the police to figure out. We're just going home."

I had to stay and help pack all day and evening. I didn't even have a chance to tip Katie off. I felt too sick and furious, and I was afraid I'd say too much to Katie. By the middle of the night, I was desperate enough to creep out of my cabin. Not wanting to get caught and maybe lose this last chance, I crawled on all fours over to Katie's window.

"Psst! Katie!" I whispered, pulling myself up onto a crate so that my face was level with the sill.

"What? Where are you? Do you know what time it is?" Katie's groggy face appeared at the screen.

"Shush! Let me in quick. I'm going to fall off this crate."

"Oh, hold on!" Katie looked over my face once I pulled myself over the sill and into the light. "You've been crying."

"I can't, I just can't go home," I sobbed, not making much sense. "My father's crazy. I hate him!"

"C'mon, Pina, come back to bed with me. We'll wake up early and get you back to your cabin."

"What if I ran away, and you hid me until after they left?'

"Pin, they wouldn't leave if you were missing."

"You're right. I just don't want to leave you. My father is making us leave this Friday!"

Kati looked stunned. After a moment, she whispered, "I don't want you to go either."

"I don't want to lose what we have," I said.

"I can't do it without you. No one to imagine with. No one for adventures," Katie said.

"You…just everything…I can't go back there, where everything's just the same! Like a cookie cutter…all the ugly stuff…all the church dresses and the noisy trains, and, and…alone…I'll be all alone!" I was pounding her bed.

"Shush. Come back to bed. Maybe we'll dream up a solution."

"What if we told your father everything,

everything we know with the notes and formulas and dreams, all the dreams…?"

"And all the stuff we know that clears him. Maybe he would pay us." Katie was grasping at straws.

"Huh?"

"Well, if it shows that he's innocent…I don't know, perhaps he would be grateful."

"Tomorrow, we'll do it all tomorrow." I snuggled into Katie's side.

It was so cozy and safe next to Katie, I didn't dare start talking about why next year would be different. Maybe I'd never get up the nerve to tell her how I felt, but I was too upset to risk everything now.

My father must have gone fishing at the crack of dawn. From where I was dozing, half-awake in Katie's bed, I heard his tackle jangling against the pole and bait box, and I smelled his cigarette. He usually went directly back to his room when he was out early, so there was little chance he would discover me here in Katie's bed, rather than my own.

He wasn't the only one with things on his mind apparently. Doc, who must have been sitting on the porch, let the screen door slam accidentally when he bolted out to catch my father. I heard their conversation as though in a dream, impossible to tell how much was real.

"Barney, hold on."

"Doc, uh, Ron, we've got to talk," said my father.

"Yeah, Barney. I hear you're leaving, suddenly."

"That's true. I've gotten messages from a certain criminal element. You've got to understand. I'm scared for my life and for my family. Here and in Italy."

"What do you mean?" said Doc. "You have nothing to fear. You didn't do anything."

"Except find the ring and the finger. I'm not a doctor or a lawyer. I'm just a nice, Italian fellow, and we know what New Englanders think about us."

"Barney, this is 1959. It's not prohibition or—"

"But the other Italians are saying stuff…do you see what I mean?"

"The other Italians? Oh, his father, Fifi Gallo. I don't know much about him, I only knew his son."

"Thugs, all of them! I should have gone to the police. What are you so scared of, Ron?"

"You have to understand how bad this looks for me, Barney! Regina was my girlfriend, and she was attacked while we were at camp together. She was at the sister camp around the cove. They could say I killed Butch to avenge her. It looks like Bud and his uncle, Reginald Lawyer, could have been involved—"

"Then, let the police sort it out."

"Well, Barney, I have news for you. Maine police don't like downstate docs and lawyers and old money. They'll never get to the bottom of this. I want to figure more out before we go to them."

"No deal."

"How can I convince you?"

"You can't!"

"You know, Barney, your daughter is brilliant and talented," said Doc.

"Leave her out of this."

"Wouldn't you want the best for her?"

"Of course I do. She'll go to college and—"

"She could go on to Smith or Wellesley and the Sorbonne. Just think, Barney. Why not make that possible now?" said Doc.

"You trying to bribe me?" Barney said.

"No, just telling you how much she has done for

Katie, and how she would help Katie advance if they were in the same school. Cheaper than my hiring tutors at the Albert Academy—"

"This feels a lot like strong-arming."

"What do you say, Barney? I can do the Academy. The girls would be ecstatic and Pina would be a shoe-in, given my involvement for the Foundation for the Sister Schools, and then she could help Katie get ahead. If my father had been able to do for you what I'm proposing for Pina…just think, Barney, your college could have been Yale, and then Med School. You could have been a doc like you wanted to be, like your great grandfather."

"You mean, instead of a measly insurance underwriter," said my father.

Doc continued, holding up his hand, "Stop! I don't mean to insult you, Barney. You would have been brilliant, and unlike you, Pina has a real chance. Get her away from the nuns. Let her have her castles in Sicily. Let her go back to your family in the Belice Mountains. Let her invent something or find a cure or write the world's best novel."

"What do you want me to do?"

"Just wait about the police. Hold off. I'm not going to protect the murderer but I want to spare everyone undue pain. Reginald Lawyer, the judge, is eighty-five, rather old for jail, but…if Papa Gallo did it, Joe and I will get him the best defense. His daughter was brutally attacked. Jeremiah doesn't deserve to lose work and clients if the police start combing the property or raise suspicions about him. But…I give you my word…I, too, want to see justice done," Doc said.

He continued, "Leave Pina here with us for now. I'll find someone in Portland to have her IQ tested.

I think she has some other extraordinary gifts, but I'm getting ahead of myself. I'll start working on the application for the Academy."

I started to stir for real. I could smell the muffins from the dining hall. It was later than I thought. If I stayed in bed any longer with Katie, I'd really be in trouble with my father. I had a vague recollection of a conversation I overheard between my father and Doc, but I couldn't tell if it was just a dream. I felt well rested at last, as though I had been sleeping soundly and contentedly all night.

"Katie, I've gotta go," I whispered.

"Let's find my father later and tell him everything. Did you dream up a solution?"

"Well, you know, I feel like something good is going to happen," I said, sensing a certain *deja-vu*.

"Really?"

"I don't know. I just feel really different this morning."

"C'mon, you have to go before they see you," said Katie.

I was barely out of Katie's cabin when I heard, "Where were you?" My father stood smiling at me from the doorway of our cabin.

"Uh, I got up real early and went to see if Katie was awake yet."

"Come here, honey. How would you like to go to school with Katie?"

I couldn't believe I was hearing this. Every fantasy I'd ever imagined was actually coming true. I ran into my father's arms.

I pushed myself into his warm chest and mumbled through my tears, "I...uh...that would be so great. But...it costs way too much."

"Don't you worry about it. Doc and I have a plan."

"Really?" I pulled back to look my father in the eye.

"Come give me another hug. I've got to go get washed up. We'll talk later."

"Does Katie know? Can I tell her?"

"You'll have plenty of time."

"But tomorrow…"

"Your mother and I know how much you want to stay, and Doc McGuilvry has offered to let you stay with Katie."

"Really?" I was hooting and doing cartwheels in the pine needles. I stumbled and fell over in the dirt, still laughing, just laughing and laughing.

My father's grin made the sun come up in my heart.

Chapter Twenty-four

GOOD NEWS

I left my father standing there in the doorway of our cabin and ran immediately to Katie's window. I woke her up again, but this time I wasn't in a panic, just hysterical with happiness.

Katie was only half-awake, so when I told her I was going to stay, she thought I was still planning on hiding out until my parents left.

"No, Katie. I mean stay here with you."

"Pin, you're crazy. You can't, sweetie," she said, still groggy.

"Oh yes, yes, indeedie! Your dad just worked magic with my dad."

Katie rubbed her eyes and said, "Okay, I am really awake now. What are you talking about?"

"It's real," I said. "Your dad and my father agreed to let me stay for the rest of the summer with you! Hot damn!"

She bolted out of bed and tore out of her cabin, still dressed in her nightie. Outside, she threw her arms around me and swung me around in a broad circle. We were both giggling uncontrollably.

"Guess what else," I goaded her.

"More?"

"C'mon guess, what would be even cooler?"

"Don't know." She wrinkled her face. "A date

with the Everly Brothers? I give up."

"Well...how would you like a roommate at Albert?"

"Huh?" Katie scrunched up her face in confusion. When she finally put it all together, she lifted me off the ground and let out whoops of joy. "Really? You're not dreaming?"

"Nope. It's the real thing. Can you believe it?" I said.

"C'mere then. I've gotta kiss you."

I sucked in a breath of anticipation, and then I felt Katie's soft lips on my forehead. She pulled away and continued to dance around with joy.

"Wait a minute." Katie stopped dancing and spun around to face me. "But what about the money? I mean...your dad's job...can he pay for this?" Katie looked embarrassed.

I explained that her father and mine had worked something out, that Doc would be taking care of my schooling.

Katie covered her mouth, suddenly looking anxious. "A bribe?" Her voice was barely a squeak.

Now I felt confused, too. We were convinced that Katie's father hadn't killed Butch. But then why was he being so generous, unless he had something to cover up? Why would my dad accept it?

The balloon of joy in my chest had started to lose its air. Before we could speculate further, Dr. McGuilvry walked up to us, beaming. Despite my fears, I threw my arms around his neck. I just knew he would explain things in a way that made sense. At least, that's what I hoped.

Dr. McGuilvry kissed me on the cheek and said, "I thought this would make you happy, both of you."

"Oh, Dr. McGuilvry. Thank you so much. You don't know what this means to me," I said. "I mean, I hope it's okay."

"Yes, it is. I think I do know how important it is to you. We'll make a deal. You help Katie avoid distractions, make sure she doesn't get lost in her chem set and forget her other studies, and I'll send the two of you to the same college too."

"Huh? I know you like Pina, but that's a lot of money," Katie said, chewing on her lip. The two of us shared a worried look.

"Don't you worry about that," said Doc.

Katie mumbled something under her breath, but then found her voice, "Sounds like a bribe…"

Doc pulled at his collar, looking like he was about to choke. Standing out there in the open area between guest cabins, he looked as if a whole courtroom had accused him of murder. His flush grew darker and darker. He looked at Katie, his top lip almost curled. For a moment, I thought he was going to smack her.

When Doc spoke, his voice was low but severe, "Dammit, I didn't touch Butch."

Katie started to run up to her father, stopped abruptly in her tracks. She had a conflicted look on her face, and I wondered if she was remembering the strange encounter we had witnessed between Doc and Joe Gallo. We were all definitely going to have that big conversation soon, get the facts out in the open.

I gave Doc the gentlest look I could muster and said, "Dr. McGuilvry, we know for sure you're not guilty."

I told Doc it was a long story, but that we knew he was innocent. "I dreamt about the night Butch was killed. I was Billy in the dream, and we were saying we had to keep you out of it."

"Who? How do you know for sure they were talking about me?" Doc asked.

"They said Ron."

"Who said?"

"The voices…Kevin and Peter. I didn't see faces, but I'm pretty sure it was them. They said things like, 'the others are out cold,' and that they had used 'Peter's stuff' and that it had really 'worked.' Then Katie and I found a paper marked 'sleeping powder invented by Peter' in the old science cabin."

Katie picked up where I had left off. "And Pina saw the fire and the sheets and the masks, and we know Roger was really bullying Billy." Katie said. "Dad, what is it?"

Katie's dad had a thoughtful, far-off look on his face, "You mentioned Roger…what did these voices say about Roger?"

"They said something about how Billy owed Kevin and Peter and Wolfgang for keeping Roger away from him."

"And Roger and Butch?" Doc's voice was thunderous.

"Are you angry with us? We proved you didn't do it," Katie said to her father, sounding a bit put out.

"Puzzled. Just puzzled." But Doc seemed different now that we'd told him our secrets, like gone in a way. Something else was definitely on his mind, and I knew we had put it there. I was scared, not that he might be angry with us. I was afraid we had made things worse than they already were by dragging up all this messy stuff from the past.

I started to feel sick. I was on a roller coaster today. First, I got the best news I could possibly ever get: Katie and I would be together. Magic happened! I was at the top of the world. Then, I was reminded of the hellhole my dreams had dragged everyone into, especially Doc, my benefactor.

Would any of us be in this mess if it weren't for my dreams? Maybe they really were devilish.

Chapter Twenty-Five

TRUE CONFESSIONS

After our conversation, Dr. McGuilvry slinked away to make phone calls. Katie and I were really getting good at tailing him. We passed behind the dining hall so Doc wouldn't see us as he walked in front. We followed him past the main house and the old carriage house, and even got down on our knees to crawl along the base of the screen porch, where Joe was lounging in an Adirondack chair.

We overheard Doc's voice, "Joe, listen. I need to know everything you remember about Roger."

"What is this…jealousy or protection twenty years too late?"

"No, no. It's hard to explain, but Roger may have had something to do with Butch."

"I don't think Roger was exactly Butch's type. Wrong gender to start with."

"Just think about it and come see me later. I've got to get back to the girls." Doc paused for a moment. "I am sorry."

"What?" Joe sounded really surprised.

"I really didn't understand."

"Ron, let it go."

"I did care."

"Twenty years ago."

"I do care, Joe."

Katie's face scrunched up. I wondered, too, just how much Doc cared, but we had to sneak back to the cabin before Katie's father beat us there. We made it back in plenty of time to smooth our hair and settle in the easy chairs. Doc came into the heated sitting room, carrying our logbook as well as the breakfast we had all skipped.

Katie, Doc, and I nibbled on muffins as we paged through the log.

"Pina, what can you tell me about your dreams? It's important that you give me every detail," Doc said.

"Well, I already told a lot of this to Katie, but… one of my first dreams was in the boys' latrine. I saw Roger. He was a tall guy, and he was pressing Billy up against the wall. Kind of…uh, pressing into him. Billy was crying. Saying he wouldn't tell. Then, another big guy with a deep voice came in and yelled for Roger to stop bothering little kids."

"Go on. I know it's scary," said Doc.

"It seemed real scary when I dreamt it. Like Roger and the other guy were going to fight. Roger was… real vulgar. He called the other guy 'stud' and said he thought he would be too busy 'balling chickies.'" I blushed. "Sorry, those were his words. Do you think that was Butch? He was real smooth, real cocky. But he did protect Billy." I took in a sharp breath, feeling a bit overwhelmed.

"You're doing great, Pina. Perhaps it was Butch," said Doc.

"Should we make Pina dream?" Katie asked, "Dad, what would be helpful to know?" Katie seemed to be going back and forth, once angry with her father for all his secrets and then wanting to help him.

"Are you willing to try this? To let me hypnotize

you?" Doc asked me.

"Well…I guess so. You're the doctor, anyway. If anything bad happens to me, you could save me."

"I won't let anything bad happen," Doc promised, "Here, lie down here and look at me. Okay. Good. Follow my finger. Okay?"

"Yup," I said.

"Can you feel the heat of the fire?"

"Mmm. Sort of."

"Keep your eyes closed. See the oranges and the reds, smell the pine and the smoke…"

"Yes. I hear the crackling."

"Good. Anything else?"

Doc's full head of white hair clouded over, no part, no strands, just a flat white surface. It moved and wrinkled. I pulled at my white shirt…no, something white. A sheet. I pulled it away from me, asking if I had to wear it. I was so hot. It stuck to me, and I couldn't breathe very well. Sweat dripped down my face and into my eyes. I couldn't see. It felt like my face was in a funeral mask. Then, I heard voices, low and gravelly, and sliding footsteps.

One voice said, *"What's that? I hear something over there."*

Another voice, *"Who's got the knife? And the tools? Peter?"*

"Shut up! Ssh, really. There's Butch. Get him!" said several voices.

Screams, I heard screams, and a slow scuffle. I smelled sweat, and felt pulled into the middle of a huddle. Hot bodies towered above me. I was going down between crotches and knees.

Voices said, *"You, you're gonna lose it. We'll cut your balls off."*

One shrill voice said, *"Who's that? Give me back the knife, you mongrel. Whose balls?"*

"Don't you dare run off. You've got work to do, Billy Boy," a crazed voice said.

Then blood curdling screams.

"No, no I won't! Don't touch me! I need to tell. Stop! Stop! You're hurting me. Don't, don't."

I knew I was coming back. I knew I had been dreaming or hypnotized this time. Still, I thrashed and clawed my way awake.

"Pina, you're here with me, Doc McGuilvry and Katie. Wake up. That's it, that's it. You're okay. I'll hold you. Do you know where you are?"

"Yes, sort of," I answered, my voice trembling, "That was too horrible."

Doc and Katie eased me back into consciousness, then gave me a moment alone. I was lying on the divan in the sitting room. I was exhausted and a bit scared. This time, though, it wasn't the mere fact that I was dreaming, that I'd had these visions, that made me feel crazed. This time, it was the knowledge I'd gained in the dream that terrified me. I was starting to piece it all together, but I wasn't totally clear-headed. My ribs felt a bit bruised and my hands real achy, as if I'd been twisting a trowel or unscrewing a stubborn pickle jar lid.

Still, for the first time, a part of me felt strangely good. Maybe I had an important job to do. Maybe my dreaming had to happen, as if it was my responsibility, now, as I got older. It wouldn't rule my life. I'd have to see if I could control it.

After fifteen minutes or so, Katie came back into the sitting room and sat by me. By now, I was sitting up and really craving sweets. Doc had left the cabin with the same thoughtful look on his face, promising to get us ice cream.

He came back with spoons and bowls under his sturdy arm, his hand clasping the sweating gallon container against his chest. He scrambled a bit to balance his load as he tried to open the door. I laughed at the sight of this tall and dignified man with a woman's apron around his middle. The momentary relief from all this cloak and dagger stuff felt really good and safe.

"So here's a couple of bowls of butter crunch," Doc said, as he finished scooping our ice cream. The half-melted liquid was dribbled on his apron and down the sides of the bowls.

"Thanks, Dad," Katie said.

"Doctor, I think I was Billy in this one," I told him.

"Go slow."

"I kept on thinking we should stop. Not my dream, but what was happening. Billy wanted to stop it."

I was feeling much more together, much clearer after my rest and the sugar from the ice cream.

I kept recounting for Doc. "All those guys, your friends, had gathered supposedly to scare Butch. Peter held the knife to threaten Butch, when someone else, I think Roger, came on the scene. I think Butch pried the knife out of Peter's hands and swung at Roger. Roger got cut, just a little prick really...a small gash. He was wearing a plaid shirt. Then...I think Roger and Butch struggled for the knife, and Butch fell."

I continued to describe the dream. Roger was like a wild man, a monster. His eyes were red, and he was impossibly strong. My voice sounded like it was getting smaller and smaller. I felt tiny, like I was in an *Alice's*

Adventures in Wonderland scene. I was beginning to shrink into a tiny dot way back behind my eyes and somewhere deep in my chest.

I dug my nails into my palms to stop this feeling of fading to ground myself back in the real world. I was okay. I could do this.

I continued summing up the rest of my dream for Doc. Roger, the madman, stabbed Butch dead. He turned on the other guys, threatened them. Demanded they start cutting off Butch's hands. He was going to dismember the body, cut it into tiny pieces and scatter them so they wouldn't be found. Peter, Kevin, and Wolfie managed to break free. They tried to pull me, pull Billy, away with them, but Roger was too fast. That's where the dream goes black. I felt like I was dead. I think Billy is dead.

"That's it, Doc," I said.

"No more. I'll sit with you two for a while, but I just want you to rest. No chatting. I'm shutting the shades. Understood, girls?"

Chapter Twenty-six

MORE TRUE CONFESSIONS

Katie and I slept until after lunch. We picked at some snacks and then we were ready for some air.

We were just leaving her cabin, wanting to sit out in the sun and bake, when we saw someone approaching. It was Joe, looking really handsome in a British tennis sweater, the real kind, and white linen slacks.

We had to figure out a plan quickly. Katie's mom was probably playing Bridge or listening to Lara Scatterwahl, an old New Englander, play the piano in the main lodge. Since Joe was coming towards the dining hall, he had probably seen Doc hitting a few balls with the machine on the tennis court in front of the hall. They would probably come back here.

We dropped down off the stoop to find our dugout under the cabin porch. It was a quiet day; there were no lawnmowers going, and no one was lining the tennis court. Sound would be perfect. We knew they wouldn't go into the sitting room and risk not seeing Catherine, Katie's mom, if she came along the path.

I braced myself. When was I going to find the courage to talk to Katie? What was going on between her father and Joe had obvious consequences for Katie and me. I was sweating as much with anticipation as with the closeness. There was barely enough vertical space under the floorboards to sit up.

Within a few minutes, we heard their footsteps above our heads. Two men starting speaking: Doc and Joe. They shared memories, saying it was painful, but necessary. Doc admitted that he had had his head in the sand in those days and didn't know kids were being bullied and preyed upon, nor did he have any idea Butch was hitting on Regina, Joe's sister. He sounded kind of pathetic, like he was hiding from himself.

Doc continued, "You and Kevin and Peter protected me. You kept the dark side of things away from me. But I guess I blamed myself. Your sister was gorgeous, and I think she loved me. She wanted me, and couldn't understand why I wouldn't touch her. She just thought I was too Catholic."

"Do I want to know this? Spare me the details," Joe said.

"Yes, you do, Joe. I was confused. I liked her, but I didn't. I couldn't. I had no appetite for…dammit, Joe, I had no sexual urge for her or any girl."

"Some of us mature later."

"Enough sarcasm. I had a feeling Butch was hitting on her. At least maybe someone would get her excited."

"And you?"

"Joe, that time."

"What time?" said Joe.

"C'mon, you know, that time we snuck out late in the canoe and went to the island. You helped me out of the canoe and touched my side. I got so excited. I joked how you were so much the gentleman, and I… hugged you." Doc said.

"Oh, that time? Yes, I remember. I hugged you

back, then I kissed you, and you were hard. I could feel it."

"We fell over into the sand. We snuggled for hours, until almost dawn."

"Ron, we did more than snuggle. You always denied it."

"Okay. I touched you and let you touch me. I felt…alive. I've never felt that way…before or since."

Katie sat straight up, almost hitting her head. Her cheeks were flushed, and kept on getting darker. She looked over at me in the dim light, looking as if she were holding her breath and would explode any second. I put my fingers to my lips as much to silence myself as her. I had never heard anything like that before. Two men…touching each other?

Katie's chest started to heave up and down. I was afraid she would sob out loud. I grabbed her wrist and shook my head.

I whispered, "Wait."

The two men upstairs continued.

"Are you sure about all that? How you felt?" Joe asked.

"Don't make this harder," said Doc.

"I didn't know what I was doing," said Joe.

"Ah, who's backing out now?"

"I mean I hadn't any experience."

"But we found each other, and somehow knew what to do," said Doc.

"Yes, that once. You never let me after that."

Doc's voice was gentle. "But you never stopped trying. I wanted you, but I hated myself. That was queer. I relived that scene every night, feeling you with me, your mouth on me. Jesus, Joe, I've never been so excited and…in love."

"And now? Why tell me now?" Joe said.

"Don't get me wrong. I made choices I knew I had to make. I love my wife in my own way, and my family. But I also know I loved you and wanted you, and I hated myself for it."

"I was scared too, but I would have walked off into the sunset with you. I was convinced I had lost your friendship, that I had offended you. I thought you were having sex with my sister. So I figured I could make up for the queer offense by going after the guy who tried to molest her," Joe said. "I felt obligated to trash Butch."

"I knew nothing, not even that that had happened."

"Why now?"

"Butch's death…did you guys do it?" Doc asked.

"Ron, we were all drugged."

"How was Roger involved?"

"No idea. I told you, Roger was too busy bullying boys."

"But in Pina's dreams, Roger and Butch had a fight, and Roger threatened Billy that he would come and get him if he told. Joe, I've got to know what Roger did to you."

"Tried. Damned near succeeded. Is this some kind of vicarious thrill, or what?"

"Come here. Please let me hold you."

"Why?" asked Joe.

"God, Joe. Let me hold you in my arms. Why wasn't I there to protect you? Why, why, so many things."

"Shush. Just be quiet. I love you. You excite me even now. I'd kiss you now, but I won't play with you, your marriage, your family."

"Just hold me a little longer," said Ron.

"And you've never…"

"No, I was too busy in my life. I wouldn't let myself go there. We could go to that island."

"It wouldn't be wise," Joe said, "and it would be even harder to lose you for a second time…now that I've found you."

"I don't know what will happen in my life after this murder stuff. What I'll do…"

"Ron, shush. I'll tell you about Roger. I think part of you wants to know if Roger and I had something going. Absolutely not. He was repulsive. Roger threatened me once…cornered me in the dark with a knife. He said it was a warning…or a tease, whichever way I wanted it. He knew I was homosexual. Well, I got away, and I was so mortified I vomited. I didn't understand it. I started to have dreams about Roger."

"Joe, dreams…they're…it didn't mean…I am truly sorry, Joe."

"I haven't relived that story in ages. Spent some quality time in counseling over it. Now, why did you want me to tell you?" Joe said.

"Do you think he knew about us? My daughter, Katie, and Pina, talked about a dream where Roger called Butch 'Romeo.'"

"So, you're thinking Roger targeted Butch and me."

"And why not me?"

"Jealous?"

"No, seriously, from Pina's dream. Joe, you have to understand, these are no ordinary dreams. Experts studying this call it extraordinary knowing. They could be very, very real. To hear Pina tell it, it sounded like Roger may have killed Butch."

"Oh, I think there's some more investigating to

be done. We need to keep our heads together on this." Joe coughed and then chuckled. "No, I'm serious."

"Yes…Did Roger ever come back to bug you again?"

"No. I made good and sure I was never alone," Joe said.

"Like when you would sneak into my bed."

"Yes. Even if I had to sleep next to you on the floor."

"As you said, all of this needs more investigating."

"Ron, who's teasing now?"

"I'm not. But in the one case, I know we can rally the troops and get phone numbers. Track down the key players from camp. In the other case, I know what my feelings are. I don't know about my courage or whether or not I'm willing to inflict that sort of pain on others, on my family, but I do know how I feel."

"Ron…"

"No, I'm not going to lie anymore. That goes for you too."

"What?"

"Get your father. I know he's here."

Chapter Twenty-seven

AN URGENT TALK WITH KATIE

I had no choice now. I had to talk to Katie. I was afraid her father's story would reveal too much about my feelings and our love story. But Katie was in pain, and I had to comfort her.

As soon as the screen door slammed above us, I held Katie close and stroked her head. I asked her where she wanted to go to talk. We crawled out from our dugout, grabbed blankets from the cabin, and made our way to the rec hall in silence.

The late afternoon sun magnified and expanded through the back windows, warming the floor of the rec hall. The vacuum-like silence there felt safe.

"How could he...?" said Katie as soon as we were camped on the floor.

Katie sobbed, mumbling that her father was really a queer. She pounded the floor and kept on screaming, "Why?"

I wasn't sure what to say. "It sounds like they were really good friends."

"Yeah," she said. "But good friends don't touch each other that way."

"Sounds like they fell in love. I mean, it didn't sound like a dirty movie," I said.

Katie threw me a look that said, "A lot you know."

I put my hand on her shoulder and tried softly to

dry a tear about to cascade over her cheekbone.

"Katie, he married your mom. He must have loved her, and he certainly loves you. And I've seen him kiss your mom."

"God, if anybody finds out," Katie said. "They'll make fun of him! He'll lose patients. What will they do to me at the Academy? I mean, he's not Liberace. What makes him think he can get away with it?"

"He's not talking about getting away with anything," I said.

Katie was up on her elbow, staring down at me, saying, "Oh, yeah? My father wanted to go to that island and kiss Joe!"

Man! I wanted to kiss Katie to shut her up. I knew that would have been it, curtains, end of show, if I kissed Katie. This was not the right moment. I had mush for brains. She was just so exciting when she was riled up. I had to focus and let myself feel what I would have felt if it had been my father. My father? A queer?

I settled down and reminded Katie that Joe said he wouldn't upset Katie's family. She cried again on my shoulder while I patted her on the back. I was so afraid of being romantic that the gesture came out more like burping a baby.

Finally, I pushed Katie up and looked at her from two feet away. "You can't do anything now. He hasn't changed in any way towards you. He's loving and generous and kind. I like him…and Joe!"

I went on to explain that her mom was already looney tunes, no offense. If Katie told her, it might push Mrs. McGuilvry over the edge.

Katie stopped sniffling. She told me I was right. She kept on saying it was a shock.

I guess it was. It would have been hard to picture

her dad in Greenwich Village, wearing a motorcycle jacket and tight dungarees.

My father had to drive us through Greenwich Village one time, through the homosexual neighborhoods. There were men in make-up and men in long, chiffon-like scarves. My father had made smooching noises and called them faggots.

I didn't think it was big news, like Khrushchev or nuclear test sites. Just strange. I didn't think of myself like that, down there in the Village. I just wanted to be a Beatnik, an artist or a musician. I was planning on sneaking down there as soon as I was sixteen to listen to music, dressed in a cape and dungarees, and a beret.

So, Katie was right. It was a shock. Her dad wasn't like any homosexuals I could imagine.

I asked Katie that question.

"Yes. A homosexual is…is a pervert." She lowered her eyes then and shook her head, mumbling, "But maybe *I'm* just wrong."

We really did have to go to dinner, and she needed to put on a cheerleader face before seeing her family, she said. Me too, I knew I had to put on the inscrutable teenager face. That was my dad's phrase, not mine.

Chapter Twenty-eight

TRUE CONFESSIONS, FAMILY-STYLE

On my way back to the guest cabins, I was mostly silent, as was Katie. What Katie's dad had said about hiding, from himself and from others, was playing havoc with my mind.

We always joked about hiding our thoughts from our parents, but maybe I was more like Katie's father than I thought. Maybe I lacked the spinal column, as I heard him say once.

A memory of my successful cousin, Candida, flashed across my mind. In my Grammar School Graduation Memory Book, she had written, "Let your true self go out into the world and do a great deed."

I couldn't very well do that in hiding. I had to unravel the mystery at hand, as well as the mystery of my father's decision to allow me to go to school with Katie. As we neared the guest cabins, I could see him on our porch, just resting.

"Daddy."

"Yes."

"Daddy, maybe I shouldn't go to the Academy. I know you don't have the money."

"Don't you worry about that."

"But, you never accept money," I said, trying to catch my father's eye.

"Who said I accepted money?"

"Is it a bribe?'

"What are you saying?" My father glared at me as he reached over to light up a Raleigh.

"I know Dr. McGuilvry offered to pay for my schooling, and that you accepted. Why did you take the money? Were you afraid he killed Butch? But we know Doctor McGuilvry is innocent."

"You think you know so much."

"But Dad, you know I'm telling the truth! My dreams, just like Grandma, like in Sicily—that's what you said! You know this is real."

In between puffs and swirls of smoke, my father spit out small shreds of tobacco. "So?"

"*So*, I do know Doc McGuilvry didn't do it. So, why? Why the whole thing? I want it so badly—to go to Albert with Katie. But I'm afraid you've made some strange deal, and I don't know why. I'm afraid it will all fall apart, that it won't happen."

"But it will. It will because it didn't happen for me."

"Huh?"

"Look, Toots, the Doctor has contacts. He can get you scholarships to the best schools. You'll get the best. All the things I couldn't have."

"But Daddy, you did. You paid your own way to CCNY and NYU."

"I never finished. You know that." He turned away to tap his ash in the glass ashtray advertising Socony Mobil's flying horse.

"But you could have..."

"No, Pina. I'm a scared man who listened too much to my father. I lacked the courage that I see in you. You do know that I wanted to be a doctor. My father told me over and over I'd never do it, that I didn't have the *palle*, balls. I was full of myself, wanted to be like my grandmother's father, Dr. Daidone."

My father spat out *buffone* in Italian. Clown.

I'd seen this attitude in him before. I had felt it aimed at me, at times, oozing out of him. I didn't like that it could tear him down. I knew the feeling, and I didn't want anybody else to feel so small.

"But Daddy, you were a big shot. Aunt Maria told me that you performed solo violin at the Brooklyn Academy of Music."

"Yes. My father said that was for 'sissies.' So I stopped it all before his prediction had a chance to come true, before I'd be a failure. He was right. I gave up. Pina, I want more for you. I don't want to fail you anymore. I was a second-class husband and father. But, it's not too late for you."

"Daddy, you're not a—" I stopped short upon seeing my mother come through the second door to the porch, her face contorted with tears.

She was red in the face and her feet seemed to want to do opposite things: come in or go out? Maybe that's what we were all doing here, deciding whether to say what was really on our minds or just go along.

She started slowly, "I heard you from outside. You're not a second-rate husband. You've got to stop this kind of talk."

"Mommy, what are you doing here?"

"Telling your father to stop being angry with himself. Stop doing what you've always done…quitting before things turn bad. Quit before you even get going. You're angry, and you pull away from us. You cheat us, not just yourself. Look, remember the violin?"

"Giusy, please stop."

"No, for once! Your daughter tried to surprise

you. Polished your old violin, the Steiner that belonged to your maestro. She glued and restrung, all wrong, mind you, but she worked so hard, for days just to get it ready for your birthday. She was so pro—"

"Giusy—"

"Let me finish! She thought maybe, just maybe, you could play it for us, just once. She wanted so badly to hear you play."

"Mommy, stop! He'll be angry."

"No! Enough anger and secrets. Why wouldn't you play for your family?"

I remembered this well. I was absolutely crushed. I wanted to know who my father really was. When I handed the violin to him on his birthday, with a red ribbon tied around the violin itself, I held my breath. Not out of fear. It was enormous for me. I had done the impossible, I thought. I put back together my father's dried-up, dismantled violin. Above all, I was offering my father the way back in. The way to reclaim his past glory, or so I thought.

The silence lasted what seemed like an eternity before he took the violin. Everything stood still. Without a word, he threw it, hurled it the length of the basement stairs. His face, almost blood red, seemed frozen as he stalked from the room. As a kid, I wondered where his soul had gone.

I remembered my mother muttering something under her breath after my father left the room.

"Hate," she had said. That was the only word I caught.

I misunderstood. I thought she was saying he hated me, and I crumbled. I fell to my knees and bawled on the kitchen linoleum.

I carried that hate in me because I never

understood what I had done.

My mother's voice interrupted my flashbacks. She was saying, "I couldn't tell Pina. Couldn't tell her that her hero, her beloved Daddy was scared. There, I've said it. Now, enough! I want you to let your daughter, our daughter, go to that Academy. But on one condition: you must play the violin again. Only if you have the courage. The same courage you're asking of your daughter, to go off with the wealthier girls, to go off to New England and old money, to make it in a world that hasn't been hers. I fell in love with you, the musician. You who, in the midst of poverty, touched my soul with your music. You never believed that I truly believed in you! Come back to me. Back to us."

"Giusy, will you let it go? Will you let Pina go? Whatever it takes, I want this for her."

"Do you want it for all of us?"

"Yes." My father's voice was low and shaky.

My mother pushed aside her second drenched hankie.

"Pina, come, let me get your hair out of your eyes." She pulled me close to her. "I love you, Sweetie, and I'll miss you. I hate to let you go, but I won't hold you back."

"I can go to school with Katie?"

"Yes, but don't start coming home with airs." She laughed through her tears.

"Daddy, will you play the violin for us someday?"

"Yes, I promise."

I told them I'd like to take a walk before dinner. I just wanted some cool air before I met them in the dining hall.

I couldn't believe how like my father I was. I flashed back to my earlier rambling thoughts, thoughts about lacking courage. About remaining silent when truth was demanding to be heard. About taking the easy way out...bribes...trade-offs. My father's mystery made sense now.

It seemed like all my choices lay right in front of me.

On one hand, stood my father, a conservative, small man who threw away his gift for a mediocre life in a mediocre geographical setting. A big fish in a little pond. All the relatives and neighbors came to him for advice, he did everyone's income tax, and at parties, he recited chapter and verse from a good many books. A big deal. We were intuitively connected, and I knew I loved him.

On the other hand, there was Doc, bold looking, tall, and rugged. Selectively out-spoken about appropriate convictions. He wielded a great deal of power, and he stood ready to open doors for me. Big schools, big names, big opportunities among the wealthy and famous. He, too, had thrown away something of value.

Back when I was that little kid with the rejected red-ribboned violin, I asked where my father's soul had gone. Maybe I had lost mine too? I lacked the guts to tell Katie what was really going on for me. If I couldn't tell her, even at the risk of losing her, I would lose my gift of loving, my way of holding on to life. Maybe forever.

Ha! Was the Academy the right thing for me? Who was I kidding?

I would be shunned. The lesbo. The queer.

The other choice? Going back to Queens? I'd accept the status quo, shirk my dreams and my responsibility?

Like my father, I could be a big fish in a little pond. I could easily get good grades. I wouldn't even have to work hard. I'd be one of the most comfortable residents in a run-down neighborhood. I would be a model citizen. I would gag in silence.

Right now, I really did have to silence myself. My parents were waiting, so again, I would go in hiding.

Chapter Twenty-nine

LULLABY OF DREAMLAND

After dinner, I was falling asleep on my feet. I swore to my parents I was going to our cabin and immediately get in bed and this time I was telling the truth. I flashed Katie a sign: I put my head on my hand, like a pillow, and closed my eyes. She understood.

The next morning, the sun filtering through the thin shades awakened me even before my father lit a fire. I pulled on heavy dungarees, a long-sleeved polo shirt, and my gray, boatneck sweater. I was off into the crisp morning air that announced mid-August.

I hurried to go hang out in the rec hall. Things got all hushed there, and the windows stood silent witness to so many years of secrets. I was still tired. I hadn't counted on dreaming, but I was beginning to see the dream right in front of my eyes while I was still awake, like a film projector going, on and off. I thought it wouldn't be about bloody hands or violence, maybe just violins.

I never knew why Dad was so mad. It made sense now. I remember staying away from him for a week. I hated him, but I felt ugly too. My gift was wrong. I was wrong. I was so sleepy lying here in the sun, dust particles dancing in front of me, and there was a musical voice, a funny accent.

"No, *not Cortina, not Corleone, Cremona. The best. I used to have one, you know, the real one, the one by Stradivari. Yes, yes, I was a big maestro. I play at la Scala in Milano. For Enrico, I play. In old days, people pay to hear and breathe, respire, and live, vive. Then, no more. I go from Italia. Bastiano, Barney, I come to find you, in East New York. You, my little virtuoso, I bring you to Enrico where you a star, my stella. And then, pooh—you stop! You give up. You stop the sweet sounds, la musica dolce cause you tired. I tell you, tired, pooh pooh! I spit. You coward. Where the grand artist in you? I turn my back on you. Pooh!*

So ha! You hold my second-class violin. They took my pride, my Strad from me. A shame! I give you my birthright, mia musica, musica d'Italia! You play again, eh? So you say. If...big if you play again, you bring me back to life. But, I don't hold my breath. Pooh! Coward. My son, you betray me. Traitor!"

I wiped my hands. I was wet and sticky, and my head was pounding with a strange music. I didn't recognize it, but then...slowly...some more notes... Vesta la Giubba. My father used to sing it, said Caruso taught it to him. Just like he used to say he knew the endings to movies, because he wrote the story. Now, somehow, I knew the haunting, driving notes. There was also something from Bach, the Concerto in F Minor.

Then I rubbed my eyes, and I knew, yes, I did really know that my father hadn't been lying. He did know Caruso, his Maestro told me in this dream.

So this was my father...a man who was being preened for greatness...a man who came so close, and then turned his back on it. No wonder he threw the violin. But I didn't know. So my father was to play again. He would bring the memory of his Maestro back to life. But first, I had to succeed at Albert Academy for him.

I couldn't play any instrument. I couldn't sing. Maybe…just maybe, I could help the doc with more details and dreams. Maybe I could figure out why my father was still afraid, especially at this point, the day before they were leaving. It wasn't of failure, then, but…of what? I had to get out of the rec hall. I had to go find Katie.

Chapter Thirty

A REDEMPTION STORY BEGINS

As I was about to cut over from the rec hall to the road, I saw Katie running towards me from the other direction.

"Katie, did you just get up?"

Katie rubbed her eyes and yawned

"Yeah. I was dead last night. Things cool with your folks?"

"Yup! Super cool. I talked to them yesterday," I told her.

"And? Can you really stay?"

"Uh huh. And we will definitely be at Snobsville Academy together."

"Holy cow! C'mere, roommate!" Katie wrapped her arms around me so tight she lifted me off the ground.

"Yeah," I said to the top of her head. "Wouldn't that be a real killer!"

Katie and I were done with this mystery business. We were ready to get back to our regular lives and promises of the future. We decided to tell her dad as much as we could, and then let the adults figure it out. Anxious just to be goofy teenagers again, we stumbled over each other in our attempt to get back to her cabin as quickly as possible. We still had time before breakfast.

⁂

"Hey Dad, we have to talk to you," said Katie as we approached her cabin, "Oh, sorry!" She finally noticed Joe Gallo was also sitting on the porch. Judging from the looks on Joe's and Dr. McGuilvry's faces, we were obviously interrupting something important.

"Sure, but I've only got about five minutes," Doc said.

Still puffing from our run, I was glad to spit out the last of my info for Doc.

"Okay. I'll be quick. I forgot to tell you one dream. I was Billy, and I had blood on my hands. I think I cut Butch's hands. There, that's it," I said. I rubbed my own hands together, as if I had just washed them of this drama.

"Mmm," was all Doc said.

"Oh, no," I said, remembering. "There's another thing. I was trying to wash the blood off when I walked into the water and almost drowned."

"Hmm. There was a story about a boy who tried to drown himself at the end of the season…" Doc coughed as he sat up straighter. He seemed to be thinking about something else. Then, he extended his hand to Joe to make the introductions he'd skipped when we first saw them together a few days before.

"Ah, Joe, this is my daughter, Katie, and her friend, Pina. Girls, this is an old friend from camp, Joe Gallo."

"Regina's brother? But, you're the real Joe Gallo, the journalist? Wow!" I sounded like a fool, but I didn't quite know what to say. Katie hung back and was silent.

"Yes. Glad to meet you, too, Pina," Joe said.

"I'm sorry. It's that my father, Mr. Mazzini, is acting strange, and maybe he's scared…Mr. Gallo, your father? Your father is…I mean…my father made a deal, I think, and…"

Katie's father cut me off. "No, Pina, I convinced your father you deserve it. This was a 'deal' between your father and me. No one else."

"But he's got to play again," I said.

"I don't understand. Can someone explain?" Joe said.

I said, "My father wants me to go to this good school, kind of like going in his place. To live up to his dreams? My mother says if he wants me to have the courage to reach outside my element, he has to redeem himself by playing the violin again. They say he could have been a great violinist. He says he's a coward."

"Okay. What has that got to do with my father?" said Joe.

"I think your father scared my father. I'm not sure how, but now he's desperate to get away from here."

"I'll fix my father. He's going to redeem himself. My father's got friends in Italy, violinmakers, maestri. He could definitely help. Not sure exactly how," said Joe, combing his wavy hair with his manicured fingers. "Sorry he's been a problem. I didn't want him to come here, to Maine, but he thought the murder might point to him and that maybe he could solve it. I've been trying to keep him at the hotel down the road, but I see he's been lurking around here at Owl Lake. Sorry."

"Oh…it's like my dream…" I said, "I dreamt something like this would happen…"

"Hmm. I'll see what I can do." Joe glanced over at Doc, eyebrows raised.

"Wow! That's great," I said, and turned to Katie's dad. "Seriously, Doc, I need to get out of this murder business. All of you adults, you all sort it out. It's too much."

"You're right. You've given us all the details. We'll take it from here." Katie's dad nodded.

"Doc, and Mr. Gallo, is there anything you can say to help my father calm down?"

"Please, call me Joe. I can do that. My own father has to stop this bullying and shaming once and for all."

I thought now we'd be free of this intrigue and adult drama. I needed to spend more time with Katie. I could see by her silence and her arms nearly glued straight to her sides that she was still really upset about the conversation between her father and Joe the day before.

While we were still talking about my father, Jeremiah came to get Doc and Joe. He had called, wanting them all to meet, along with Bud and Fifi in the Lodge's poolroom. Katie and I managed to get there before the men by sneaking around through the icehouse to hole up in the loft overhanging the racks of cue sticks and chalk.

I have no idea why I dragged Katie there, when I really just wanted to be alone with Katie. Why couldn't I just leave the murder business up to the adults?

It was a very important meeting. That became clear quickly. We learned that Jeremiah had buried the bones, and that all of the men had dug the bones back up for Doc and Fifi. The bones needed to be tested to see if they were human and cut with a knife or another tool by the doctor and the Mafioso, based on their professional expertise. Bud would take the ring back to his family to make sure it belonged Butch. Then they spoke about Doc and Joe going to Portland or Boston to locate Peter and Kevin and Billy to find out Roger's name. Katie and I wondered how much of their trip was really intended to research former campers, or each other.

After everyone else vacated the poolroom, Ron slid the heavy cross-beamed barn door shut, leaving him alone with Joe, the scent of chalk, and old hay. Not to mention Katie and me hiding out in the loft.

"So what about Bud? Anything left there?" asked Joe.

"Seriously? There was never anything—" said Doc.

"You tried to claim that about us, too."

"Touché," said Doc.

"I wish," Joe said with a big grin.

"You have to talk to your father. No funny business from now on. We'll get enough information to clear us all, and we'll turn it over to the police. Then, we can sort through what we have to do about us."

"You're serious this time, Ron?"

"I believe I am."

"Says the man holding the bones."

"Come here."

"Put the bones down first. I want to be the only one in your arms," said Joe.

"Am I serious enough now?" said Ron.

"Just hold me."

Up in the loft, I held Katie's mouth closed with one hand, and patted her shoulder with the other. Warm tears rolled across my knuckles. We heard the creaking of the barn-type door rolling on its wheels and the dull thud as it banged against the heavy frame. They left. Only then could I let Katie sob whole-heartedly.

Chapter Thirty-one

KITTY KISSES

After witnessing the scene from the loft, we hung out with my folks, who were leaving the next day. Katie wasn't really ready to be with her father. My parents took us out to Naples to walk around Long Lake and take in a boardwalk-type atmosphere. The setting sun was beautiful, and the ice cream was really tops. It was just what Katie and I needed.

Later that night, my parents allowed me to sleep in Katie's cabin since I had already brought my things over. I promised I would get up early to see them off.

Before going back to her cabin, Katie and I flopped down under the yellow pines, sap and all, to play with the kittens. It felt good not to think too hard about anything much. I was tired of playing sleuth. I told Katie I just wanted to savor all of Maine and the kitties and her.

I asked Katie to pass me one of the kitties, Bobbi, the one with the bobbed tail. Her fur just stood up and poked out all over. It was so stiff.

I nuzzled Bobbi close. "Aren't you just a fuzz ball, sweet kitty? Here, Katie, touch this spot, this little crook in her tail, at the end."

Our hands brushed as we petted and held the kittens. Katie's face was open and available. Bobbi the kitten curled up around her neck. I wanted to be Bobbi.

I looked up at Katie in the growing darkness. Her eyes were soft with a touch of moonlight glistening. She was looking at me. Dreamlike, I reached over to pull her head closer to mine. We were leaning in, closer and closer, when Bobbi wedged her head in between our faces, wanting some attention. I came to my senses. What was I thinking?

"Watch it! She'll adopt you," Katie said, sitting up straight.

"Like you've adopted me?" I was flustered.

We finally dragged ourselves into the cabin. I undressed in the bathroom and jumped into the bed, pulling the covers up to my chin. I clung to my edge of the bed. I almost didn't trust myself. Now that my folks were going home, my future was entirely in the hands of Katie and her family. I couldn't risk shocking her. I didn't want her to think I was a queer.

Chapter Thirty-two

TRUE CONFESSIONS - SICILIAN STYLE

I left Katie's bed really early, afraid of my instincts and anxious about my parents' upcoming departure. During the night, I wrestled with doubts about whether I was making the right decision to stay. My father wanted me to do what he couldn't. Could I achieve what everyone said I was capable of? Could I really? What did Katie really want from me? Was it the same thing I wanted?

I ran all the way to the lake. The morning mist was rising from its mirror-like surface. I spotted Joe and Fifi on the beach, sitting in a pair of Adirondack chairs. I went through the blueberries to keep out of sight, dropping behind the beach pines a few feet to the side of the two Gallos.

Joe Gallo was serious about redemption, and I thought that was just a Catholic thing. It seems everyone and everything was rising to the occasion.

In his thick accent, Fifi was almost singing the praises of the vista in front of our eyes.

I heard him say, "It make me want to settle down. This blue water, like Sicily, Lago Arancio, near Giuliana. Miracles they happen there at Lago Arancio."

"Maybe here, too. It's old Indian country, close to the gods. And over there, over those hills is Shaker land, Sabbathday Lake. Maybe miracles can happen here, if you let them." Joe seemed to be setting him up.

"What's that supposed to mean?"

"Dad, you've got some repenting to do. You did your tuff guy stuff with Barney Mazzini. You scared him good. Why?"

"No police. I don't want police."

"Hold on. Barney's not going to the police. You've shamed the man in front of his family. You and your Sicilian honor crap. You taught me to honor the family, to forgive a man who told you the truth. You want me to be real? Okay. You know I'm a homosexual. You know the man I love is Ron…I always have. I will respect his family as he has respected our family even when he thought you were up to no good, you and your mob. I want your blessing. You know him. You respect him—"

"Yes. You old enough to live any way you want long as you don't hurt nobody."

"Listen to yourself. I'm asking to hold up my head, no shame. I'm also asking you to help Barney do the same, win back the respect of his family."

"*Santo cielo*! Holy Heavens! And how?"

"Reassure him you're not going to rough him up, number one. Then, your connections in Italy. I want you to get Barney's violin from his wife. I want you to get it to Cremona. It's a Stradivari, and have the artisans in Italy repair it so it will play again like the nineteenth century piece it is. Then you take Barney to Sicily and get him the best Maestro."

"I don't understand."

"Babbo, he's got to play again. It's what he needs to hold his head up again. You need to be the good protector, the good-hearted man, you started out as."

"Giuseppe, I like to be here. It's like I say,

something clean and holy happens here. Okay. I'll figure out. You be good to the family of Ron. Come, embrace your old papa."

❧ ❧ ❧ ❧

When I arrived back up at my parents' cabin, they were in the final stages of packing the car. I waited, kicking through pine needles behind the cabin. As I was inhaling that dreamy Maine scent, I heard the sound of footsteps.

Fifi Gallo. His rolling gait was a bit cocky, a bit old and soft. He was wearing a kind of ascot and a smile.

He was almost singing, "Ciao."

Gallo approached my mother, tipping his hat and extending his hand. My mother gave him an icy stare. She said nothing, just stood there with her bags next to the trunk of the Rambler.

Fifi Gallo continued, "Mi dispiace. I am sorry. I was afraid, and I make your husband scared. Missus, I'm not a bad man. I don't want to scare you."

"I don't know what you want from me."

"To forgive me, and your man's violin."

"My husband's violin?"

"I will aid him. I will make a repair in Italy. Like new. I take him, and you if you like, to Italian maestri. He will play again better than at the Brooklyn Academy of Music. I heard him, one time, long time ago. He will be our virtuoso. What do you think?"

"I don't know what he will say, but let me see."

"It's a surprise, don't tell him. Shush. Here is Barney. Buongiorno."

"More of the same?" said my father.

"I come to wish you a good trip, and I say I'm sorry. I want only the best for you. I mean you no harm. Old wise guy ways…they are difficult to change! Forgive me!"

"Why?" asked my father.

Fifi explained that his son, Joe, made him realize he had disrespected my father. Fifi's heart was heavy with shame. He had only the best of wishes for my family, and asked forgiveness.

I came around to the front of the cabin as soon as Fifi ambled off. Fifi's proposal just made my dilemma murkier. If my father was going to run after his dream, what about me? If he became the violinist he once was, he wouldn't be ostracized, like I would if I followed *my* dreams. My dreams made me a queer.

My face was wet with tears I didn't know were coming. My mother told me she'd miss me too. She reminded me to mind my elders and to help out by tidying up, as well as a whole bunch of other, trivial things. I knew she expressed her concern, worry, and love this way.

My father had his trademark cigarette hanging out of the corner of his mouth. He looked down at the ground as he pulled it away from his lips. I could tell that he was uncomfortable with this goodbye. We had so many conversations that never took place out loud. I hugged him hard, and managed to whisper, "I love you."

Chapter Thirty-three

MORE ANSWERS

It seemed Mr. Gallo was on his best behavior. He managed to get the doc alone, just resting on one of the golf greens, chewing on a blade of grass and contemplating Sebago Lake in the distance. He'd be chewing on a lot more in a minute. Katie and I were just on the other side of the mini sand trap and the row of pines close to the rec hall.

"Mr. Gallo!" said Doc.

"Just Fifi. You know, you like a son to me too."

"I'm sorry?" asked the doc.

"I know things. Joe, he don't think I do. You may not be a specialist of the heart."

"A cardiologist? I'm not."

"You very smart in the ways of the heart. My son's heart. I want only the best for Joe. He tell me he only love two men in his life: me and you. Good company."

"I don't know what to say," said Doc. "I thought you came over here to find out what my colleague, the pathologist, said about the bones."

"First, I say my piece. My son, he's a good man. He brings no shame on you."

"Of course Joe is a good man. What is this about?"

"Don't hurt my son."

"I'm not in the business of hurting people."

"You think I am. I'm a different man. I come here, and things, the odor, the arbors, trees, it takes me back to my home, the Belice, in Sicily. The sticky stuff of the tree sap, it stick in my hair when I'm a boy. I go round all day with the odor in my mind. I sit in school or church, I see myself, I imagine myself in the tree. Free. Here, same thing. I'm free. I don't have to be a wise guy. I see my face as a boy come back at me in the Lake, like Lago Arancio in Sicilia. I like my boy face."

This draw of the land, I too felt it. The softness of Katie's face, a fleeting tenderness around her mouth, her watery eyes, all told me she knew exactly what Fifi was talking about, and she was sensing it in this moment too. His acceptance of Doc as the only other man in Joe's life also seemed to move her.

Doc and Fifi kept talking. They said the experts they had consulted agreed that a short, sharp blade had cut the hands, not by a professional, but by a shaky, inexperienced hand.

"Well, the girl, Pina, she say she cut the hands?"

"In her dream, Billy did."

Fifi sighed and lifted his hand in the Italian gesture meaning, *what to do*? He asked Doc not to tell Joe about their conversation. Doc agreed and said he and Joe had work to do in the archives, and that they awaited news from Bud. Bud was checking with his uncle to verify the ring and to get the full names of the other campers.

⁂

I was becoming quite the expert on eavesdropping on Doc and Joe together. Katie and I were privy to occasional sweet talk. I watched Katie carefully to judge just how much she squirmed when she heard them exchange terms of endearment and whether or not she turned away if Doc stroked Joe's hair.

She also complained a lot more about her mom these days, saying that her mom was never around. If we counted all the times she spent at Bridge or singing *Ramona* with Laura Scatterwahl, the Grande Dame of New England, at the piano in the main house, Katie's mom was more like a ghost coming back to her cabin for an occasional haunt. She was even planning an overnight at the Poland Springs Mineral Spa.

It was clear that Katie liked Fifi. He made the two of us smile. She got teary-eyed when Fifi told her father he was like a son to him. She had asked me if I thought that meant Fifi really accepted Doc's connection with Joe. I shrugged to play it safe. She no longer referred to Joe as the pervert.

We were minding our own business, just playing croquet close to the main house, when we saw Doc and Joe go by. Despite ourselves, we went to sit outside the sitting room window where the phone was located.

The phone rang. Doc took the call on the first ring. The tension was palpable even through the window. We couldn't make out much just from hearing Doc's end of the conversation, but afterwards he recounted the whole call to Joe. According to Dr. McGuilvry, Bud said that his father identified the ring as Butch's and named the key players by their family names: Roger Brown, Billy Collins, Wolfgang Holthaus, Peter Shattuck, and Kevin Coe.

We heard Doc settling in in the wicker rocker as he continued to fill Joe in.

"Yeah, according to Bud's uncle, Roger had been detained several times by the cops."

"And they never had enough evidence? Seems fishy," Joe said.

"The whole thing is. Not only that, earlier charges of sodomy, abuse, and endangerment of a minor were expunged from his record. Then, he really picked on the wrong kid. Apparently the child of someone influential. Anyway, that's what the judge said."

"Yeah?" Joe sounded impatient.

"But nothing. Not a word. No mention of Roger in the system."

"C'mon, Ron. What do you mean, nothing?"

"Beats me. Bud said his uncle seemed to be fudging but finally admitted that the Feds got involved."

"Well, it's got to be that the Feds told him to forget everything to do with this case," Joe said.

"Right. Bud did say that files disappeared. There wasn't even anything to verify the little his uncle had told him."

Through the window, we saw Joe pacing the length of the sitting room. He scratched his forehead, rubbed his chin, and let out a sigh, saying, "Now we have the Witness Protection program?"

"So whose kid was important enough? That doesn't work, unless—"

"The Feds wanted the person whose kid he abused more than they wanted Roger."

Doc was on his feet: the two reflections in the wavy windowpanes of Doc and Joe became one. Hugs and slaps on the back and belly laughs soon turned to "Holy shit! It's a big name gangster."

Katie's eyes lit up, but the question she was eager to have answered dealt with Witness Protection and not queer love.

Chapter Thirty-four

FAMILY REUNION

After an uneventful evening, Katie and I slept undisturbed by kittens, tickling, or any temptation on my part. I had washed and thrown myself under the covers, faking sleep, when Katie crawled in. I was becoming a skilled hugger of the edge of the bed.

Late morning, Joe found Ron, who was lounging in an Adirondack chair on the grassy knoll overlooking Owl Lake with a Sylvester-grin on his face. Needless to say, Katie and I were in hot pursuit. We felt a bit magnetized to Joe and the doctor's new relationship. It drew each of us differently. Katie was obsessed with understanding more about her father. I knew they held answers to more than one question. One I still had to work out. The big one about Katie and me.

"Heck, you seem chipper," said Joe. "There's my father coming towards you with a big grin on his face. Wait a minute, what's going on?"

"As I've always told you, your father loves you," said Ron.

"Oh, and now you love him?"

"Like a son!" Ron smoothed back his hair in what seemed to be a new gesture.

Fifi greeted both Joe and Ron with much affection, embracing each of them. Joe and the doctor seemed to be flirting, teasing each other about being brothers. Fifi saw that they were playing, and laughed a big, Sicilian guffaw.

I felt Katie shift her weight on the side of me. I turned towards her and caught her smiling a bit when Fifi laughed.

"They're like two little boys teasing each other in front of Daddy," she whispered to me in a chiding sort of way.

Doc informed Fifi of his phone call regarding Roger, and all that he had learned. Chiefly, that Roger was a child molester. Joe said he would start searching police and print archives through his reporter connections. Fifi insisted that he had other connections who could crash through dead-ends, even barriers set up by the Feds. Fifi said it sounded like a mob thing, that maybe this pervert also had info on a big Mafioso.

I stole another glance at Katie. Here was that word pervert again. I wondered if she saw the difference between Roger and Joe and her dad. They were not perverts, and I had to have the courage to argue this point with her. For now, she seemed caught up in the FBI story.

"Do you know something? Does this ring a bell?" Doc asked Fifi.

"I just say if the hurt kid's papa is in the family, the papa get all of his boys after this monster Roger. That was the way."

"So the Feds?" said Ron.

"Maybe, Roger, he sing, how you say, he rats on everyone, if he had something on someone to sell out, and then the Feds, they take good care of him. Some place nice with a new name, new suit, new face, if necessary," said Fifi.

"So, he's dead or he's dead as Roger Brown," said

Katie's dad.

"I'd say dead as Roger Brown," Joe said.

They agreed that Fifi should enlist his gumbas in search of this important mobster whose son had been abused by Roger.

After Fifi's departure, accented with Italian words and warm embraces, Joe said to Ron, "Well, you two are chummy."

"He knows everything and gives us his blessing," said Ron, grinning.

"Yes?" Joe was also smirking.

"We've got some figuring out to do. Suffice it to say, he has accepted me and you."

"And you? Have *you* accepted us?" said Joe.

"I do care. First I have to unravel my life, not just the life of Butch and Roger."

"You'll get to my chapter this time? Or, will it be a closed book again?" asked Joe.

"I promise you. You are in my life and will continue to be. I have to do what's right by everyone. Especially you." Ron leaned over to run his hand through Joe's hair.

"I believe you," said Joe, pressing into Ron's touch.

"*Ti voglio bene*. I love you!" said Ron, obviously practicing the little Italian he knew.

They walked off arm in arm.

Katie immediately turned to me and said, "We could find something that belonged to Roger. See if you can pick up anything about his new identity."

I agreed, but I was hesitant about something else. I searched Katie's face and body language for some clue as to what she was feeling. Doc had said some alarming things in that conversation, like he wanted to unravel his life.

"Katie?" I said, waiting for a reaction.

She merely shrugged. "I don't know."

"They're not the perverts, Katie." I softened my look and held my breath. Nothing.

After Katie's lack of response, I let it go again. We were on our feet, beginning to walk up the hill away from the beach.

"Do we have anything that belongs to Roger?" Katie asked me again.

"Let's see. The knife. No. The notes? No. The shirt…the shirt!"

"Right, where is the shirt?" she asked.

We rummaged through her father's drawers to find it. We sat looking at it, passing it back and forth until Katie found it: an old camper's label, R.B. Pretty worn, still visible.

After a couple of hours, Doc came back to the cabin with Fifi in tow. I told him I wanted to put the shirt on to see if I could feel anything.

"I need to do this, even though it does make my skin crawl." I was halfway into the shirt, half-buttoned in the wrong holes. As the shirt came in contact with my skin, I started to feel strange.

"I feel dirty," I said. "I think I'm going to upchuck. Watch out!" I said, running out of the cabin. Everyone followed, wanting to help, but I just stood there with my mouth hanging open and dry.

"What is it?" said Doc.

"I…I don't know. Those were someone else's words. I didn't think them or anything, it just came out," I said. "Something—or someone—was starting to take over in me."

"Chuck, it's gooda name?" Fifi pulled on Doc's

sleeve.

"No, Fifi. Upchuck is slang for vomit."

"But, I say Chuck, he's a gooda name," insisted Fifi.

As they spoke, I was still fighting sickness. I knew it was important to keep the shirt on. I breathed deeply and cleared my mind.

"You know, I think so, too," I said, joining Doc's and Mr. Gallo's conversation.

"Anything else?" asked Doc.

"Maybe, steak or roast or meat?" questioned Fifi. "Did the voice make you say these words, too?"

"Stop! Everyone," I said. "It really feels slimy, like bad meat. Mr. Gallo, did you say meat?"

"Yes," said Fifi, "I make a little joke, maybe yes, maybe no."

"Maybe no joke, Mr. Gallo," I said. "Maybe it's really supposed to mean meat."

Fifi grew quite interested in the shirt. He said he would take it to Italy, that he knew a woman, a witch, who could feel an article of clothing and tell things about its owner.

"Are you all right? Pina, can you hear me? You're here with me, Dr. McGuilvry."

"Get me out. Let me out. I'll claw my way out of this hole." I was leaving, but not from my dream, yet.

"Fifi, help me stand her up and shake her. Pina, you're here with us outside my cabin," said Doc, grabbing me under the arms.

"Free?" I said, slowly looking around.

I was half-awake, however awake enough to see Fifi and to sense an old current flowing between us. Ancient, like the cave dwellers and the Normans were to Sicily. Old like the scent of garlic on my grandma's

     Dolores Maggiore

breath as she jiggled me on her foot and blew gentle kisses that magically flew over the language barrier. Fifi was conveying something more than grandfatherly caring.

I started to come back to awareness. "I think I'm okay." I looked down at my hands. "But why am I so dirty?"

Katie snapped back, "Because you were clawing in the dirt to escape. Let's get out of here. Dad, can we just go sit somewhere calm? Please!"

Katie was already standing. I couldn't quite read her face—nor was I in the right frame of mind.

Chapter Thirty-five

RESEARCH

After a short snooze on Katie's bed, tucked in the crook of her arm, I woke up smiling. I was still dressed in my own somewhat soiled tennis shirt and madras shorts. Katie startled upon seeing her dad peek his head in.

"No more!" she screamed, but Doc just wanted to let us know he was finally going to the library with Joe, and that Fifi was actually on his way to Sicily to consult with the psychics.

As he was walking away, I heard Doc say he would be back before too long to receive a call from Bud. Katie and I would have to be ready to get to the phone.

Katie didn't say much as we walked over to play a game of croquet next to the main house. When I tried to stop her from tripping over loose rocks by the croquet post, she shrugged away from me. I asked if the humidity was getting to her too, but she merely grunted. I wondered if this was a good time to be eavesdropping.

We were ready to take up our post by the window when we saw Doc and Joe, walking side-by-side. We were in position and ready to glean any useful information that might leak through the porous calking of the window by the phone.

The phone call started, and Katie and I leaned in close. Most of what Bud was relating to Doc must have been old news, because Doc seemed to be impatient to get on with the call. Then, I could hear Doc shifting his sizeable weight and muffling some of the words that followed. Katie shot up from her crouched position and caught a glimpse of Joe kind of doing a dance around Ron, attempting to pull the receiver away.

"I think Joe and I are going to have to go to libraries in Portland. Maybe Boston," said Doc to Bud. "Catherine?…She's not doing well again. Kind of drifting. She spends her days staring at the hills on the other side of the lake, talking about when she was a girl on the porch at Star Island."

With that, Doc ended the conversation, claiming he was needed elsewhere.

I realized Katie was crouched over on her side and crying. I tried to hold her and tell her it would be okay, but she twisted away from me. We needed to go, but she refused to leave. I was afraid she would burst into the house and force her father to tell her what was going on with her mother.

Doc was still talking to Joe. "She looked at me the other day and made me promise I'd leave her at Star Island. Some mumble jumble about going 'with the tides' and 'following the stars.' I scheduled neurological and psychological tests in Portland for her next Friday."

Doc cleared his throat. We heard him put his bulk into the wingback chair and saw Joe's shadow merge into his. Katie and I sprung up and saw Joe massaging Doc's shoulders.

Katie couldn't be stopped. When she saw them in that close embrace, she bolted.

I heard the screen door clack shut, Doc's strange cough, and Katie's shrill voice yelling, "Tell me!"

At Katie's loud introduction, Joe sprang away from Doc. This left Dr. McGuilvry wide open to Katie's pummeling fists. He wrapped his arms around her, trapping her hands against him, and buried his head in her hair. Joe passed away from the window, and again I heard the dry clack of the screen door.

Doc spoke softly. "Honey, look at me. I don't blame you for being angry. I do have to talk to you. Your mom's not well."

Katie barked out, "So? I know that. But Joe?"

"Wait, everything in due time. Your mom told me she just wants to go away to Star Island and just 'dream,' she says. The doctors have to do special tests to see what's really going on. They may recommend total rest," Doc said.

"Maybe she's going crazy because of you and Joe. Dad, are you…are you homosexual?"

"Oh, Katie…" Doc paused. I heard that cough again and Katie's renewed sobs.

"It's a long story, and I don't want to lie to you," Doc said, then paused for a few seconds. "Your mom's disorder doesn't have anything to do with Joe, nor does he play a role in your mom's wish to go away. I love your mom, Katie. I always have."

"But you love Joe more," Katie snapped.

"I don't know if you can understand this, but it just happened. Years ago. I do love Joe, like a brother. Like a partner with whom I share a great many things. I don't quite understand it myself, but I won't lie to you any more…or to myself."

"What's going to happen?" Katie said.

"I don't really know. I love you, you know that?

And you do come first."

Katie pushed away from her father, looking as if she were about to vomit.

"I'm out of here," she screamed as she bolted.

When I heard Katie slam the screen door, I jumped to my feet and tried to catch up with her.

Turning back to look at me, her face contorted as she screamed, "I hate him. Just leave me alone, all of you."

Doc followed Katie. He stopped short when he saw me attempting to hold her. His hair looked more like Einstein's than Don Everly's, and his shirtfront and face were drenched.

I raised my eyes to him and attempted a smile. "Sorry."

Dr. McGuilvry lowered his eyes and sighed. Once he had pulled everything back inside, he told me he and Joe would be leaving for a few days. He would call often to keep us up-to-date on new details.

"Do you know what's going on, Pina?" Doc asked.

"Yes," I confessed.

He suggested Katie and I get pizza from town tonight so we wouldn't have to go to the dining room. Doc hugged me.

I held on tight. "I don't think you're a bad guy."

"Watch the mail." He changed the subject gruffly. "Fifi Gallo may send postcards from Italy. You two should read them."

Chapter Thirty-six

QUESTIONS AND ANSWERS FROM BEYOND

Carrying the pizza in one hand, I knocked gently on Katie's door. She looked up from under the comforter and eyed the pizza box greedily. I think that was the best reception I could have hoped for.

I said, "I'm sorry."

She mumbled, "I don't want to talk."

With that, she started singing "Tall Paul." We both really hated that song, but it did change the topic.

I agreed to play a cutthroat game of Monopoly or Clue, which couldn't have been too challenging since we both fell asleep sprawled over Boardwalk and Free Parking.

We spent the next two days lounging and swimming, not putting too much into words. We weren't touching as much either. I had tried to put my arms around Katie once and my hand almost froze from the cold shoulder she gave me. We chatted a bit with Katie's mom, if hazy, monosyllabic words count as conversation.

On the third day, we received a letter from Fifi, marked "importante." He sent it from Sperlinga in Sicily where he met with a "strega," a seer.

He wrote that she had handled the shirt and said, "Old blood, old meat." Then she repeated herself, "meat."

Fifi wrote out an exact phrase that the *strega* had said to him, *cio che cerca e carne*. He said we must listen to what the Italian sounded like phonetically: cho kay chair ka kar nay. Joe would be able to pronounce it in Italian, according to Fifi. The phrase meant, "You're looking for meat."

Katie seemed mildly interested. She spent her time looking at old family pictures and reminiscing about her father taking her to the park and pushing her higher and higher on the swings. Sometimes, she said, he would bring her to his office and let her play Nurse.

I tried to tell her none of that was gone. He was still that same Doc.

"Yeah, but I'm no longer that little girl," she said.

I took Doc's call, later that day, since Katie didn't feel like speaking to him. He gave me the update: one of his camp buddies, Kevin Coe, a World War Two hero, had been hospitalized with a mental break at the hospital where Dr. Walter Freeman performed ice pick lobotomies. Mentally, Coe was basically a child. The hospital kept him on as a grounds worker.

Katie was sulking after this call, but wanted to let her mom know that her dad was okay and due to return from Boston soon. We tiptoed in, figuring we'd leave a note. For once, Katie's mom was actually in the cabin.

"I'm awake." She didn't turn to look at us from her chair near the window. She just continued blowing smoke rings at the ceiling.

"Right. You don't usually sleep well when he's gone."

"Always gone. But I'll be gone too..." Mrs. McGuilvry twirled the pink, satin ribbon on her nightgown as she continued. "Your father? Always, I let him go, and I have lived inside, deep inside." She looked down at her breasts where the ribbon tie to her gown now lay.

"Katie, leave her be." I tugged Katie's sleeve, just wanting to end this painful scene.

"You girls are fine. Girls are always fine. Come visit me, won't you? I need the Star, and the water. I see myself on the porch. You, too, you'll see me. I have always loved that rocker. I just go back…and forth, just back…and forth, closer to the water and back away… from the water. It's so blue, you know."

"Let it be," I said to Katie. "She's talking about Star Island."

"Yeah, a Star Island of the mind." Katie wore a mask, now, a real angry one.

"Is the real one like a sanatorium?"

"No! It's…a rest home or a boarding house," Katie snapped at me. "I am bored with her. She can just drop dead! I'm the one who needs a rest."

Katie pushed me out the door.

Chapter Thirty-seven

VILAGGI OF BURGO AND GIULIANA - WITCH/ WHICH MAFIA

I continued to have dreams, although now they were all of meals. I saw steaks, and roasts, and chopped meat in my dreams. Smelled them cooking too, and saw blood, deep, red-brown, greasy blood. Something was definitely brewing. A witch's stew perhaps.

More letters came from Fifi. The latest told us he was in the villages near my ancestral home. A contact with another seer confirmed the importance of the shirt.

This one also said, "What you are looking for is meat."

She emphasized the word for meat in Italian, *carne*. According to the seer, this was the name of the person who had done very evil things to children in America, especially to the child of the boss of bosses. She said this evil person was still alive.

Katie looked at the pictures Fifi sent and expressed a bit more interest in the clues he was giving. She actually took a call from her father and choked out "I love you" at the end of the call. He promised to return the next day and take us for a seaplane ride.

The next day, Katie greeted me with something resembling a smile. She actually tore open the letter from Fifi in Giuliana. He cut to the chase from the start:

the victimized child was the son of big boss Propiziano. The FBI arrested this big boss shortly after his son's molester blew the whistle on him. The seer told Fifi that the molester who ratted on Propiziano used to be known as Roger Brown. The seer said he was still alive.

After Fifi's letter, Katie said she needed to tell me something, and asked me just to listen. She settled down beside me on her porch, the closest she had been to me in a few days, and said she had been trying to understand about Joe

"My dad always kept their framed picture on his desk. It was the two of them, real handsome and young. They were, well, like they had their arms around each other's shoulders, and they kind of were looking into each other's eyes."

"Katie, it's...they're like us," I said, trying to figure out how freely I should speak.

"Oh, you think so?" She looked over the top of the sunglasses she was wearing, more for effect since we were indoors.

She put her head in her hands a second, and said, "It's weird. My mother was always talking about how special Joe was back then. Do you think she knew?"

"I don't know. I do know they've been best buddies. They've been hanging out since they were nine or ten, like us," I said.

Oh, crumb. If I kept talking like this, there would be nowhere to go but all the way into the heart of the matter: the matter of our heart. I took a safe detour.

"Joe is kind of...well...he sort of lisps. My neighbor Vinny had a piano teacher, Mr. Kraus. He dyed his hair and lisped, and kids teased him."

"Because of his hair?"

"Katie, get with it. He was a queer."

"That sounds strange. 'My dad is a queer.'"

"How about, 'Pina is a queer. She's being a queer with Katie.'" I said it like it was a joke…testing the waters.

"Stop!"

"C'mon, Katie. I'm teasing you." Obviously, I had opened the can of worms. "It was sad. The piano teacher was really a nice man. He was kind and sad."

"Did he have a boyfriend?"

"No. He lived all alone."

"What do you think will happen to my dad? Will he be all alone?" Katie's face began to soften. She smiled, barely.

"Of course not," I said, risking a bit more excitement. "We'll be with him."

"We'll be at school, and you just have a crush on Joe," Katie said.

"I do like Joe. I hope he and your dad do work it out. I feel bad for your mom, but she's living in her head. She keeps going further and further away."

I wondered if I really would be at school with Katie with all this drama going on. Maybe I should just resign myself that it probably wouldn't happen. I had just ducked the big conversation again, but I felt the pressure rising.

If I didn't blow, Katie would.

Katie took off her sunglasses with a slow, deliberate movement. She had a far-off look on her face. She had gone someplace in her head.

She mumbled, "Uh huh." Then she stood up and left the cabin.

After our chat, Katie seemed to feel a bit better. She found several excuses to go to the main house to see if there had been a call from her father. Nothing.

Chapter Thirty-eight

TWO GIRLS AND A FLOAT

Day four, no activity, no phone call from Doc. I longed for a distraction or a crisis.

I had to talk to Katie. We had come so far, learned so much about ourselves and the case...and now nothing. No more talk about our conversation last night.

We swam out to the float and lay on our stomachs, dripping and breathing heavily from swimming hard.

I tugged on Katie's arm and said, "Listen. We can't just lie around every day and go swimming. I mean, the float is warm, yeah, the pine is filling my head, loons are cooing, and I'm in..." I hesitated, on the verge of saying love.

Katie raised her head to meet my gaze.

"That's lovely." She choked out, rolling her eyes.

I frowned at her. "You know we've got to call your dad about Fifi and my dreams with the meat."

Katie sighed. "It's all so crazy, and the other dreams, too! Maybe we're in one of those strange zones like in Bermuda."

"C'mon, Katie, we're not disappearing," I responded.

"Maybe we should, or go to Boston to meet my father and Joe."

"You know, a moment ago we were talking about

something, and now you want to dream about Boston?" I snapped at her.

"Hold on. I just want to talk to my dad about regular stuff. Not dreams or bloody hands," Katie whined. "I'm actually tired of these dreams."

"What? All right," I said. "We can dream about happy places tonight."

As if I had a choice. I rubbed my temple, which had started to throb with annoyance.

"I just wanna swim back now and talk to my dad. You can come if you want." She threw the words back over her shoulder as she jumped into the water and swam away.

I had no clue what was bugging Katie today, other than not hearing from her dad. Last night, she almost seemed to be coming to terms with things. I thought that maybe she and her mom had seen something coming all along. Now, I just knew I had to race back to shore with her.

Back on dry land, Katie zoomed to the phone, pushing me aside in the process. She was still dripping from the lake. What is up with her?

"Hi, Daddy, I miss you," Katie almost whimpered in a voice I wasn't used to hearing from her. I leaned in close so I could listen in.

"Everything okay?" inquired Doc.

"Yeah, I guess. Fifi's has written us some letters, all about '*carne*.' Dad, that's meat in Italian and now Pina's been dreaming about meat. I just want you to come home."

"I know, honey. I'll be home tomorrow night. Joe already called his father, so we've got all the same information, but thanks." Doc sounded pressured. "We'll talk more then."

"Good bye and kisses to Pina," was Doc's parting note.

Katie hung up the phone and dashed back out the screen door. I chased after her.

"Hey Katie," I teased, pulling her back by the belt once I caught up to her.

Katie twisted away from me, slapping at my hand.

"Stop!" She whined.

"You know," I pushed her further, "Your dad said, 'kisses to Pina.' Well...?"

Katie rolled her eyes, "Huh?"

I risked asking, "What's the matter? Your dad's coming home; he's taking us out for a seaplane ride. And, we're going to plan a happy dream, together."

Kicking up pine needles, Katie answered, "I think I just want to go to sleep early. In my father's bed."

"What?" I screeched, pulling her back to look at me. Her closed face said it all. Silence.

"But Katie!" It sounded like I was begging and maybe I was. "Tell me what's going on," I asked again, trying to touch her arm gently. She pulled away so quickly, I expected her arm to detach at the shoulder and just be left hanging in my hand.

My astonishment didn't last for long.

Katie spun on me, shouting, "It's all about you, Pina. Pina this, Pina that. Well, forget it! I'm sick of your dreams. My own father—all he cares about is how special you are."

I was caught completely off guard. I kept trying to get a but in between her sobs.

Finally, I got out, "But you liked that I was special. You even said you wanted in on the dreams."

"That was then," Katie replied. She tore off the braided weed ring I had woven for her, "and I don't want this stupid thing. It's just a weed! You're the prize rose. So that makes me a common weed. Just ordinary!"

"No! You're my sweet violet, or even my four-leaf clover," I said desperately, through the tears. "Don't throw away my ring!"

"Yeah right," she responded, "Your this and your that. Your dreams and your queerness, and I don't want any more. No queers, no dreams. I'm losing everything to you! Everybody's leaving me—my father, my mother, my me. Maybe I'd even rather be at Camp Maidenfern!"

I knew we had crossed a line. Camp Maidenfern! Katie hated me. She'd rather be with those snobs, all nails and boobs.

Did I dare ask her if she meant it? No. She was steaming like I've never seen. But give up my dreams? They're me. Queer, that's me too. I started really sobbing.

Katie made one final comment as we reached her cabin, "You can sleep in my bed; I'll sleep in my mother's room."

The screen door snapped shut in my face.

Chapter Thirty-nine

LOST

The day after my fight with Katie, I sat in the heat of the rec hall. She still wouldn't talk to me, wouldn't even look at me. I was by myself, for once.

Well, that was a figure of speech, since most of the time even when I was by myself, I was not truly alone… or myself. I was sleeping and dreaming so frequently, it was becoming very confusing.

I thought about it. Who am I? Could I be many selves? I was tired, and the closeness of the dusty rec hall was making me even sleepier. The last thing I wanted to do was dream. Maybe dream with Katie, dream of Katie, dream Everly Brothers type of dreaming, but no special dreams. I didn't want to be another person again.

I caught my reflection in the panes of warped glass. Or was the glass just fine, and I was warped? My reflection revealed a confused face staring back at me. The whole mess felt like a crazy tapestry, like a woven rug. I had thought Katie and I were weaving together. Were we really unraveling, thread by shredded thread? I *was* the warped one. I was a queer.

I was confused. Yeah, I just wanted to have fun, be with Katie, breathe in the deep, rich smells of Maine. Bury myself in pine needles and blueberries.

No murders, no dreams, no seriousness. But now, no Katie. I was totally abandoned, thrown away.

I'd just call my folks, tell them the Academy thing wouldn't work. It was just too hard. I'd be expected to be a rich girl. I'd miss them too much. What else could I do?

Once I settled on the obvious, I hurried to leave the rec hall. The heavy air was making me feel claustrophobic and queasy, like my stomach was rising up. I didn't know if I could hold it, and everything else, in place. I ran to the main house, and luckily, I was able to have the sitting room and the phone all to myself. I asked the operator to place a call to my parents' number in New York. She said she'd call me back as soon as she had the line.

I tried to get my voice back to normal. This had to make perfect sense to my folks, fit in with the way they think.

The truth would never fly. "Yes, hello, Mommy and Daddy…yes, I'm coming home because the person I love doesn't want me because I'm queer and I have funny dreams."

At best, I'd get, "Don't be ridiculous."

I did sound pathetic. I felt pathetic. The phone ringing startled me. The operator told me the trunk lines for New York were all busy. I should try later.

I'd have to talk to Doc, tell him I couldn't go to Albert Academy. I tried Joe's number in Boston. Doc answered the phone, sheepishly muttering something about missing the plane. I couldn't hold back the tears any longer.

I wailed, "Doc, I need your help! I don't think I can dream anymore. The dreams are making me too twisted."

Doc put on his physician's voice. "Tell me why." Then, he softened. "Honey, take a deep breath."

His warm, soothing words just made me melt, and I continued to blubber.

"I want to be normal. I want Katie to be my friend."

"But," he said, "you are extraordinary. Katie loves you. We all do. Have you two been fighting?"

"No, not really," I lied. "It's…well, Doc, you want me to get the answers about Roger. That's not normal. I'm not a detective. I just want to be liked for me, not for the *Ripley's Believe It Or Not* stuff."

"Oh, sweet Pina," Doc crooned, "Honey, we do love you for you. And yes, I do believe you have answers, and those answers are important. In your future, this gift of yours will be all the more important. You know about my research, right?"

I leaned away from the mouthpiece to blow my nose.

"Yes," I answered.

"Well," he continued, "I'm going to write a report on you, and if you agree, we'll talk about these dreams to doctors and students alike. What do you say?"

"So people will study my dreams?" I asked. "You mean you're studying me?"

Doc coughed.

His answer had several false starts, "Uh…well… it's not like…looking under a microscope. Yes, in a way, you could say I'm studying you, but the truth is, you're showing me things, important things only you can show me."

I didn't want to offend Doc, but I had to know. "It almost feels like a trap. People only want me to be this special dream person, and what if I stop? Would people still want me? So are people using me?" In a small voice, I dared to say, "Are you just using me, Doc?"

"Oh, Pina! I am sorry," apologized Doc. "I guess it could look like that, but if you say stop, we will. I want this for you, for your future I know where you can go with this."

I couldn't stop the burn in my chest and the sick feeling in my stomach. I had to tell him.

"Now, I'm really scared Katie wants me to quit. She thinks I've taken you away from her. She won't talk to me, doesn't even care if I come into the cabin to sleep or not. She said flat out no more dreams! She even said, no more us!"

I couldn't take it anymore. I told Doc the whole story of my love for Katie and our conversations about being queers. I was so desperate. I could feel myself flush. Thank God, he couldn't see me.

When I was done, Doc said really softly, "Thank you for trusting me with that. I can't tell you what to do, only what I wish for you. I know it is hard for you now, Pina, but I do not think you should give up your dreams. They are your heritage. I also know you will benefit a lot of people, now and in the future. But I will respect your choice."

I broke down some more when I told him about the Academy. I really didn't think I could go. I couldn't be there with Katie and just be friends. That would be the killer.

He listened quietly. I thanked him, mumbled that I loved him, and had a lot more thinking to do. He promised again that he would be back tomorrow and asked me to tell Katie. I would pass along the message, if she would even listen to me.

I had to go to the beach. I needed water to wash away my tears…to feel light and clean again. It really was high time for me to go jump in the lake. I watched the slight lapping of water at the edge of the sand. The water came in crystal clear, and then mixed a little with the sand it kicked up as it rolled away and grew cloudy. Moments later, it came back again, farther up the sand. It was constantly coming.

So, I thought, me too, I'm coming…I'm becoming. I'm in the action of becoming. I can't go all the way back to being just a run-of-the-mill Catholic girl in Queens, New York. Not in love, not a queer, not open to dreaming. I can't go back.

So, I got washed in the lake. But then, I thought I've gotta go back, gotta give this up. It was someone else's dream, the dreams, the Academy, the queerness. This was no dream. It was a nightmare.

I had to figure out what I would say to Katie. I wouldn't know until I was in front of her. But how could I live without Katie…our dreams together, our school, our future? Like living with one lung, one eye, no heart!

Without my dreams? One lung, one eye, no soul! I can't grow another heart. Without my soul I couldn't even be. I didn't like these choices. Who would want me without a heart or worse, without a soul? I wouldn't even want myself.

God, I was pathetic. I sounded like I belonged in the *Wizard of Oz*.

The phone call to my parents never happened. The operator hadn't called back. I wasn't thinking clearly. I never went back and called again.

Another day came—and almost went—in silence. I was sick. I didn't go to meals. I couldn't sit down opposite her, and eat, in silence. Her father hadn't returned yet.

This morning, I didn't even get a hi from her. I couldn't take it much longer or I might have to take it forever. Whichever, I had to speak to her before bedtime.

I had to go home to Queens where I belonged. Didn't I? I would tell her, and phone my folks once I had done that.

Chapter Forty

THE CONVERSATION WITH KATIE

I waited outside the dining hall after lunch. I hoped Katie wouldn't make a scene in front of other guests. I approached her and quietly asked her if we could talk some place private. She agreed, despite the grimace of panic that flashed across her face. I wasn't feeling all that courageous myself.

We found a quiet spot under one of our favorite yellow pines. The kittens seemed to sense the seriousness of this meeting, and they tried to distract us with their antics but I plodded on.

"I've been doing a lot of thinking...and crying," I began. "I know I love you, and..."

Katie was already in tears. God, what was she thinking?

I continued slowly before my sobs could silence me. "I love you, and I've never meant to take things or people away from you. Sometimes, I didn't tell you the whole story about a dream, because...well, I was afraid it would come to this. You would think I was too uncool, too psycho. I did think of you as my Katie, but that's because you're the only person, only thing, I ever had kind of all to me...except my dreams."

I paused.

"I didn't tell you the whole story of my love either...for the same reason. And you, as I expected, ended up rejecting me, because I was a queer and psycho. Just too much! So this isn't right for me. I've got to go home. This isn't right for me. I can't be queer. I can't make it at the Academy. I can't betray my parents."

I sobbed loud and hard, but I tried to continue.

Katie motioned for me to let her speak.

She spoke just above a whisper. "I love you, too. But how can you love me, Pin, when you've got everything else…everyone else?"

I rambled on, missing the part where she said she loved me.

"Here in Maine, you've been my world and if we continued, it would be a queer world. This world also holds my family, my roots, my dreams for our future, and my dreams…the other dreams. They're all me, just like all the things that are you, in your own special way. Things that I would never take away from you. I can't love you without your passion for science or your teasing…even your kitten craze!

"I can't be anyone other than me: queerness and dreams included. I wouldn't be me, without that stuff. I wouldn't like me, and neither would you. There I said it. I want you, I need you, and I won't ever again be less than all of me."

Jeez, I sounded like a recording. A bad one.

Katie spoke, "Oh. I really, really do want all of you and your world: pasta and pizza and Puccini. And your dreams. Even the scary ones. All of it…my dad's queerness and ours. Our big dream that we were going to plan together. You still want to?"

Katie leaned into me and shook me gently by the shoulders.

I was shocked. "Yeah, I do, really. Please, I wanna hold you. I've missed you so much. I thought my life was over. But…you'll really be able to stand the crazies, the worst of the worst dreams?"

I saw her face just soften.

"C'mere," she said. "I want to hold you, all of you."

We hugged and hugged and cried and cried. We even walked, sashayed back to her cabin hip to hip, holding hands. We fell over each other into a bed of dried needles behind her cabin. Katie pulled me against her, her blue eyes pulling me in even deeper, and found my lips.

We kissed, and our lips parted. We clung to each other, lost in our world for hours.

After a while, we picked ourselves up from the pine needles and freshened up in time for lunch. After we had an unbelievably silly lunch with Katie's mom, Catherine, Mrs. McGuilvry went off to her scheduled overnight mineral spa treatment at nearby Poland Springs. Claudia was charged with looking in on us. We assured everyone we would be fine, just fine.

I skipped down the dining hall steps singing Buddy Holly's *Everyday*. I was throwing Sylvester-grins at Katie.

"Love like yours will surely come my way…"

Back in the stuffy cabin, we shed extra layers of clothing as the day heated up in all ways. We stretched out on the cushy porch furniture and dialed Katie's powerful transistor to WVNJ to listen to a mixture of R&B and folk. *In the Still of the Night* was playing, and I darn near swooned.

Katie was speaking openly and tearfully about her dad. She explained that the night I had said he was a queer like us, she started to put things together. She began to see that her dad and Joe fit together in a way her mom and dad didn't. She said she had no idea what was going to happen, but…she couldn't hide what she was beginning to understand for her dad as well as for herself and me.

Katie leaned over to take my hand. She said, "I feel blessed. Like the time during communion, I felt like Jesus talked to me. Not talked, but totally there, like how it is between us. I think it's that way for them too."

I joked, "You love God that way?"

"Not love, not like girlfriend, boyfriend, but like there's no beginning, no end; you don't start here, and I start there. It's almost like you and I are one."

"So you and God are one?" I asked.

"Not God, but something…you know my mother is always talking about God and saying her Rosary, and going to the Legion of Mary like she's some saint, but I think she just gets lost. It's like when she smokes her cigarettes at the little, round lace-covered table, I don't know what she's thinking. I call her, and she doesn't answer. I shake her, and she's not there. She has this funny look in her eye, and sometimes, the cigarette is actually burning her fingers. I cry because she is… like dead. My father comes in and tells me to go cry upstairs, and that my mom needs to go see the doctor. It's so scary, and I feel all alone."

"I never knew that. Come here," I said, pulling Katie's chair closer.

"No, listen first. I never talk about you and me. It's…it's why it's so special. It's like today. It's as if I belong. I'm together, joined, attached, like you and I are one."

"I think I love you, like love," I said wholeheartedly, without blushing this time.

"Just hold me and hold me and hold me." Katie stood up and pulled me with her into her bedroom. She held me close, stroked my head, and kissed my eyes. "I'm so sorry for those three days. I was so scared."

We inched towards her soft bed where she brushed my lips with hers and kissed me, pulling my lips gently apart. I kissed her lips and her whole face. She leaned her whole body into mine, setting off tingling sensations in every inch of me. My hand found its way under her shirt, to her breast.

Her eyes said, "Yes."

After making out for an hour, we planned our dream, which was rather freewheeling, given our smitten state.

"Ready?" I said.

"Yeah. Just let me get the really soft blanket. Did you douse the fire? I can smell it," Katie said.

"First," I said. "Set the alarm. It's ten now. Say, three."

"The bewitching hour." Katie bared her teeth in a vampire-like grin.

We decided on a travel dream. Maybe we would meet in Europe or maybe in Northampton, Massachusetts at Smith. We'd be in college together.

⁂

"Wake up, Katie! The alarm went off," I said amidst a gigantic yawn.

We recounted our dreams to each other. Katie said that she had been in Boston in Harvard Yard eating ice cream at Brigham's with her dad who was on call at the local hospital, and someone was sick.

I said that they were operating on my brain,

looking inside my head. I scratched my head at the mere thought. Katie insisted that her dad was probably called to assist in the procedure. I laughed that she probably just went on eating her ice cream; I would have laughed at just about anything. Our make-up relieved me so. It had given me my life back.

"Okay. Let's plan dream, part two," said Katie. "I bring you ice cream. My father stitches up your head. All our dreams come true."

"Like, ice cream for life?"

"No, silly, us two. Together, doing good things, helping others," Katie said, sitting up tall in the bed, shoulders back, chin up.

"Helping others to love one another," I said.

"Yeah. Oh, we can put Joe in the dream."

"Yes. My folks and your mom and all the families. Happy again."

"You think we can finish this by morning?" Katie said.

"Sure!" I answered with a big grin.

In less than five minutes, I was aware of Katie's snoring. Then, my eyes fell shut, and our real dream began.

Chapter Forty-one

THE DREAM

Ijust love when you come over for lunch," I said. I was dressed in a white smock and had a nametag on my breast pocket. My long hair hung straight, almost board-like, parted in the middle. The room held files and projectors. The air seemed hygienically sealed in.

"Rescue me from work! Come give me a hug. How's the conference coming?" Katie said. She wore an ecru, jewel-necked, cashmere sweater and a long equestrian-looking tweed skirt. Her short dark hair was somewhat two-toned in points.

"Super. But your father is a bit tight-fisted with the early Army contracts."

"He'll come around. He always does," Katie said, pulling a piece of fuzz off my shoulder.

"Look, just look! I've always loved this view of Sebago. I never thought we'd see it any other way except from the golf course," I said, pointing to the stripe of blue past the two pavilions. *"Seriously, were you able to think beyond the camp, the latrine, the rec hall?"*

"Me, no," Katie said. *"But you, I think you always knew, at some level."*

The dream ended with my talking about being paid to do research and set up the clinic, apparently a sleep or dream study clinic. Katie had studied in

Zurich, probably psychology, and ran the women's clinic.

"*It was a dream, huh!*" said Katie. "*And the part of 'they lived happily ever after'…*"

"*It is, and it's all coming true. What do you think, Joe will write it all?*"

"*Dammit! You can't even trust your dreams to co-write it with Joe?*" said Katie for the umpteenth time. "*Our lobster is ready. Want to eat in the sleep chambers?*"

"*If you promise not to fall asleep on me…*"

❧❧❧❧

"But our deal, our lobster. I am asleep, or I was," said Katie.

"Lobster for breakfast?" I answered.

"Where are we? Are we still at the sleep clinic?" Katie looked at me, shaking her head as she spoke my name.

"In your cabin," I said.

"What year? I mean, well…how old are we?" Katie held her head.

"Look at me," I said, holding her head. "Look, you're sixteen. We are in Maine, but I know we will do all the things we dreamed someday," I said.

"Like I'll run the women's clinic, and you the sleep clinic?"

"Wow! Katie, you did dream the same dream I did," I said.

I tousled Katie's undyed hair. I laughed, thinking about the streaks in her butchy haircut in the dream. I shared the image with her, and she agreed the cut was not becoming.

"So. It's real, some time, not the haircut, but this

clinic place, here on this site? What if we mess it up?" Katie asked.

"We won't." I grabbed Katie and shook her, shouting, "We did it; we seeded the dream, and we will seed our future!"

"Watch it, you're dumping me off the bed—in the here and now!" Katie laughed, a full-belly laugh for the first time in a long time.

"Yeah!"

Chapter Forty-two

JAIL HOUSE BLUES ITALIAN-STYLE

It was so cozy under the comforter and in the comfort of our shared dreams that we lounged about in bed for a while. The sun celebrated with us by lighting up the whole cabin, warming it earlier than usual. Eau de Balsam, as I sometimes called the aroma of Maine, bathed us in its incense. I thought I had lost this paradise.

Katie was more interested in the nectar of the gods rather than their throne right now, since our lobster lunch had only existed in dreamland. She scooted off to breakfast with Claudia, our babysitter who hadn't checked in on us at all. Katie promised to return with some goodies for me.

My body was in shock. I had prepared for the worst: ready to give up Katie, the Academy, my dreams, and my queerness. Instead, I had been given so many things that I had wanted for so long. I felt soft and mushy…good mushy.

In case my folks had gotten any calls from the operator, I would try to call them today to tell them all was fine and that I missed them. Ditto for Doc, who was supposed to get back that afternoon. We'd have to phone this morning to catch him and Joe before they flew out of Boston.

Katie returned with muffins and sausages and a

rhubarb jam kiss. I was soon ready to call Doc from the main house. Once we got there, I found a letter from Fifi in the office mail basket.

Fifi enclosed a postcard of Palermo, which Katie and I devoured with our eyes: beautiful old mountains, some like smokestacks rising out of the Mediterranean, castles, and cathedrals. Katie oohed and aahed over the deep blue water.

Then, we prepared to do battle with Fifi's written English. As best we could make out, Fifi was telling us he went to jail, but not to worry, just as a visitor to Mr. Propiziano.

Propiziano—another extended Mazzini family name. I guess there were bad guys in my family—a far distant branch of the family. Fifi had mentioned names of other people he had visited in Sicily that also sounded familiar to me.

My focus became fuzzy for a few seconds as an overwhelming sense of familiarity and family subsumed me. I could smell the heart-warming, chocolate-chestnut scent of my Aunt Maria and all her sisters. I still felt her smile, and I knew that some of these people Fifi mentioned did really belong to me.

Katie nudged me to keep on deciphering Fifi's writing.

He said he told Mr. Propiziano that Francesca Arcuri of Giuliana had sent him. That's why Propiziano was willing to talk to him—in English so the Guardia wouldn't understand. Propiziano confirmed that Roger Brown had victimized his son and then ratted him out to the FBI. Propiziano confessed in a roundabout way that he wanted to track down Brown and have him put out of his misery, but no one was able to find the man.

Then I said to Katie, "Crap! He spilled the beans."

Katie wisecracked, "I don't see any beans; I see meat."

I didn't laugh, but explained that when Fifi asked Propiziano if he knew anybody named "meat" or "carne," he tipped off Propiziano to Brown's new identity. Provo's guys might be out to get Fifi right now. They would assume he wanted to eliminate the new Brown, but according to Fifi, in Mobster Ethics, that prize belonged to Propiziano and the Boys: Fifi would have to go.

We immediately called the operator from the phone in the main house to place a call to Doc. Katie's greeting to her dad was bubbly, but real. She even inquired about Joe, who returned her greeting from somewhere in the background. I took turns with Katie relating Fifi's news, and then quietly explained that I believed all was resolved. Doc said he had a lot to tell both of us, but they had to finish a few errands before heading to the airport. He was almost sure they could catch a plane into Portland airport later that day.

Chapter Forty-three

WHAT DOES IT ALL MEAN?

After the call, Katie and I chatted a bit more about Fifi. We decided to ask the cook or one of the waitresses to pack us a picnic lunch so we could spend the rest of the day at the beach, before her mom's return from the spa.

Equipped with sandwiches and wrapped in towels, we took the path through the woods to the beach. We stopped every so often to laugh or just to make goo-goo eyes. It took us longer than usual to get down to the beach.

Since our sunbathing days would soon come to an end, we slathered Johnson's baby oil on each other. I tickled Katie as I slipped some under the straps of her green plaid bathing suit. She traced the front outline of my stretchy racing suit. I caught her finger and pretended to lick it.

After a half-hour of serious attempts at tanning, which only resulted in rosy burns, Katie sat up and said, "So, what do I tell my dad?"

Not quite ready to touch an already touchy subject, I said, "You mean what do you ask your dad?"

"Yeah," she said, puffing out her breath. "I do not want to know about their sex life."

"Yuck! I can't picture my folks either. I mean—"

"I meant my father and Joe." Katie started to

make circles in the sand with a dried reed. Sand stuck to the back of her greasy hand.

"Are you afraid your folks will divorce?" I asked.

"Well, he better take care of my mother first." Katie turned towards me. "Wouldn't he do that first?"

"I know you're scared, for your mom, I mean."

I reached across to Katie's hand and got a handful of sand.

We both laughed and took a break from the conversation. It was time for cooling off. We pushed each other up, slipped on racing caps, and tripped over each other getting to the dock. We dove in at the same time and raced to the water system pipe in this man-made lake. It was only a few strokes away, and we were quickly refreshed and degreased.

I drew her dripping face towards me and kissed her gently. She started to pull away, afraid there were other guests on the shore. Everyone must have been at lunch. She kissed me back. A lot.

When we finished our bath and dried off, we sat and ate our BLTs, dripping mayo and bits of farm-grown tomatoes down our suits, licking up the mess and laughing. We chatted a bit more about Katie's dad.

Katie said she understood his attraction to Joe more and more and confessed to actually liking Joe a lot.

"They're like us." She smiled as she twirled a strand of my sandy hair. "I know how my feelings have grown…and grown and grown." She laughed and started to tickle me.

We hugged and sat with our arms around each other's burning shoulders. Katie's soft voice broke through the languid stillness of the air.

"It's hard not to know what will happen."

I whole-heartedly agreed.

Our early evening was spent eating with Katie's mom, who had returned from the spa in good spirits, looking relaxed and smelling delightful. There had been a call from Doc saying they couldn't get out of Boston that day.

Katie was disappointed, but said that it bought her some time to find the right questions and words for her father. Exhausted and burned, we kissed only once or twice and kept a short distance away from each other's flaming skin under the crisp, thin sheet.

Chapter Forty-four

MORE JAILHOUSE BLUES

Our bodies had gravitated towards each other in the night. I just loved spooning. It automatically threw the switch, drawing me deeper into dreamland. I let myself go there, anticipating pleasant dreams.

"Chili? I'll give you chili...down your pants."

"Huh? Here's a blanket, Pina. Go back to sleep." I heard Katie's voice, but all I pictured were gray, cement walls and iron bars. The smell of dirty bodies, male bodies filled my nostrils, and I felt a man's penis against my thigh.

"Who's 'cornuto?' You'll cuckold me! Ha! Get off me. Shut the hell up with your corny and corn balls."

Another violent dream. Crud. This time, I might be able to control it.

"You won't get me tonight. I'll get myself put in the hole."

I would scream for the guard. I'd get myself out of there. I struggled and twisted and kicked.

"Wake up. Wake up! Please!" Katie was shaking me.

"Where? Who are they? They beat me up." I clasped my chest with my hands.

"Here, let me wash your face. It'll wake you up." Katie tried to scrub my face.

I ripped at my mouth. There was a familiar smell on this gag. I had to stop it.

"*You can't suffocate me. No gags.*"

"Pina, Pina! It's Katie. I'm taking care of you. Where were you?"

Katie succeeded in waking me. I could see my dream more clearly from this distance. I was in jail, where a lot of rough, ugly men with long, dirty hair were fighting, pulling each other, clearing the way to me. Two grisly-looking guys like sumo wrestlers were about to pounce on me. Men were screaming, fists and feet were flying. They called me 'Corny' and 'Cornuto' and 'Chili.'

This was not the dream I had anticipated, but I knew there were clues within. When Katie asked me if I meant "chili con carne," everything started to come together: Fifi insisting on the word carne or meat, and something else having to do with the shirt.

I remember when I put on the shirt, and I felt so sick. Fifi didn't understand the word "upchuck." He said chuck was a good name, and then something about a roast or meat.

I was trying to recall images from my dream. The denim shirt I was wearing. I was on my stomach, and for just a minute, I could see my back, the back of my shirt. It read C- A- R-N...I couldn't read the rest.

Guards with guns and clubs got me out of there before it was too late, but I continued to hear taunts and screams of "big man's brown nose" and "I'll show you brown." That's all I could remember.

"Well, this guy, the guy I think killed Butch. That was him in jail."

"Who's in jail?"

"Roger Brown's in jail...I think." I said, a bit

exasperated that Katie wasn't following me.

"So this guy is in jail, and other guys are beating up on him. His name is Carn-something, and he's the 'big man's brown nose'." Katie was piecing it together.

"I'm confused." I had to admit it.

"Yeah. Me too."

By now, we were fully awake. We decided to get up and start the day, which promised a bit of rain by the looks of the gray sky. It was already about seven, but the fog was darkish. That usually meant a real downpour. The only good thing about that was the smell of balsam and pine that the rain seemed to bounce back up in our faces.

Chapter Forty-five

DOC'S RETURN

Doc arrived very late that afternoon, to Katie's relief. He seemed delighted to hear the two of us giggling as we all carried his bags in from the rental car.

He hugged Katie really hard and whispered, "I love you so much."

He explained that the delay in coming back was due to bad weather. He told us about the new contacts they had made, contacts which seemed to clarify a lot about the case, as well as clear Doc's and Fifi's names.

Doc came over to me on the porch and lifted me off the floor, telling me how glad he was that I had made good choices. I was aware of Joe's absence.

Catherine came out of the sitting room, eyeing Doc as if her were a stranger. He hugged her and kissed her on the cheek.

She mumbled, "My stranger," and disappeared back into the sitting room, a trail of Kent smoke following like a scarf stretched out in the breeze.

Holding on to Katie on the porch love seat, Doc summarized some more details he had gleaned. He told us about a story from a Colby, Maine newspaper in '43 about the suicide of Billy Collins. Just the way I had dreamt it – walking into the water. It had really felt like I was trying to wash away my guilt, to get to the clean water.

I left knowing Katie and Dr. McGuilvry needed to talk. Joe was checking into a room at the main house. I could just collapse in the Adirondack sofa in front of the dining hall.

There was still some time before lunch when Katie came bounding up from behind me. Katie's talk with her father had lit up her face and put a sparkle in her eyes. She was gorgeous: dimples fully exposed, freckles dancing on her high cheekbones, a rosy glow all over.

She sat down in the green springy chair next to me, and her words seemed to tumble out. She explained to her dad how scared she was at first that he and Joe were like Roger, perverts, and how furious she was at him for doing this to her mother…and her.

"Pin, he started crying and kept on saying he was so sorry."

"Wow…" I said, afraid to say too much or too little.

"Yeah. He told me he and Joe were attached—in friendship and in love—like you and me."

"Wow! Cool daddy-o!"

"Yeah! He really did say that…then, I was crying, really sobbing, too." Katie scrunched up her face. "I shouldn't have, but I asked if he ever loved my mother. He said he did, very much. He started to sniffle again when he said he could never admit to anyone that he liked boys, not even to himself."

"Hmm. I know about that…" I mumbled.

"He was convinced, he said, that his parents would disown him, that he'd be thrown out of school and the church."

"I was afraid, too. Oh, crumb, Katie…I'm still

afraid of what my parents might do."

"Oh, Pin, they wouldn't, would they? God…he did say a part of him died, and he tried to bury that part in work. I told him I was so sad I missed out on the parts he had to hide."

"Katie." I started to shake my head and squeezed my eyes real hard not to cry. "I don't want to hide."

"I can't miss out on you, any part of you, Pina." Katie reached for me, mumbling, "My dad said when people hide one part of themselves, other parts get hidden. I can't let you disappear. Please don't…"

Katie looked around, checking to make sure we were alone, and then hugged me hard.

"I hugged him too, a long time," she said, wiping her nose on the back of her hand. "Everything was real quiet and a soft rain was falling. My dad and I just sat there getting drenched."

I held Katie's face, just to look into her eyes.

"I love you," I said. "I really do."

Chapter Forty-six

THE PRIEST AND THE SHRINK

Joe was coming down the path from the main house, a smile on his face, as we exited from the dining hall. Dressed in a slicker over his blue oxford shirt and his tennis sweater, he could have been one of the Kingston Trio. When we entered the McGuilvry cabin, Catherine's face lit up as she greeted Joe, and he hugged her. They exchanged some very friendly words, to our surprise. Katie and I just threw each other the raised eyebrow look.

Joe said we could listen to the tape from their sessions with the former campers, in his spacious room in the main house if we wanted, but Doc assured us the cabin would be fine. Catherine was expected as a fourth for Bridge at the house, so we took over the sitting room.

Doc lit a fire that soon cracked and released its sappy aroma to the room. Joe made small talk with Katie and myself while Doc went to get a notebook and tea for all of us.

Joe leaned over and took Katie's hand. He told her she was so brave; he hoped they could be friends.

She turned a few shades of crimson as she said, "Yes."

Joe leaned out of his easy chair to rub my shoulder, and congratulated me for interpreting his father's broken-English scribble. I laughed. I really liked Joe.

When Doc returned, we sipped our tea and Joe readied the tape. Before he hit play, he explained that we would hear Peter Shattuck, now a priest, and Wolfgang Holthaus, now a psychiatrist, on the tape. They had been the two counselors who were present the night Butch was killed.

I listened very closely to the tape of Peter Shattuck telling the gist of the story:

"Billy couldn't hurt a fly. He, of all people, wanted to intimidate Butch. We were going to threaten to cut off Butch's privates if he didn't leave the girls alone. If he didn't confess to attacking Regina. Cockamamie idea. We were doing it for Ron and Regina, and to show Butch he couldn't keep getting away with his perversions," explained Peter.

"Billy had the knife, but Roger took it and cut Butch once. A small jab. But then, Roger got nicked. His eyes went wild, and he started ripping off his clothes and brandishing the knife. Butch was bleeding, and the last thing I saw was Roger trying to grab Billy. I ran. I heard screams, but I kept on running. I got to the road and must have only been there about five or ten minutes when Wolfie showed up. He was bone white, and bleeding a bit from a small cut. He started vomiting. He said he wanted to get drunk and get laid. He put his hand on my throat and swore we wouldn't talk about this."

Then Wolfgang was speaking on the tape. "I stayed long enough to see Roger grasp Billy and hold a knife to his throat. Butch made some crude remark about Roger. Something to the effect of how he, Butch, should have included Roger in his repertoire of victims.

Then, there was some more blood coming from Butch. I made one attempt to grab Billy, but I got cut. Then, there was total chaos. Blood and flashes of the knife and blood-curdling screams. I ran for my life."

Wolfgang went on to say that Peter and he had contacted the police in later years without revealing sources and asked about a potential child molester in certain neighborhoods. There wasn't any trace of Roger, and no one had reported Butch's death. They couldn't report the murder themselves, because they hadn't actually seen him killed. They said they pushed on with the police, claiming that Wolfgang had dreams, and that maybe the police could contact a psychic. In the end, it came down to this: no body, no murder.

It was hard to listen to the recordings. Doc and Joe stopped the tape several times, worried that the stories were too graphic, but Katie and I told them to continue. By the end, Katie's eyes were rather glazed, and I had heard enough. In a way, we knew all this, not the precise details, but the gist.

Katie and I just wanted to forget about the case for a while. Doc came up with a brilliant solution. He needed to have a long talk with Catherine, so maybe we'd like it if he dropped us off at the Spa to eat dinner. He would pick us up afterwards.

Katie and I exchanged a long look. She started to pout, and I tugged at her arm, reminding her it was probably about the tests Catherine had to have. I heard a gentle sigh of relief, and saw an enthusiastic nod of approval.

Doc also said he had an apology. He had promised to take us to Naples to go on a seaplane ride over Long Lake. He suggested we do that tomorrow after breakfast. We could eat lunch there on the boardwalk.

All of us let out one huge cheer.

Joe said he'd see us in the morning. He had started to write bits and pieces of this story, and wondered if he could interview us. Where it would end up, he didn't know, but we would definitely have starring roles.

I was beside myself with joy. Two days ago, I was going to go back in hiding. To bland old Queens. To be emotionally buried among the less-than-famous and wealthy, and to be a star disciple of the Holy Conservative Church. Today, I stood exposed, although not naked, on the road to the Albert Academy. A budding sleuth, and a soon-to-be star interviewee. I said as much out loud, and Katie gave me a friendly shove.

Most important, I was in love!

Chapter Forty-seven

CUTS OF BEEF

Doc dropped us at the Spa on Route 302 and said he'd pick us up in about two hours. Mrs. Robinson, the owner, was there; our families and Marge Robinson were well acquainted. Everyone knew we'd be safe in her care.

We sat in the corner booth overlooking the lake, and Katie started to giggle. Her smile seemed to stretch from ear to ear as she went on and on about her father and how kind he was to her. I had to cut her off to double-check on her order. She nodded yes to our traditional lobster roll and chocolate malted.

The lobster rolls here were incredible, tons of really fresh chunk lobster from the claws on a bun with grilled sides, not like the frankfurter buns at home. They used a combination mayonnaise and lemon dressing that squirted all over your face with each bite; a ritual part of the meal was licking our fingers clean after.

When Marge approached for our order, Katie asked for the lobster roll.

I barked, "Chuck chopped!"

"Wha?" said Katie, squinting at me. "You said a lobster roll."

"Honey, what do you want?" said Marge.

"Chuck chop, chop chuck!"

I continued to shout. After my initial shock at having those words pop out of mouth, I started to get it. I was meant to say them.

Marge was so kind as she explained, "We have hamburger, and it's all good, maybe even sirloin, I'll check. But be patient, love," she said, kneeling down by my side. She exchanged a look with Katie and tiptoed away.

"What is wrong? You love lobster." Katie leaned across the formica tabletop until she was about an inch away from my nose.

"Chch…chu…" I tried to speak.

Clearly, I was not okay. Something had grabbed my insides and my vocal chords and everything came out in choppy monosyllables.

"I don't know. I don't know why I said that," I said, but I thought I had a clue.

"What, what did you say?" Katie placed her hand on mine.

"Chuck."

"Who's Chuck?"

"No, it's meat. My mother won't buy the expensive meat. I always have to get it at the store, and they have to do it special. I always forget how it's said, like 'chopped chuck' or 'chuck chopped' or 'chop chop.' I opened my mouth to say Lobster, and that came out."

"Did you hear what you just said when I asked you who chuck was? That's the answer, right? Chuck. It's a name, maybe a name we need to know."

That was all Katie said. Her eyes stayed fixed on me. Once, I might have been afraid she was feeling sorry for me, but now, I knew it was love, and she was just taking me in…all of me.

It was already late when Doc picked us up. We did get to eat lobster rolls, and Marge joked about the lobster rolls being so good, some people actually get tongue-tied.

Katie was excited to break the news of chuck chopped. She told her part of the story, leaving out her embarrassment. I said I thought it was like the dreams, and it made sense. It was a variation on meat or carne.

Katie jumped in to say, "But chuck—that's the important part." She reminded us of Fifi's misunderstanding of the word upchuck.

Doc nodded approval and said we'd have plenty of time to talk about it more tomorrow on our way to Naples. For now, the return trip to the cabin lasted less than five minutes in pitch black and silence.

Doc made us tiptoe into the cabin, putting his finger to his lips. He was going to sleep in his sitting room instead of the bedroom. Katie flashed him a bug-eyed look and asked if her mother was okay. Doc merely said she was angry about having to have tests. I don't think he meant to roll his eyes, but I could see he had had enough talking for the day.

Katie and I cuddled and fell asleep immediately.

We were up early and finished breakfast just as quickly. Joe joined us outside the dining hall. Doc emerged and told us Catherine wouldn't be coming.

We were on our way and driving slowly through the Village of Raymond with its eighteenth century grange and some Shaker looking buildings painted white with green shutters. The buildings seemed embraced by bog land, which soon led to small lakes and outlets of Sebago Lake on our left as we headed west.

There were still small dairy farms and what we

called truck farms in New York, farms producing mainly salad stuff, tomatoes, beets, carrots, cabbage, and herbs. Occasionally a deer would run down from a hillside to disappear in a grove of tall pines or birches.

We passed the sign for L.L.Bean with its neat painting of a fisherman in an Old Town canoe and soon after arrived in Naples, a small town swarming with tourists and campers alike. The big deal was Long Lake, a deep, velvety blue home to graceful white yachts, seaplanes, and fishing boats for hire.

Doc and Joe held our hands as we stepped off the dock onto the pontoons of the seaplane. Katie let out a nervous giggle as the plane jostled us back and forth to our seats. Doc finally took Joe's hand to help him on and smiled back at us.

We were airborne, doing dips over shaded coves, and lily pad ponds framed by the White Mountains along the New Hampshire border. We laughed as our stomachs did flips when the plane dropped close to the surface of the water. After a half-hour, we braced ourselves for the bouncy landing on the white-capped lake. The noise of the engine had been deafening, but we could hear the sweet sound of calmer waters lapping against the dock.

We got our land legs back and crossed over the main street to the boardwalk side. Gift shops selling balsam sachet bags, shells, and bottle openers shaped like lobster claws lined the boardwalk. A few restaurants resembled riverboats and sternwheelers. I liked the white one that was a retired mail boat, low-slung and homey. That's where we were going to eat.

There were only about ten tables, pine and coated with Spar Varnish. Portholes still worked, and waiters looked like old time sailors, wearing middies and white twill bell-bottoms.

Katie pulled her dad aside. My antennae were up. Katie's asides were not too subtle, more like two-by-fours. The doc's whispers sounded like a PA system. Just the same, I knew that Katie was on board with me. I wasn't afraid any more that she'd ditch me.

I overheard her say, "Dad, maybe I can ask for hamburgers?"

"You want to trigger the same thing that happened at the Spa? Might work, Sweetie. Leave it to me," said Doc.

"Hey, you McGuilvrys," said Joe. "C'mon. We're starving. Listen, order for me and I'll run to call Papa Gallo. It's been a while."

❧❧❧❧

The sailor waiter seated us immediately at a window table. Through the porthole, grasses swirling in the soft eddies caught my eye. I started to get lost in the circles when I heard Doc order.

"Two Tom Collins, a Salisbury steak – and are your burgers chopped sirloin or chopped chuck? I think I prefer the chuck."

"What exactly is chuck?" said Katie.

"A cut of meat. There are a few different cuts used for hamburgers: top round, sirloin, and chuck. They chop it or grind it," Doc explained.

That was when I felt my eyes dart back and forth.

The waiter asked me what I would like – and then, I heard myself say, "Chuck! Dropped chuck, no chopped chuck. Butch, no chuck chopped. Chuck chopped Butch. Chop chop. I'm going to upchuck. Chuckle chuckle! That's what I want. Chuck. 'What you want is meat, carne,' right? Right? Chuck Carney."

"I got it," I said. I spoke through a cotton-like gauze in my mouth. "I know what's happening. I'm going to be okay."

Okay, but still not up to eating meat, or really anything after the plane ride. Yeah, but this place was famous for its blueberry pies and ice cream.

I sat licking my butter crunch ice cream, holding one of Katie's hands under the table. I had answers now; they didn't have me. Plus, I had Katie. I also had big enough ears to hear Doc and Joe, who just returned.

"Did she really say Chuck Carney?" Joe asked. "My father said the same thing. He's our man."

"She certainly did."

Joe loosened his shirt collar as he explained the details of the phone call with his father.

"Fifi went to jail to see the Mafioso who Roger Brown sold out and whose son he abused. He accidentally—"

"Accidentally?" said Ron with a smirk.

"Yes. Accidentally tipped off Propiziano to the name Carne, Roger Brown's alias. I all but drew a picture for my father of the obvious hangman's noose he had knotted for Roger and himself.

"He mimicked Pina saying, 'Ima Upchuck Carney.' So, I put that together with the witch's message 'Cio che cerca e carne,' and again, it spelled out, 'What you want is Carney, Chuck Carney.'"

"Goodness," said Doc, "We have to verify that and go to the Judge."

Chapter Forty-eight

BACK TO THE BOOKS

Doc and Joe took us with them to the Portland Library on Forrest Avenue. For us, it was a great outing to the older part of Portland. For Doc and Joe, it meant more research. We checked in with them every once in a while, got the research report, and went back outside to explore the neighborhood. I knew they would find answers. I could quit this intrigue business.

We were in the library on one of our check-in missions. Katie was reading historical plaques on the wall, while I ran my fingers along long rows of old books. Out of the corner of my eye, I saw Joe pull Doc aside. Even though I was officially off the case, I moved closer to eavesdrop.

Joe held a book in his hands. "This Portland branch is not a bad library. Listen to this: '*Chuck Carney, 30, recent resident of West Memphis, Arkansas, arrested in Kansas City in a series of child molestation cases. Little information was available at time of press.*'"

"When was that?" asked Doc.

"1949. Hold on. Here's 1950: '*Carney sentenced for child abduction and aggravated assault.*'"

Katie and I stepped closer, right up to the heavy pine desk where Doc and Joe sat. We wanted the scoop too.

"Where is he incarcerated? How long?" Doc said.

"Hold on," said Joe. "Uh…fifteen years. Can't find where."

"There aren't any more articles on him," said Doc. "Do you think the FBI buried him again?"

"No clue. C'mon, we've got to call the Judge and pick up Fifi at the airport," said Joe, and we all started to make our way out of the library.

"Mentioning my father to Judge Lawyer might work wonders," Joe continued as we walked, "if the Judge thinks Carney's death might cause a scandal. If my father is suspected of planting the 'accidental' slip—"

"*If* Carney is still Carney, hasn't changed his name to something else by now, and if he's rotting in jail someplace," said Doc.

"Well, it doesn't take a brain surgeon to know that if we discovered this info, the mob won't be far behind."

Doc mused, "So. Pick up your father, establish a gag order—so to speak—and contact Judge Lawyer with the full exposé."

Katie and I waited in the car with Doc at Portland's tiny airport, while Joe ran to get Fifi. Fifi appeared tan and rested. Settling himself in the car, he gave us all Italian kisses on both cheeks, followed by a soft pinch.

He immediately started telling Joe in Italian what happened with Propiziano, or the 'boss of bosses.' Joe made him speak English so we could all understand.

Fifi had spread the word among his old friends to be on the lookout for anyone from Propiziano's family who might be looking for Fifi to eliminate him before he could get to Carney. Joe said he would call Judge Lawyer to explain in a non-incriminating way what had happened.

We arrived at the phone company in time for Joe to place a call to the Judge. While he talked, the rest of us roamed around this cool old building. We all kept one eye on Joe, and we could see his body tense up as he informed the Judge that Butch's bones had surfaced in Owl Lake.

From the sound of things, the Judge grew more curious about Chuck Carney. Joe was telling him about the newspaper clippings describing Carney's last crime and sentencing.

Joe explained that it was Propiziano's child Brown had assaulted, and Brown who had sold out Propiziano to the Feds.

Joe hung up the phone and rushed over to fill us in. Apparently, the Judge believed Fifi innocent of Butch's murder. The Judge also said that perhaps he needed Fifi's services again to obtain a confession from Chuck Carney/Roger Brown regarding Butch's murder. The Judge promised to find out where Carney was locked up and have the man put in solitary, in order to protect Carney from a potential attack by Propiziano's men.

Chapter Forty-nine

IN RETIREMENT

I was enjoying my vacation. My detective services were, for the moment, unneeded. I relished my semi-retirement, since it gave me more time to spend with Katie. Katie no longer believed she was a weed. Thank god. We would need to find her a new ring, or a cigar band, to replace the old, weedy wildflower one.

One morning, one of the waitresses came to get me from Katie's porch for a phone call at the main house. The phone call from my mother interrupted my musings on Katie's ring. My mother was actually giggling when I answered the phone.

She had me on pins and needles as she told me a long and winding story about my father's violin, which a Mafioso errand boy had picked up for repair.

Several times, I shouted "Mom!" to get her to speed up her story.

Finally, I got the full details. Fifi had promised to have my father's violin repaired and to get Maestri to retrain my father. Was my mom gutsy! She hinted that she darn near threatened divorce if my father didn't grab this second chance at success in music and in life.

Holy moly! Everything was jiving: the folks were cool; I was off duty and going steady with Katie. I still kept my ear to the ground and cut a sharp eye for any movement of the key players in the case.

Joe seemed to be on a mission early one morning, tracking down Doc on the cabin porch. I put my ear to the thin wall and my eye to the knothole.

"Judge Lawyer called," said Joe. "He's found out that Chuck Carney is in jail up at Sing Sing. The Judge told the warden the whole story. They need something that leads to a confession. The plan is to use my father's reputation to scare Carney." Joe grinned and shook his head at the mention of his father's reputation. "My father said if this works, he'll take us all to Italy someday. You, me, Catherine, Katie, Pina, and of course Pina's folks."

"You're kidding," said Doc. "He's got that much extra cash?"

"Apparently. Never spent a dime of what Judge Lawyer had given him back in the day. He also referred vaguely to a promise he made Pina's mom. Something about making a new Italian man out of Barney," said Joe.

"Well, I'll be, but he means he'll make a new, good Italian man out of himself," said Doc.

❧ ❧ ❧ ❧

I liked learning all the details of the case and not having to do the legwork. Actually, Katie and I had already done the legwork: our legs were just fine, thank you.

Fifi did visit Carney at Sing Sing, wearing a wire taped to his chest. We listened to the recording afterwards. Fifi introduced himself, and alluded to a big friend in jail in Italy, an important man who was very interested in finding Carney.

Carney said he didn't give a damn. "Sonnabitch! Whaddya want? Who the blazes are you? Gallo…I don't know you, stupid wop. Oh…Christ," Carney said.

"Yes. You know my name. You know my daughter, and my son. You see, I get curious too, especially when they find someone in that lake in Maine."

Fifi explained that when the others had found Butch's bones in the lake, they thought Fifi had killed Butch. It was a reasonable assumption since Fifi had every reason to dislike Butch after he assaulted Regina. So, Fifi wanted Carney, otherwise Fifi might go to jail for Butch's murder.

Fifi said, "*Mi dispiace.* Sorry you so stupido, Mr. Carney. This Propiziano, he got friends here, in jails too. He's still furious that he go to jail 'cause you gave him up. You, the same person who do bad things to his son. Word's out in many jails that Mr. Propiziano looks for this rat. You see, if you die, Mr. Carney, you cannot confess about the bones. The police still think I kill this Butch."

"What's that got to do with me?" said Carney.

Fifi explained that he knew Carney liked to paint, and that Fifi had friends in high places who could arrange for a person to have a cell in a higher security jail. A cell with windows and yards looking out on trees and water. Jails where Carney's old name Brown would never surface.

Carney finally expressed some interest, especially when Fifi said he was about to leave empty-handed and leave Carney to rot in that jail…or he could call the warden for—

"A little confession…and then, where to find the bones, the parts that go with the hands," Fifi suggested.

"Go to the bog to find the body. Have a good

time. Who do I talk to?" Carne said.

"Just speak more loud in the microphone," said Fifi.

The tape did the trick. Chuck Carney confessed after Fifi's fine portrayal of a thug. Judge Lawyer managed to clear the names of all of our loved ones.

Joe showed us the note Fifi got from the Judge. Carney claimed Butch's death was an accident at first. That he got cut, grabbed the knife, and cut Butch. They struggled, Butch got stabbed, almost fatally, and Roger, heavily drugged, panicked, killed Butch, and made Billy cut off the corpse's hands and weigh them down in a tire.

Chapter Fifty

SICILIAN DREAMS

Katie and I just wanted to celebrate. We made Doc buy us some bubbly cider to toast everyone, including, and especially Fifi. Since we would be leaving soon, we asked if we could celebrate in the rec hall, a kind of good-bye. We reconvened back on Katie's porch after dinner.

We were packed to go. Doc and Joe carried the cider and lanterns that they would light once we got inside the hall. Katie and I had flashlights that we played up and down as we walked. Somewhere along the way, we shut off the flashlights to view the stars against the crisp, black night

Once inside, lit by railroad lanterns, we named the shadows that seemed to prance across the walls. Joe and Doc, back here in the rec hall for the first time together since 1939, read their names from the wall and joked that the shadows were figments of their former selves.

"Here's to Roger's confession." I raised my glass to Katie, Doc, and Joe.

Our glasses caught the reflection of the dancing flames. We clinked them together in a festive circle and shouted enough "Yeas" to scare away any real spirits.

"Dad, I know you're a good man," said Katie. "But I was afraid."

We toasted Doc's innocence.

"Maybe now I can stop dreaming," I said.

"No," they all shouted.

Katie's look said it all. I felt accepted just as I was.

Doc and Joe danced a victory dance with us. We all hugged and closed the front doors gently as we exited the hall, probably for the last time.

As we walked back to Katie's cabin holding hands, Katie whispered, "You can definitely continue dreaming about weddings."

We kissed Joe goodnight before he went off to his room at the main house, and hugged Doc a long time before we crept into Katie's bed.

"Kiss me goodnight," Katie said, and I felt her soft lips on mine.

I was tired but ecstatic. We had solved the case; Katie and I were going to go to the Academy together; Joe was delightful; Doc was innocent. Yeah, there were things that had to be worked out, but…Katie loved me, and neither one of us was rushing into things we weren't ready for…yet.

I shut my eyes and allowed myself to float, anchored only by the feel of Katie's arm grazing against mine. I drifted into a dream. The aroma of San Marzano tomatoes wafted in, and I was out to the world.

❧❧❧❧

"*A tavola, fa presto,*" said my father. "*C'mon, Giuseppina, sit down at the table quickly!*"

"*Daddy, stop yelling. You know I hate it when you call me that. It's Mommy's name. It's so Italian! I'm Pina.*"

I knew I was dreaming, a dream that made sense

in a way. This scene had actually happened several times in real life at home.

In the dream, I was back in eighth grade introduction to Latin, and someone was saying, "*When in Rome…*"

Roman monuments flashed by, but my father was saying we were on a bus in Sicily. I saw a gigantic smokestack-like peak that seemed to be half in water, half on a city street. Someone shouted out in an authentic Italian accent, "*Monte Pelegrino.*"

I was rocking back and forth, bumping over a bad road. My father, wearing a camel hair sports jacket over his shoulders, hummed "Volare," and said we'd get off in Giuliana, our village.

"*But, I'm supposed to be at the Academy. Did you kidnap me to stop me from going?*"

"*Honey, just enjoy La Dolce Vita. Two weeks visiting your forebears in Giuliana.*"

"*Dad, stop joking. I haven't been anywhere for two weeks. Stop! Stop! Aiuto! Help! Fermi! Stop the bus! Aiuto! Help!*"

"Wake up! What's going on?" Katie was poking me.

I sat up in bed.

"You were shouting *Fermi, fermi,*" Katie explained. "What's that mean?"

"Stop the bus," I said. "I think the dream was telling me something."

"Yeah, that you shouldn't eat pizza before bed. I'm tired. I'm going back to bed."

I heard Katie's breathing slow back down. I was left tossing and turning. The dream had frightened me. I hadn't made a choice to turn my back on my parents. I was not turning my back on my parents!

I remember Katie's last word before she started sawing logs.

"Pizza."

"Yeah, *abizz*, as my father says."

❧ ❧ ❧ ❧

"Good morning, girls!" Doc knocked on Katie's bedroom door, humming something about a red, red robin.

"Morning," said Katie, half-awake. "You're all dressed up?" I felt Katie raise herself up on her elbow, and the cozy, morning softness disappeared. "Going someplace again with Mom the way she is?" Katie asked, frowning.

"Just because I put a bow-tie on? Besides, we may all go together," said Doc.

Joe poked his head in from the porch. He was also smiling. "Yes, girls, my father is so pleased about how things turned out that he wants to take everyone to Italy next summer."

"Everyone?" asked Katie.

"Everyone," said Joe.

"Ha, ha, Pina. You and your dream!" said Katie. "Pina had a dream she was in Italy with her father."

Joe tapped his forehead and spread his hands to say, "Of course! That makes sense. There's some deal my father worked out with your mother and father. Babbo is going to have your dad's violin repaired and your dad will have lessons in Italy from the Maestri."

"Yahoo! Thank you, Mr. Gallo!" I said. "Will we see your dad soon to thank him?"

"You'll probably see more of my dad that you might want," said Joe. "He really likes you two. I think you're hot stuff too!"

I started to blush and kind of glared at Katie so she'd say something nice to Joe.

"We really do like you." Katie's voice trailed off in embarrassment, in shyness?

I laughed then and whooped it up. I was going to Albert and eventually my ancestral home.

Chapter Fifty-one

HARD TALK

That tense look on Doc's face made me want to get up out of bed and take off. I thought I would wander around the grounds, find some of the newly born kitties to play with. As I got ready to leave, I saw Joe raise his eyebrows at Doc in silent communication. I hurried to get dressed and follow Joe out of the cabin. Only, I was going to stay put under the cabin window, maybe try to hear some of Katie's and Doc's conversation. Something was brewing.

"Katie, honey, we need to talk," said Doc easing himself onto the porch glider. "Come sit next to me. You know your Mom is sick. She's been diagnosed as dissociative. Usually, it just means that someone tunes out, more or less, from what's going on around them. Sometimes, in more complicated circumstances, the person seems to have different personalities and may even behave in ways that other people can't recognize them."

"Dad, Pina tunes out all the time!"

"This is different, sweetie. Your mom is detaching more and more from us. It's okay to cry. Come, let me hug you," Doc said.

I heard the glider squeak as Doc shifted his weight to hold Katie.

"This is so unfair!" Katie protested.

"It must be lonely for you at times, given your mother's condition. I'm trying to do something about that now. Your Mom has decided to stay by herself on Star Island. She says it's best. With your going away to school, I believe it's best too. She does love you, you know."

"I know that. I wish she wasn't so sad. But, I'm really angry." After a few seconds, Katie asked in a shaky voice, "Is it me?"

"Oh, honey, no. This has been going on for a long time. I'm so sorry I couldn't drag myself away from work to keep you better company."

"Dad, I know you've tried."

"Not hard enough, and not just with you."

"Oh, Dad, I don't know, but you kept being mean to Joe at the beginning. I get that he's much more than a friend. Dad, I think you love Joe the way I love Pina. We're almost sisters, but if she were a guy, I'd be going steady with her."

"Well, yes, like that," said Doc.

"I love you. It's okay."

"Come here, honey. What did I do to deserve you?"

I could hear Doc stand up and draw Katie to him. I heard Katie's muffled sobs as Doc continued to hold her close.

"Your mom…we'll go visit her."

Katie sat back down and slid her chair closer to where Doc usually sat.

"Wait, I'm confused. You mean she's not just going for a long visit?" Katie asked, after blowing her nose.

"No. She wants to spend the rest of her days on Star. She wants to compose music," said Doc.

"Oh, if only she could play again. Then we could go listen to her play." Katie clapped her hands together once, before adding, "But she really wants to be by herself, like forever? So…it's like a divorce?"

"Oh, honey. Yes and no. Your mom has been in her own world in a way for a long time. Maybe I have too," said Doc.

"When is she leaving?" Katie asked.

"Any day now. Soon as she's packed."

"Oh."

I could hear Katie choke back a sob.

"I know it's a lot to think about. She wants you to go with her for a few days," said Doc.

"Jesus! This isn't fair. Do I get a say?" Katie sighed heavily. "How long?"

"Joe and I will pick you up–with Pina if you like, after the weekend. Is that better? Katie, she's your mom."

"Shoot, Dad, I know that. I'm just ticked off. You and Joe, what's that gonna be? I mean…that long trip this summer…like you were living together." I heard Katie blow her nose. "What you said about me being lonely, I guess you were talking for yourself too. I think you were lonely. Joe keeps you company, he pays attention to you, and you let him tease you."

Doc sniffled.

"Will he live with us?" asked Katie.

"We think so. You know, there are people who are not crazy about this idea."

"Tough!"

"That's my girl! But I'm serious."

"Then that's their problem."

"I'm so glad I don't have that problem anymore," said Doc. "I used to, you know."

"Does Mom know?'

"I think so. She seems to want it this way."

"Yeah, she always seemed to love Uncle Joe. She used to tell me he was such a dear friend to you, Dad, more than you knew."

"Well, I'll be…" said Doc. "Give me a hug, sweetie."

"Yeah, a big one. Can I tell Joe we talked?" said Katie.

"Yes. Yes. Tell him all you want."

❧❧❧❧

Almost on cue, Joe had drifted by on the path when Doc started the conversation with Katie. Now he stood on the shuffleboard court, stick in hand, narrowing his gaze at the distant triangle. It was the focus of someone about to ace a shot.

Katie, giddy with her father's permission to say whatever she wanted to Joe, ran across the court doing pirouettes and plies. I had escaped my hideout and joined in the antics.

"Hey, what are you two goofballs doing?" Joe leaned on his stick.

"Oh, Joe, well… looking for you. We just wanted to make sure you knew we liked you," I said, sneaking a peek over at Katie, who winked. She probably knew I had eavesdropped on her talk with her father.

"I never doubted it, but it means a lot," Joe said, motioning for us to sit down. "What's this really about?"

"Well, for me," said Katie. "I want to let you know I don't feel bad. I mean I'm not angry about my mother."

"Why should you be, Katie? Your Mom doesn't

want to stay here."

"No, I mean, like uh, well, you know, like Pina and me, and you and," Katie babbled.

"She means if you and her dad get married." I said.

Joe started to correct me. "You know that's not possible."

"Oh yes," I said. "In Greenwich Village."

"How do you know this?" Joe laughed, thumping us lightly on our backs.

"Well, Pina has a neighbor named Dolores who married a girl in Greenwich Village," said Katie.

"Oh, and you think Ron and I should get married?" Joe was laughing even harder now.

"Yeah! Yes! Both of us do," said Katie, who quickly added, "But, Joe, I don't blame you for my mother. My dad said he and my mom, well, it's kind of like a divorce."

"I mean you know Katie's mom is strange. I'm sorry, Kat, but it's true. Your dad is always alone." I gave my version of her parents' divorce.

"He's been weird with you, Joe. I think because he was afraid to show you how much he cared," said Katie.

"Like Katie used to pick on me, right, Katie?" I said.

"Yeah. Even my mother knew how special you were for my dad. She told me."

"Hmm. Well, I like your mom," said Joe. "She's an artist, not strange."

"Well, artists sometimes get real strange when they don't do their art. Like my father and his violin," I said.

"Sometimes, we call that depression," said Joe.

"Yes, that's like my mother, too, only even more."

"Yes, but it seems your dad seems will be happy now. He'll be in Italy, speaking Italian, and I'm sure his professors will like him; my father says your dad is talented," said Joe.

I really livened up at the thought of my father. "Yeah. He's like my old dad. He always used to take me places with him and showed me canaries and how they sang like real people. He was always so happy with music. A long time ago, he took me to buy a canary for his mom on Fulton Street in Brooklyn on Mother's Day. He named that bird Caruso."

"Well, I think he will have us singing like canaries to accompany him on his violin. You know when they hold the memorial for Butch, he'll play Mozart's Requiem," said Joe. "In the meantime, Katie, your mom will be practicing her solos on Star Island. You can do some piano while you're there too."

I watched Katie frown as Joe spoke. This was the first time someone other than Doc mentioned Katie leaving Maine with her mom.

Joe noticed the look, too. "Think I said too much." Joe stood and patted us on our shoulders. "It's only a few days; you'll manage."

After Joe had disappeared around the edge of the tennis court, I turned Katie towards me. She buried her face in her hands.

"Katie, I heard. I was listening under the window," I said.

"No," she sobbed. "They're getting a divorce. I have to go with her. She's looney-tunes."

I looked around to see if anybody was coming and squished next to her in the double Adirondack. I put my arms around her.

"Katie, it's just for a few days."

"She's so darn selfish. Crud!"

"Sweetie, your dad said he'd pick you up with me and Joe after the weekend."

"Yeah, yeah. But…but he'll feel guilty and…and…" Katie wiped her nose on her sleeve and looked at me. "You think he'll break up with Joe, or make me live on Star?"

I shook her. "Katie, dammit, we're going to Albert. He's not going to make you live with her. She's sick, can't you see?"

She sniffled. "Yeah, but he didn't say when! Who knows how long I could be trapped there?"

"You'll see. It will all work out. C'mere…" I rocked Katie back and forth, fighting back my own fears. I hadn't been alone, without Katie, in two months. I could feel the loneliness creeping in my every pore as I tried to fill Katie up with love and courage. We sat there rocking and rocking until the lunch set started to arrive.

Chapter Fifty-two

MOM AND DAD BID ME ADIEU

My parents had come back up to Maine as a surprise send-off before we left for Albert. I wasn't totally thrilled since I wouldn't be staying with Katie for a week, just as she was about to leave for Star with her mom.

I tried my best to get along and not argue with my mother, but she was watching me like a hawk. Actually, I think it was more that her little gosling was escaping from under her wing.

There really was so much I was grateful for, when it came to my mom, namely how she dealt with Fifi and my father. I was allowing myself to see that she was pretty cool.

I walked with her to the lake. The wind was up, and the aroma of pine needles wasn't as heady as it had once been in July. My mom was wearing a windbreaker and smoothing her wispy hair behind her ears.

I took her by the arm. "You know, Mommy, you're really being so great."

"What, dear?"

I knew she was probably just trying to get me to repeat it, but I didn't care.

"Mom, you're tops in my book," I said.

We crunched along the gravel and pine needles for several more minutes in silence. I peeked up at my mother. She was crying.

"I love you." She sniffled. "I'm going to miss you."

"Well, you've got me now!" I pulled her along to the row of metal springy chairs atop the hill.

I knew I needed to say more. We must have both been at a loss for the right words.

"I'm so proud of you…" my mother said. The words seemed to echo back at us from the lake. It was nice to hear them. I was totally fuchsia by the time she said, "You were so lady-like and polite with those old folks I saw you with earlier."

I was about to say something jerky to cut through my embarrassment. I stopped myself and just squeezed her hand. I smiled at Mom and thanked her. I told her how much I appreciated her for letting me go to Albert and then, I just gave in to what I really wanted to say.

"Mom, thanks, thanks, for being my mom." Her eyes reddened once again. "I really admire your courage, getting Daddy to do this musical training."

She pulled out her embroidery. I patted it flat to admire it. I felt like we had never done so well together. Maybe my folks were not so bad.

She asked nonchalantly, "You going to miss Katie?'

I started to panic; this was usually the way a hard conversation started. One where she would tell me everything I was doing wrong if I wanted to be a good girl. I started to tell myself it was all a set-up. I didn't have the guts for that fight.

I told the truth. "Yeah. It's been like having a sister."

My mother continued to work on her piece, smoothing it and counting. I could leave the comment there. No more; no less. My mother smiled and turned her face up in the direction of the sun.

After a few more rows, she giggled. "C'mon, let's go get some fudge."

We walked back to the Lodge quietly, arm in arm.

When my father saw us coming back up the hill from the beach, he called out to me.

"C'mon, Toots, I'll take you for a malted."

I kissed my mom and grabbed my father's arm. We walked in silence, me in my mocs, him in his topsiders, to the spa.

I leaned across the table and with my dry hand squeezed my dad's hand a bit.

"You know, Dad, I am really proud of you." I paused a minute. This was hard. "I know sometimes I say Queens is ugly, and why do we have to live in such a boring place. You and I have had arguments about the church and narrow-minded people."

"So, Toots, you want to have a fight now?"

"No. I don't want you to think I'm turning my back on you and Mommy."

"I don't."

My father reached out with a napkin and wiped the malted from my chin. He smiled and brushed my cheek with his fingers. "I'm so proud of you and what you've done. Your grandmother would be proud too."

He changed the subject so the tear in his eye would not cascade down his cheek. "I see your girlfriend is going to leave us to go visit with her mom on Star Island. You going to miss her?"

I could feel myself stiffen. I looked away from him, pretending to check out a man passing by. Where was my father going with this question? God, I've got to bolt.

My thoughts were interrupted by my father's saying, "Nice girl. I've always liked Katie. Respectful too."

I peeked a glance at him sideways. He wasn't starting anything. I had to relax. He liked her. That was the important thing. He wasn't asking anything. No need to talk about queerness now.

I smiled at my dad. "Yeah. She's got to help her mom. Her mom wants to stay and do music on Star. Kind of wish I could play."

"You want more gifts?" He joked, pinching my cheek.

I would be sad to see them go home, but at the same time, I needed them to leave. I was getting a bit scared about Albert. It all seemed mixed up. Life was good but not tidy, kind of out of sync – like we all have to figure out how and where to fit in.

Chapter Fifty-three

KATIE LEAVES

It was a hard morning to face our last day together. I managed to sneak back over to Katie's cabin from my parents'. We snuggled a bit longer than our usual morning ritual. I would see Katie in a few days, but after spending almost every minute together all summer, even this separation seemed enormous.

In the chill of the early New England fall, we pulled the comforter around our legs and retold each other the story of our summer. We laughed about early June and how we felt like imitation Nancy Drews. Now we were the real thing in many ways.

I wished we could have just gone from celebrating Carney's confession straight to the beginning of our life at the Academy; our sleuthing work was over.

"So glad you chose me," Katie said, as she buried her head in my arms.

"No. My grandmothers chose you for me!"

We sat like that until our tears risked flooding the bed. Doc was almost ready.

I watched as Doc put Katie's suitcase in the car taking her to Star Island, a good hour-and-a-half away. Her leaving, this time, was totally different from those times at the beginning of the summer when she would run away from me or wouldn't show for our morning ritual at the rec hall. I trusted she wanted to see me as much as I did her.

I started to wonder about the call I had tried to place to my parents, when I had decided to tell them I wouldn't go to the Academy. What would have happened if it had gone through? And Katie? And the real me?

Chapter Fifty-four

DREAMS OF SICILY

I was alone, really alone for the first time in my life. Katie would be gone for another day at Star, my parents had just left, and Doc and Joe were hanging around Portsmouth, not too far from Star Island. They would pick Katie up tomorrow.

I decided not to go to Star. It would have meant an extra trip back and forth for Doc, so I opted to stay in the main house rather than risk being alone with my dreams in Katie's cabin. The rooms upstairs in the 1825 house were cozy with gingham touches everywhere.

Propped up in my four-poster bed, I flipped through some brochures from Albert, checked the reading list, and gawked at a book of photos of Sicily. Maybe I shouldn't have done all three, since it only increased my need to be in one spot: either in a book, lost in some literary setting, or at Albert. Or in Sicily.

When I found myself dropping the books and losing my place, I shut out the light with the fringed lampshade. The wallpaper with illustrations of carriages and eighteenth century French ladies caught some light from the road, and I could almost imagine slipping into the paper to live in those times, but my eyes couldn't stay open long enough to get very deep.

Just the same, the carriages must have transported me to Sicily, famous for its *Carrozze* with donkeys. I almost smelled donkey poop, masked by the aroma of thick tomato *sugo* with *salsicce*.

In my dream, I was finally in Giuliana, my grandmothers' village! It really was a dream, growing from the ground up: my roots were here. My dreams came from here; they brought me back here…now… now that I accepted them, with their good news and their less than good news. The hard stuff seemed to be over, and everyone was celebrating, everyone and everything felt connected, like one.

The sun lit everything, making the off-white stones of this medieval hilltop village glistening gems. My father was with me again, and the stones we walked on sparkled back up at us. The walls held us snuggly in their brilliance. Walking through archways felt like we were putting on a cape of diamonds. The castle towering above was the biggest jewel of all. Here, the earth felt like it was stepping its way up to the sky.

My dad took my hand and said, "You okay? The steps are steep."

"Yes. These the originals?"

"Yup, the same ones your Grandfather Pietro and my mother Francesca walked up a long time ago. Your grandfather used to play hooky and his mother Vincenza would come looking for him here." My father was grinning from ear to ear as he sifted the grit through his fingers. I saw a tear glisten on his cheek.

In another segment of my dream, I followed Doc and Joe to witness new life unfold in their relationship.

"*Che bella giornata! Giuseppi! Oh what a beautiful day!*" said Ron

"*Where did you learn that?*" said Joe.

"*I heard that woman leaning out her window say it. The sun, the warmth, I'm sold.*"

"Yes. The sun – o sole mio!" said Joe, trying to sing the old Italian song.

"Stop!" said Ron. *"I'm serious. I feel so good."*

"Right. But it's not only the sun. Ron, you have a new warmth."

"It's you," said Ron, slipping his arm through Joe's as they strolled down Via Garibaldi.

"Just like Italian men. See, there is a certain joie de vivre about you." Joe turned and looked at Ron with a broad grin.

"You again," said Ron. *"La dolce vita – I do know how to say that."*

"But it's in you! See, you're smiling." Joe touched Ron's cheek ever so lightly.

"I see all these people smiling, laughing, touching; the men, the women, holding hands."

"Maybe they're like us…" Joe laughed.

"No, I'm serious."

"Then take my hand, Ron. They'd never know…"

"I can do that."

It almost sounded like Ron was reciting poetry. His doctor's voice was gone; he walked differently; he almost hummed.

"I feel the touch of these uneven cobbles on my feet, I brush the stone walls, and they give up their dust where many generations of shoulders have brushed. Let's go through this archway. Oh, it's almost painful, such grace! Look at it! How it opens onto the piazza behind the big church."

"La cattedrale!" said Joe. *"Yes, you're so right. Here, under the arch, they say maybe Barney's mother lived in that house and probably her mother before her."*

"Even Giuseppina, Pina's mom, always so afraid people would know she was Italian." Joe pointed down

the narrow alley. *"Look down in the doorways. She's showing those women how to do that stitch, of course they would. They're giving her cake and coffee!"*

"Everyone seems transformed. Even you father. He's making eyes at that woman," said Ron. *"I feel, I don't know the right word, connected. The boys laugh and touch. Old men go arm in arm. Little, stooped ladies, faces like cucuzzas, gourds, you taught me that, kiss each other, smack lips with noise! Noise!"*

"Me too! Smooch! Che me ne frega! I don't give a damn who sees, or knows!"

"Shush!" said Ron, *"You are shouting. That lady is laughing, waving her hand."*

Joe seemed almost giddy. He did a kind of dance, holding Ron's hand and yelling.

"She shouts back, 'pazzo - crazy' and I say, 'Si, pazzo inamorato, – yes, crazy in love!'"

"But she thinks you're with a woman, Joe."

"I scream, 'che me ne frega! So what! I don't give a damn!'"

❧❧❧❧

I started coming to with the smooch. I heard it; I was repeating it; I felt it!

Then I was really awake. The house dog, a big shaggy thing, had pushed open the door to my room and was licking my hand.

I saw the carriages on the wallpaper and made the three thousand mile trip back from Sicily in a few blinks of my eyes.

Holy cow! What a swell dream. But no grandmas, no murders.

What did I mean, no grandmas? It had to be

Grandma wishing everybody love and connection from her world to ours. Now I was a little less worried about Albert; she'd be watching over me, reminding me of my roots!

Yahoo! I had all the more reason to celebrate: Katie would be back today, and we would share a bed, maybe even a dream together tonight.

I threw on my new pea coat since the wind had really picked up, blowing across Sebago Lake. I sat by the side of the road, waiting for Katie's dad's Lincoln.

I reflected back on the good and the bad of the summer and wondered with some apprehension what Albert would be like. Would I fit in with those rich kids? A lot of them had already spent years there. Would they turn up their noses at my budget clothes? Well, I did have some nice stuff my mother picked up on sale when she actually took me to the Villager Shop.

I heard the car's big engine. I didn't even wait for it to pull off the road. Katie hardly let the car stop moving before she threw herself out of the car and into my arms. We hugged and hugged as if she'd been gone forever.

"God, I'm so glad to be here," she said. "She was impossible."

"Shush," I said. "You're here, c'mon."

She snuck a quick glance to see if her father was looking and planted a kiss right on my lips. My knees were water; my stomach went swimming.

"Hey, Kat, we get to sleep together tonight."

"Yeah," Katie said, her happy voice trailing off.

"What?" I asked.

"Well...my mom really is a mess."

"Yeah?" I did not want to think about Catherine McGuilvry, just Katie McGuilvry!

"And…it was like she was saying 'goodbye' forever…I just felt bad, but ticked too!"

"Uh huh. Yeah, she really is weird, but…" I was growing impatient.

"I know…" Katie said, still wearing a gloomy face, "but it's hard to just turn off the stuff with my mother. I mean, maybe I'm crazy, too. You sure… about me?"

"About you and me? Natch!" I laughed and started reciting Shakespeare. "How do I love thee?"

"Cut it out," Katie said, a small smile crossing her face. "Me too, I love you five thousand and twenty ways! But I'm absolutely dead tired."

"Bed sounds good to me…" I pretended to yawn.

We raced each other to her cabin, and yelled good night to Doc, who came in and asked for a welcome home kiss. Katie and I settled in under her comforter and held our breaths to see if Doc had gone for a walk with Joe.

I placed my hands gently on Katie's shoulders, too shy to touch her. I had longed for her, and now I was almost afraid I'd break her; she was crystal, she was gossamer. She took my face in her hands and kissed me deeply.

"I missed you so much," she said.

"I love you, Katie." I bathed our faces in salty tears. I felt so moved, as if nature had placed me in trance. I lost myself in Katie.

When I awoke a few hours later, I had no memory of what we had done. We were both totally naked, wrapped around each other. I couldn't tell at first whose arms were which. I thought to myself, this must be bliss.

Katie nuzzled me and stretched groggily. She

opened her eyes, as if I were her siren and she had finally heard my call.

"Don't say anything," I murmured.

After a few twists and turns, we looked at each other. It was the middle of the night, and we were wide-awake. Just the same, we were unwilling to waste the rest of the night on Monopoly or cards. We decided to stay in a kind of dreamland.

"Let's plan a happy dream together first," said Katie.

"Right. Should we dream about your mom, make her happy? Star really is good for her."

"You mean it's like Heaven? She seemed the happiest sitting in a rocking chair, reading and looking out at the water."

"Well, maybe that's where she'll always be for you. I mean in your heart," I said.

"Yes, but I want to dream the ideal mother." Katie's face seemed soft and rested as she said, "I know that's not who my mom is, but that's who I want her to be, and that's who she really wants to be."

"Uh huh. Tell me what the ideal mom is like," I said.

"Well, first, she would hold me in her lap, in a rocking chair."

As Katie started describing her ideal mother, I began to drift off. "Uh huh."

Katie spoke really softly. "She would be looking at me with a smile on her face and real soft, smiling eyes. She would touch my cheek with her soft hand with sort of plain, shiny nails, and she would hum and rock and call me her 'wonder child' sent by the angels.

"Pina, Pina, you're sleeping..." Katie's warm body and her gentle breathing seemed to form a cozy rocker for me. I drifted off again.

Hush-a-bye, don't you cry, go to sleep, my little baby…I was moving my lips, but…

I felt myself being rocked in a big, 1920's wicker rocking chair, greenish and light orange. Italian lullaby sounds floated by. I knew this rocker from my home in Queens, but the melody and the sounds were different now. I floated back and forth in dreamland.

"Pina! Pina! Wake up!" said Katie.

"Huh? Yeah. I'm awake. What is it?"

"Well, you were humming to me like my ideal mother – a song about ponies," Katie said.

"I don't know any songs about ponies," I said. "How did it go?"

"Hush-a-bye, don't you cry, go to sleep, my little baby. When you wake—" Katie started to sing.

"You will find all the pretty little ponies." I continued the song.

"I thought you said you didn't know it," said Katie.

"I didn't, but now I do. Wait…Your mom taught it to me."

Katie looked at me as if I was bananas. "No, she didn't."

"Oh Katie, it must have been your mother. In my dream, there was this tall, thin woman who rocked us and hummed, and she had this kind of light, gauzy scarf that blew in the wind—" I said.

"and she wrapped it around both of us and stroked our faces—" Katie continued.

"and she smiled and smiled—" so did I.

"and I could hear the sound of little waves on pebbles…" we both said, "and we were really floating in the water—"

"but no, then we were on the shore, kind of

grown up, waving," I said, in tears.

"and the woman…yes, yes, my mom. She floated off and then turned and waved." Katie sighed. "Oh Pina, I think it was my happy dream."

I smiled back at Katie. "Kind of a message: She'll be okay."

Chapter Fifty-five

ANOTHER DREAM

Another night, our last night in Maine in Katie's cabin. We were excited but tired.

Lying in bed together, Katie urged me to plan a shared dream. "About school, then college–of course, we'll go to the same college, right, then back to Maine to work…right? Swear!"

"Whoa!" I said. "Katie, I just wanna sleep, but okay, I swear! Now, go to sleep. Just one question: will you marry me?" I giggled, but somehow I was dead serious.

"Yes!" Katie nuzzled my neck, and in a soft voice, she added, "Maybe someday…"

Soon, there were only voices from my dream.

"I, Pina, take this woman, Katie, to be my lawfully wedded wife."

Ooh, she's gorgeous in that gauzy scarf, and she folds it around my face with her long, thin hands, and a kind of clear, shiny nail polish and she rocks me, and we float…

"I do. I, Katie McGuilvry, take you Pina Mazzini…"

She rocks me and with her smiling eyes caresses me and touches my cheek with her long, thin soft fingers with the sort of plain, shiny nail polish…

"We witness and bless your union…"

"We hold the rings we have held for each other…"

"Ron, as my witness, I bring you dreams for your daughter Katie, my spouse and for your spouse."

"Joe, as you bring me your dreams of our work together..."

Joe the perfect witness and observer, Joe who will tell our stories and engrave our dreams.

"I now pronounce you Man and Man."

"I do, you do, they do do do do!"

"Pina! Pina! Wake up. What's the do, do?" Katie asked as she shook me. "You've been saying, 'I do, you do, they do do do.'"

"Oh, Katie, it was the dream of our wedding – in ten years. Guess what else?"

"We were pregnant?" said Katie.

"No, not yet. Your dad and Joe got married with us! I heard bells, but I don't remember anything else. Isn't it great? You were so beautiful, and we were both doing the ideal mother thing for each other," I said.

"Oh, Pin, I love you! It's a dream come true."

"Like a nightmare has become a beautiful vision. I do love you, Katie!" I closed my eyes and made a wish.

Chapter Fifty-six

GOOD BYES TO SUMMER - SEE YOU IN MY DREAMS

We were up at first light, running around Katie's bedroom, wrapped in blankets against the really chilly air. Fall was here in Maine. Our suitcases lay gaping open, ready for just a few more items. We had already packed some heavier things, like the gorgeous Fair Isle sweaters from the Bridgton collegiate shop, a surprise from Doc and Joe.

Chocolate and cookies found their way in, thanks to my mom and dad who had stopped at the Shaker Bakery at Sabbathday Lake before they left. Other unexpected last minute gifts included the camera Doc gave Katie and the leather notebook Joe presented me to record our memories and dreams. In a way, our tears at the thought of leaving were also unexpected. They were salty and mixed with joy and sadness.

School would start in four days, and we were ready, sort of. For now, we were set to jump in the car and share a few more happy tears with Doc and Joe. Miles and farms and shops rolled by, escorting us along the route to the airport an hour away.

❧ ❧ ❧ ❧

We were now waiting for our flight to Andover

at the Portland airport. The down-home feeling in this tiny terminal was perfect for our good-byes.

"Will you send me letters, too?" Joe asked me.

"Of course. When will you start writing the article about this?"

"Well…Ron and I have a lot to plan," said Joe.

"Hmm. Yes. According to my dream, you do," I said.

"You're asking a lot of questions for this early in the morning. Lots of coffee in your dreams last night, Pina?" Doc winked at me. "Come here a minute before I let you two go through the gate. I want you to write it all down. Every dream, including last night's."

"How do you know?" I asked, my eyebrows doing multiple push-ups.

"Huh? Just promise me you'll record the dreams. We can make it happen, you know. We can!" said Doc.

"Come here, girls, I love you both," said Joe.

"Love you, Joe. I love you, Dad." Katie and I said together. I said, "I mean Doc."

"Love you, my sweet Katie. Pina, I love you like a daughter. Be safe."

"We will. See you in my dreams, Doc!"

We found a note from Joe waiting for us at Albert. He said he was starting his writing at the end of the story, even though it was really just a beginning.

He wrote, "I feel like I just gave birth to two daughters, and already I had to let them go." In his letter, he continued, "Ron agrees it's just the beginning of many comings and goings and farewells and reunions."

Joe ended his brief note with Doc's dream.

"I saw Pina in my dream last night, and I saw my dream man too. I walked down the aisle with you, Joe.

They, Pina and Katie, were our witnesses, and we were theirs. Pina called you her witness-observer who would write all this. She recited the loveliest tribute to Katie as they exchanged vows. That gauze veil that Catherine used to wear, Katie and Pina enfolded each other with it and, in a dream-like manner, raised up our collective hopes and dreams."

We were sitting on the edge of Katie's bed in the dorm at Albert, our cheeks glistening with tears. I asked Katie to close her eyes while I turned around and pulled something from my back pocket. With a flourish and an abracadabra, I swirled a gauze scarf around Katie and then myself.

I lifted up both my hands and said, "To dreams! All our dreams. They really do come true!"

About the Author

Dolores grew up in Ozone Park, Queens, New York, where from the age of three she ventured away from this home on her own. While this first solo mission landed her in a nearby cathedral, her further ventures brought her to great physical and psychic distances from Ozone Park.

In addition to teaching foreign languages, and selling antiques, Dolores worked as a psychotherapist with children, teens, and couples and published reference books on lesbians and psychotherapy and child custody.

Dolores lives in Portland, OR and Borrego Springs, CA with her wife, Terrie, and Murphy, the rescue poodle, and Xander, the lynx point critic. She enjoys hiking and gardening with Terrie and Murphy and birding with Xander, from the safety of his indoor perch.

Other books by Sapphire Books Publishing

The Dreamcatcher - ISBN - 978-1-943353-67-5

High school is rarely easy, especially for a tall, somewhat gangly Native American girl. Add a sprinkle of shyness, a dash of athletic prowess, an above-average IQ, and some bizarre history that places her in the guardianship of her aunt. Then normal high school life is only an illusion.

Kai Tiva faces an uphill struggle until she runs into Riley Beth James, the extroverted class cutie, at the principal's office. Riley shows up for a newspaper interview, while Kai is summoned for punching out a classmate.

Riley is the attractive girl-next-door-type whom everyone likes. Though a fairly good student, an emerging choral star, and wildly popular, she knows she'll never live up to her older sister. She makes up for it with bravery, kindness, and a brash can-do attitude.

Their odd matchup is strengthened by curiosity, compassion, humor, and all the drama of typical teenage life. But their experiences go beyond the normal teen angst; theirs is compounded by a curious attraction to each other, and an emerging, insidious danger related to mysterious death of Kai's father.

Their emerging friendship is tested as they navigate this risky challenge. But the powerful bond forged between them has existed through past lives. The outcome this time will affect the next generation of Kai's people.

In the Direction of the Sun - ISBN - 978-1-943353-65-1

"The emotions flying between the two women who tell their story here is as dramatic as the Appalachian Trail and as tumultuous as the Atlantic Ocean. These natural elements are a perfect backdrop for the revelations of love which both repel and engage them."
 – Jewelle Gomez, author, The Gilda Stories

Steady and smart, Alex McKenzie is settled into a comfortable life in her beloved hometown of Stockbridge, MA. Everything Alex thought she knew about life and about herself changes the moment Cate Conrad blows into town like a warm breeze. Alex falls head over heels in love with the free-spirited artist and sailor but there's one problem: Cate's complicated past makes it impossible for her to open her heart completely and so she does what she's always done— she runs away. Devastated, Alex tries to heal her heart by literally walking away from her life to hike the famed Appalachian Trail while Cate takes to the water. The unexpected turn of events shows Cate and Alex how fragile life is and how love is the all that really matters.

Lavender Dreams - ISBN - 978-1-943353-59-0

When Sarah Chase got on the ferry to Bainbridge Island, she left her lover, her job, and her past behind. She didn't know that in the course of one day she would meet a woman who might be the girl of her dreams, change her career path, create a new family, and find herself in a fairytale mansion with two of the quirkiest little old ladies imaginable.

www.ingramcontent.com/pod-product-compliance
Lightning Source LLC
Chambersburg PA
CBHW051651180726
48284CB00006B/1954